ONE IN THREE

Tess Stimson is the author of eleven novels, including top ten bestseller *The Adultery Club*, and two non-fiction books, which between them have been translated into dozens of languages.

A former journalist and reporter, Stimson was appointed Professor of Creative Writing at the University of South Florida in 2002 and moved to the US. She now lives and works in Vermont with her husband Erik, their three children, and (at the last count) two cats, three fish, one gerbil and a large number of bats in the attic.

Praise for *A Mother's Secret*

'Dark. Twisty. Addictive. I couldn't put it down'
Lisa Jewell

'More chilling than *Gone Girl* and twistier than *The Girl on the Train*, this emotional, raw, dark family drama keeps you guessing until the end'　　Jane Green

'Truly gripping: the opening is heart-breaking and it never lets up, all the way to a genuinely shocking denouement'　　Alex Lake

'Such a gripping, fast-paced book. I just couldn't put it down and read it within a day!'
Short Book and Scribes

'An edge-of-your-seat-wondering-what-is-going-on great thriller!'　　Reader Review

'A must-read for all psychological thriller fans!'
Reader Review

'WOW! I could not put this down. The writing is superb'
Reader Review

For Barbi,
My Wicked-Cool Stepmother
Who'd have thought I'd get so lucky twice?

Chapter 1

The Present

His blood is all over both of us. Arterial blood, bright with oxygen. My shirt is drenched in it. It's in my mouth, in my nostrils; I breathe it in, I *taste* it. Salty and metallic, as if I've licked a rusty metal railing.

I rock back on my heels and push the hair out of my eyes. Our mortal struggle has left us both panting, gasping for breath. Ten feet away from me, she manoeuvres herself into a half-seated position, her left arm hanging uselessly at her side.

The knife lies in a glistening ruby pool between us. I don't take my eyes off her for a single second. Her gaze slides towards the blade, and then back to me.

My phone is out of reach, in my bag by the door. There's no use calling for an ambulance, anyway. He's dead. No one can lose that much blood and survive.

There are shouts outside. Running feet. The Beach House is set away from the main hotel, but sound carries across water. Someone heard the screaming. Help is coming.

I see her realise it too. Cradling her dislocated arm,

she turns quickly towards the open terrace door, weighing up her chances. It's only one floor up, there's soft sand below, but the tide is coming in, cutting off the causeway, and she's in no condition to scramble up the treacherous cliff steps. She's running out of time, anyway; the voices are right outside the door.

She looks at me, and gives a small shrug, *win some, lose some*, then leans back against the edge of the sofa, and closes her eyes.

The hubbub outside intensifies. The door shudders, and then splinters. Two men spill into the room, a press of white faces behind them. I see the shock in their eyes as the gory scene registers. One of them turns and shuts the door, but not before a mobile phone flashes in the crowd.

Now perhaps everyone will finally believe me.

CELIA MAY ROBERTS
PART 1 OF RECORDED INTERVIEW

Date:- 25/07/2020
Duration:- 41 Minutes
Location:- Burgh Island Hotel

Conducted by Officers from Devon &
Cornwall Police

POLICE   This interview is being recorded. I am Detective
          Inspector John Garrett and I'm the Senior
          Investigating Officer of the Major Crime Team
          investigating the violent death of Andrew Page
          at the Burgh Island Hotel earlier today. The date
          is Saturday the twenty-fifth of July 2020, and
          the time by my watch is 3.40 in the afternoon.
          What's your full name?

CR	Celia May Roberts.
POLICE	Thank you. And can you confirm your date of birth for me?
CR	I don't see how that's relevant.
POLICE	Just for the record, Mrs Roberts.
CR	The fourteenth of February, 1952.
POLICE	Thank you—
CR	Anything else you'd like to know about me? My shoe size? My star sign? I didn't kill my son-in-law. Instead of wasting your time with me, you should be—
POLICE	Mrs Roberts, I'm not being rude, stopping you there, but it's just important that I get the introduction bit done, so sorry to interrupt you.
CR	(Inaudible.)
POLICE	I realise this must be very upsetting for you, Mrs Roberts. Would you like a cup of tea before we continue?
CR	No, thank you. [Pause.] I'm sorry. I didn't mean

to be rude. It's just . . . we all loved Andrew very much. I can't take any of this in.

POLICE   It's all right, Mrs Roberts. We can stop at any time.

CR   I think I'd rather just get this out of the way, so I can be with my daughter and grandchildren.

POLICE   Right, then. Also present with me is . . .

POLICE   Detective Sergeant Anna Perry.

POLICE   Mrs Roberts, I know this is difficult, but if you could tell us what—

CR   Caroline killed him.

POLICE   You're referring to his current wife, Mrs Caroline Page?

CR   Yes.

POLICE   Did you actually witness—

CR   I saw that woman standing right beside him, literally red-handed. There was blood everywhere. You should be arresting—

POLICE   Was anyone else there?

5

CR   My daughter, but—

POLICE   Your daughter being Louise Page? Mr Page's
          ex-wife?

CR   Yes.

POLICE   What was she doing when you arrived?

CR   She was on the floor with Andrew. She had his
          head in her lap.

POLICE   So, just to be clear, Mrs Roberts. You didn't
          actually *see* Caroline Page stab her husband. And
          no one else was there, other than your daughter
          and Mrs Page? You didn't see anyone else go
          in or out of the Beach House?

CR   There were a couple of groundsmen outside,
          keeping everyone from going in. And of course
          a lot of people got there around the same time
          I did. We all heard the screaming – you could
          hear it halfway round the island. Min was there,
          and my son, Luke—

POLICE   But no one else was actually *in* the Beach
          House when you arrived, other than the two
          women?

CR   I told you, Caroline—

POLICE	If we could just stick to what you actually saw, Mrs Roberts. [Pause.] Perhaps we could go back to why you were all at the Burgh Island Hotel in the first place?
CR	[Pause.] My husband and I were celebrating our golden wedding anniversary.
POLICE	Congratulations.
CR	Thank you.
POLICE	So you'd organised a bit of a family get-together?
CR	Yes, we'd been planning it since last summer.
POLICE	And whose idea was it to invite your former son-in-law?
CR	Andrew is part of the family. It went without saying.
POLICE	You invited his new wife, too? How did your daughter feel about that?
CR	They've been divorced four years. This wasn't the first time they've socialised together. We all had dinner together a couple of weeks ago, after the children's school play. Louise is tougher than she looks.

7

POLICE   According to your daughter-in-law – Min, is it?
          She tells us she and your son, Luke, begged you
          not to invite Mr Page and his wife.

CR   Louise told *me* she didn't mind.

POLICE   Mrs Roberts, this was a bit more than bumping
          into one another at a school play, wasn't it? A
          whole weekend on an island at a private family
          celebration with the woman who'd run off, sorry,
          with her husband. Emotions must have been
          running high, surely?

CR   I told you, Louise *wanted* Caroline to come.

POLICE   Even though the police were called last month
          over an altercation between them?

CR   Louise said she wanted to bury the hatchet, for
          the children's sake.

POLICE   You didn't think there might be another reason
          she wanted her ex-husband and his wife there?

CR   Like what?

POLICE   Well, that's what we're trying to establish, Mrs
          Roberts. [Pause.] Did *you* have another reason
          for inviting Caroline Page and her husband, Mrs
          Roberts?

CR   (Inaudible.)

POLICE   Mrs Roberts?

CR   For heaven's sake. Hindsight is a wonderful
            thing, isn't it, Inspector?

Seven weeks before the party

Chapter 2

Louise

Everyone in the family receives a formal invitation to my mother's party. Thick vellum, Edwardian script, raised lettering, the works. Bella puts ours in pride of place on the kitchen mantelpiece, propped against the clay dog she made Andrew for Father's Day the year she turned five. He took the dog into work and showed it off to everyone, convinced she was some kind of artistic prodigy. He didn't take it with him seven years later when he left.

The embossed script follows me around the kitchen like the eyes of the *Mona Lisa*. I ignore it as I empty the dishwasher, opening cabinets and closing drawers with practised rhythm, finding comfort in the precise alignment of mugs, the orderly nesting of bowls, the military conformity of knives and forks and spoons in their segregated compartments. Everything in its place.

Everything but me.

Bagpuss winds his way around my ankles, impatient for his breakfast. I tip some dry kibble into his bowl, all he can keep down these days, and scratch him affectionately behind the ears. 'Here you go, Bags. Don't eat it too fast.'

The cat bends arthritically to his food, as old and saggy as his pink-and-white-striped namesake. I refill his water bowl, make myself a cup of tea and go outside. The air smells clean after last night's much-needed rain, but already it promises to be another warm day, unusually muggy for June. Curling up in the wicker beehive chair, which hangs from the apple tree, I tuck one foot under my bottom, and push the ground with the other. I used to hate mornings before Bella and Tolly were born, but these days I treasure this precious half-hour of peace before the world wakes up. I lean back and close my eyes. It is the only time that's truly my own.

The invitation has unsettled me more than I care to admit. My mother has sent one to Andrew and Caz, too, even though I begged her not to; now I will have to face them on my home turf, in the heart of my family.

Somehow I weathered their wedding day four years ago, energetically scouring out my kitchen cabinets as I imagined them taking their vows, scrubbing the bathroom floor as I pictured them cutting the cake, forcing the blunt lawnmower through six inches of grass as I envisioned them stepping onto the dance floor for their first dance as a married couple. Since then, I've learned the hard way to accept their presence together at school plays and sports days; I've built up a tough shell to protect myself. But this is different.

Maybe it's because it's my parents' golden wedding

anniversary, a milestone I dreamed of reaching with Andrew. Perhaps it's because Mum was the last holdout against Caz; the invitation finally brings her in from the cold. Or maybe I just need to get more sleep. I was up till two this morning marking my media students' end-of-term exams. I'd have finished more quickly if I'd let the misspellings and bad grammar go, but even though I may have fallen from the lofty heights of a weekly Fleet Street column, I still have standards.

The sun breaches the horizon, a golden band of light falling across my face. Andrew was right, I think, as I open my eyes and gaze across the rolling downs. Despite my initial doubts, I *have* come to love it here.

I can still see him standing on the low stone garden wall the day we first viewed the house nearly seventeen years ago, his arms spread wide, a joyous expression on his face as he animatedly painted a picture of our life here. Somewhere for our new baby daughter to grow up safe and happy, with the wind in her hair and grass between her toes. I was so reluctant to leave London back then; not because of my column at the *Daily Post*, which I could have written from anywhere, but because the city made me feel alive, plugged in, as if the world was at my fingertips. I hated the thought of giving it all up to live in a crumbling money pit in the middle of nowhere. But Andrew had wanted it so much, and in those days I would have given him anything he asked. It'd never occurred to me then I'd end up living here without him.

My phone buzzes in my dressing-gown pocket,

making me jump. I pull it out and swipe right, and my sister-in-law's face appears on the screen. 'Going to bed or getting up?' I ask, climbing out of the beehive chair and letting myself back into the kitchen.

'Just finished a double shift at the hospital,' Min says. 'Got home a few minutes ago.'

She looks as fresh as if she's just come back from a fortnight in Hawaii. At forty-seven, she's only four years older than me, but judging from the tiny FaceTime inset, I could pass for her mother. My mousy hair urgently needs some highlights, and my muddy blue eyes are shadowed. 'Quiet night?' I ask, propping my phone on the kitchen counter.

'Huge pile-up on the M23. Gruesome,' Min says, with relish. Her image bobs and dips as she takes her phone into her study. She puts it down, and then brandishes an envelope at the screen. 'Guess what I found on my doormat?'

I love Min. She's funny, and smart, and she makes my brother Luke very happy. But she has no boundaries, and I already know where this is going.

'Before you ask, yes, Andrew and Caz are invited,' I say, tossing another teabag into my empty mug. 'Mum wants the whole family together for her big day. And you know how much she adores Kit.'

'Well, Kit I understand, but why did Celia invite *her*?'

'Because Andrew wouldn't come without her.'

Min looks indignant. 'That woman should have the good manners to make herself scarce,' she says. 'Frankly, I can't believe Andrew's got the balls to come himself.'

16

'You can say her name, you know. She's not Voldemort.'

'Lou, why are you putting yourself through this? You don't have to play the martyr. You could put your foot down and say no to Celia.'

I don't rise to the bait. No one ever says no to my mother, including Min.

It's not that I don't appreciate Min's loyalty. I'd never have survived the brutal months after Andrew left if it wasn't for her, not with a traumatised twelve-year-old and a newborn to look after. The youngest of Min's four boys was still in nappies at the time, but she was there whenever I needed her. She took Bella to school on the mornings I simply couldn't get out of bed, made sure I ate, and helped me cope with the heart-wrenching admin of divorce: finding a decent lawyer, boxing up Andrew's stuff, going back to work. She listened patiently as I sobbed into my wineglass, trying to make sense of what had happened. And when it had looked as if I'd drown in my own despair, Min had delivered the precise dose of tough love I needed to start living again.

What she's found harder to accept is my need to finally put the past behind me and forgive Andrew. Her enduring hostility towards him is almost as exhausting as my mother's serene refusal to accept he's never coming back.

Andrew broke my heart, but it's been four years. If I don't let the bitterness go, I'll be consumed by it. He's still Bella and Tolly's father, and they love him.

Whatever Min thinks, I'm neither a martyr nor a pushover. I've learned to tolerate Caz's toxic presence in my life, because what other choice is there? The woman is married to my children's father. Her son is their half-brother. In its own twisted way, whether I like it or not, that makes her family.

'Please, Min, let it go,' I say tiredly. 'It's one weekend of my life. I think we can all get through it without killing each other.'

'We've got nearly seven weeks,' Min says, changing tack with dizzying speed. 'I've got this great diet – you'll love it. Paleo meets Weight Watchers, you'll drop a stone without even noticing. I'd lend you something of mine to wear, but you're too tall—'

I hear small footsteps upstairs, and close the kitchen door so I'm not overheard.

'Min, I'm not trying to compete with Caz. That ship has sailed. She's twenty-nine and looks like a super-model, whereas my boobs are in a race to my navel, and even my earlobes have wrinkles. I could diet my arse off and I'd still never have her cheekbones.' I sigh. 'I appreciate the pep talk, but even if I could afford a celebrity makeover, what's the point? How would breaking up Kit's family help anyone now?'

'It would put *your* family back together.'

'No. It wouldn't.'

Min's scowl fills the screen. 'You're too nice.'

I eye the invitation on the mantelpiece. Andrew and I had a deal. A deal that didn't involve accepting invitations to my parents' golden wedding celebrations, or coming anywhere near the rest of my family, for that matter. A deal he's broken, even though I told him there'd be consequences.

'Actually, Min,' I say, turning the invitation face down. 'I'm not that nice.'

Chapter 3

Caz

Angie is already jammed in our usual corner at the bar of the Chelsea Potter when I arrive. The pub is packed, with people spilling out onto the street, and it takes me several minutes to elbow my way to her side. 'That better be a double,' I say grimly, as she hands me a gin and tonic.

She raises a pierced eyebrow as I drain it in a single gulp. 'Tough day?'

'Tough week, and it's still only Thursday.' I slide onto the stool she's saved me and put my mobile on the bar in case Andy calls. 'You're not going to believe this. Tina Murdoch's going to be my liaison on the Univest account.'

Angie whistles. 'You're kidding. How the fuck did she pull that off?'

'Her career's soared since she left us and joined Univest.' I signal to the barman for another drink, twisting my long blonde hair up away from my face and securing it with a silver clip. 'What I can't get over is why Patrick's agreed to it. After she sabotaged us on

20

the Tetrotek ad campaign, you'd think he wouldn't let her within a hundred metres of the building.'

Angie reaches for a bowl of pistachios. 'If he's on board, you're stuck with it. Think you can work with her?'

'Not so far. She's nixed every idea I've presented, and already gone over my head to Patrick to complain. She's insisting on bringing in a PR consultant from outside. I almost hope he takes me off the campaign and gives it to someone else.'

'No, you don't.'

'No, I don't.' I scowl at my drink. 'I'm not going to let Tina win, but if this goes on, one of us is going to end up in a body bag.'

Tina Murdoch, my bête noire. Last time we worked together, she almost got me fired. The irony is, she's the one who gave me my big break in advertising, promoting me to a major campaign when I was only in my first year at Whitefish. She saw herself as my mentor, and made a big show of supporting the 'sisterhood' and helping young women up the ladder. Then she introduced me to Andy at an RSPCA fundraiser whose campaign Whitefish had worked on – although Andy doesn't remember that first meeting. But when Andy and I officially became an item, my relationship with Tina instantly went south. I suspect she had her eyes on him herself, but whatever it was that chapped her ass, she's had it in for me ever since.

I haven't even worked up a campaign pitch for Univest yet, let alone presented it, but Tina's insisting on a written promotional plan, copy platform details, and a full budget breakdown per territory and media format, all by the end of the month. It's impossible, and she knows it. Nolan, our Creative Director, is threatening to quit, and the rest of the creatives are on the verge of revolting. Although, as Andy dryly pointed out last night when I'd finished ranting, they're pretty revolting at the best of times.

Angie clinks her glass to mine. 'Fuck it. It's nearly Friday.'

'Yeah. Fuck it.'

She cracks open another pistachio, and tosses the shells back in the bowl. 'You in town this weekend? There's a great band playing at Borderline on Saturday night.'

I grimace. 'Can't. We're in Brighton.'

'Shit, *again*?'

'It's our weekend with the kids.'

'Can't they come up here? My sister would babysit for the night.'

'Louise won't let them.' I reach across the counter for the bowl of pistachios. 'She says they're too young to travel up on the train on their own. It's ridiculous. Bella's sixteen. At her age, I was hitching to Crete.' I sigh. 'Mind you, there's barely enough room to swing a cat in our flat, never mind find room for three kids. Kit has to bunk in with Tolly, and Bella ends up on the sofa with her shit all over the place. At least in Brighton, they have their own bedrooms.'

'Christ. I don't know how you put up with it.'

'I don't have a lot of choice. They're Andy's kids.'

Angie shoots me a look, her funky eyebrows almost disappearing into her turquoise-tipped black hair. We've been BFFs since our primary school days in Dagenham, and she knows me better than anyone, including Andy. We drifted apart a bit during our uni years, when I was at Bristol and she was studying fashion at St Martins, but we've been joined at the hip ever since I moved back to London. We couldn't be more different; I'm ambitious and driven, whereas Angie never thinks beyond the next round of drinks. Her idea of a manicure is to hack at her nails with a Stanley knife. But she knew my mother before her accident; she understands where I've come from, and what I've had to do to get to where I am. Apart from Andy and Kit, she's my only real family.

Angie knows kids were never part of my plan, never mind three of them. But Louise played a blinder when she got herself knocked up with Tolly. She nearly pulled it off, too.

'Talk of the devil,' I groan, as my mobile lights up. 'The Wicked Witch of the West.'

'What does she want?'

'God knows.' My tone is light, but I feel the familiar knot of tension in my stomach. 'It's a bit early for her usual rant. She must have hit wine o'clock ahead of schedule.'

'Ignore her, Caz. Let it go to voicemail.'

I'm tempted, but then the familiar guilt kicks in. Once the other woman, always the other woman. It doesn't matter how unreasonable Louise is, or that *she* was the reason Andy ended their marriage, not me. Somehow, I'll always owe her.

'She'll only keep calling. It's better to let her get it out of her system. Watch my bag for me, would you?' I push myself off my stool and head to the back of the pub, near the loos, where it's a little quieter. 'Hello, Louise.'

'This is the third time I've called,' Louise says sharply. 'You need to keep your phone on. You never know what might happen.'

The band around my chest tightens. Breathe, I tell myself. 'My phone *was* on—'

'Well, never mind that now. I don't have time to teach you how to be a good mother. I'm sure you've forgotten, but it's Bella's play on Saturday. She asked me to call and make sure Andrew is coming.'

Shit. It'd totally slipped my mind. 'Of course we haven't forgotten,' I fib. 'We've been looking forward to it.'

'It's at seven. You'll need to get there earlier if you want good seats.'

'Fine. We'll be there in plenty of time.'

'Min and I are planning to take them to The Coal Shed to celebrate afterwards,' Louise adds. 'A special treat, since this is her first big role.'

So much for being broke. The Coal Shed is one of the most expensive restaurants in Brighton. Louise is always nagging Andy to increase her child support, even though she works full-time herself. She seems to

24

think we're rolling in it. The only reason we can afford two homes is because I already had the Fulham flat long before Andy and I met. We'd never be able to afford it now. And our house in Brighton is mortgaged up to the hilt. Andy earns a good salary as INN's *Early Evening News* anchor, but it's not the silly money Louise seems to think it is. We're talking cable, after all. What with maintenance and child support and private school fees, she takes nearly two-thirds of everything Andy earns.

It suddenly occurs to me that this is Andy's weekend with the children anyway. I'd love nothing better than a weekend alone with Andy and Kit, but my husband would be really upset, and he'd blame me. 'Sorry, but it's our weekend, Louise,' I say politely. 'I think Andy's already made plans to take them out to dinner.'

'Well, he can change them, can't he?'

'He hasn't seen them for two weeks,' I point out. 'He wants to spend some time with them.'

'What do you care? They're not even your children,' Louise cries, all pretence at civility evaporating. 'Bella is *my* daughter. I should be the one to take her out to dinner on her big night! She'd be spending it with *both* her parents if it wasn't for you.'

'Louise, please—'

'I'll call Andrew. I should have phoned him in the first place. I don't know what I was thinking. It's the organ grinder I need to speak to, not his monkey.'

'You do that,' I snap, ending the call.

My stomach churns, and I taste acid at the back of

my throat. It's bad enough having to deal with Tina at work, but at least I can keep her out of my bedroom. There's no escaping Andy's ex-wife.

It's been more than four years since they split up, but Louise shows no signs of moving on. If anything, she's getting worse. The sniping, the mind games, the way she poisons Bella and Tolly against me, constantly guilt-tripping Andy – she just has to snap her fingers, and he comes running. And then there are the phone calls. Sometimes she's sobbing down the line, begging me to let him 'come home' to her; other times she yells abuse until I'm the one in tears when I finally hang up the phone. She's smart enough only to call me when she knows Andy's at work, or away on an assignment. She knows I can't say anything to him, or I'll look like a jealous bitch.

And what makes it so much worse is that she's nice as pie to my face. The other day, Andy even commented on how well we got on. After everything she did to him, to us, he still has no idea what she's *really* like.

To my surprise, my eyes suddenly blur. I'm so tired of the constant fighting, the running battles over money and the children. If I'd had any idea what it was going to be like, I'd have thought twice before I ever agreed to marry Andy.

No, I wouldn't. I'd walk over hot coals for my husband. Louise is a bitch, but I'm not going to let her get to me. I'm just tired, that's all.

Gathering my bag from the barstool, I fish out a twenty from my wallet and put it on the bar. 'I'm so sorry, Angie. I'm going to have to go. Louise is on the warpath, and I'd totally forgotten Bella has this play on Saturday. I'm going to have to work tonight instead, or I'll never get everything done by Monday.'

'Hey, not a problem.' Angie shrugs. 'I get it. Let's pick up next week, yeah?'

I kiss her cheek. 'You are a total star.'

'I know.' She grins. 'That cute girl by the window in green? She's been giving me the eye since I got here. You're doing me a favour.'

She blows me a kiss, and I squeeze my way through the throng of people and out onto the pavement. My phone rings again before I've even gone ten paces.

'Andy, I'm sorry,' I sigh. 'I shouldn't have hung up on Louise. It's just, it was so noisy in the pub, and I thought it'd be easier if—'

'Where the hell are you?'

'Heading towards the tube station. I should be home in half an hour—'

'You were supposed to pick up Kit at five,' Andy says tersely.

I stop still in the street. 'You said *you* were getting him.'

'I said I'd *try*,' he snaps. 'We agreed you'd collect him unless you heard otherwise, remember? And I left you a voicemail telling you I couldn't make it. Don't you check your messages?'

'Oh, God, I'm so sorry—'

'I just had a call from his child-minder when I was in the middle of taping an interview, and we're going

27

to have to redo the whole thing. Greta says she reminded you this morning? He needed to be collected on time so she could get away to her evening class.'

'Is he still with her?'

'I've asked Lily to go round and pick him up. She'll keep him next door with the twins until you get home.'

I feel like the worst mother in the world as I flag down a cab. 'I really am sorry, Andy. I should've checked my phone. I honestly thought you were—'

'It's not me you need to apologise to. Greta says she can't have him back if we're not going to pick him up on time.' I hear someone in the background calling his name. 'Look, I've got to go and redo my interview. You'll have to sort it out with Greta. And if she won't take him anymore, you'll just have to find someone else.'

Climbing into the back of the cab, I give the driver our address, staring out of the window as we head back down the King's Road. Andy didn't say this would never have happened on Louise's watch, no matter how chaotic her week, but he didn't need to. We both know that's what he was thinking.

Chapter 4

Louise

'You reminded Dad about tomorrow, right?' Bella asks.

I set Tolly's plate of spaghetti hoops in front of him, and whip Bella's cheese on toast out from under the grill. Until I get paid at the end of the month, it's this or baked beans. 'I told you, darling. Dad's out on a story all day, his phone went straight to voicemail, but I texted him *and* left a message with his secretary.'

Bella flops into a kitchen chair, the long black sleeves of her sweater trailing across her plate as she pokes suspiciously at her dinner. I don't blame her for being wary: no cheese is meant to be this yellow. 'Have we got any Worcestershire?'

I pass her the bottle. 'You need to call Caz and tell her to remind him,' she adds, smothering her food with sauce. 'He'll forget otherwise.'

'I spoke to her yesterday, and reminded her. Dad's not going to forget, darling.'

'And she definitely said they were coming?'

'She promised they'd be there.'

Bella shoots me a look. 'You *were* nice to her, weren't you, Mum?'

I hesitate. I'm civil to Andrew's second wife when I have to be, but Andrew and I always make arrangements for the children's weekend visits ourselves. Voluntarily picking up the phone, asking Caz to make sure my daughter's father didn't forget her school play, stirred dark feelings I thought I'd put behind me. I may not have been *quite* as civil to her as I should have been.

'Of course,' I say.

'Can you call her again now? Just to make sure?'

'Absolutely.' I unplug my phone from its charger on the counter. 'Make sure Tolly eats the sausages as well as the hoops. I'll be back in a minute.'

I go outside and walk down to the vegetable garden, where I can be certain I won't be overheard, and pace up and down between the broad beans, my mobile in my hand. Every time I call Caz, it feels like another surrender, the yielding of yet more precious family terrain. Asking her for her co-operation legitimises her role in the parenting of my children. But Bella needs her father to be at the play. Our divorce came at the worst possible time for her, when she was on the cusp of adolescence; every relationship she has with a man going forward will follow the template set by the one she has with Andrew. I don't want her to grow up attention-seeking and needy because he failed her.

My fingernails dig half-moons into my palms. This woman didn't even know my daughter for the first twelve years of her life. She broke up my son's family before he'd even said his first word. And yet now she has a legitimate claim on them, a half-share of their precious, swift-flowing childhoods. I've come to terms with the fact that I've lost my husband to this woman, but the thought of her mothering my children cuts straight through to my soft underbelly.

I pull up her number, but to my relief, the call goes to voicemail, and I hang up without leaving a message. I'm still seething over the fact that Caz will be the one celebrating Bella's big night with her, and I remind myself firmly that this isn't about me. Andrew will be there for Bella, which is all that really matters.

When I go back inside, Bella has disappeared upstairs, leaving her plate of untouched cheese on toast on the table. Tolly is crawling around on the floor, trying to feed his sausages to Bagpuss.

'Leave him alone,' I scold, rescuing the cat and depositing him on the ancient, hair-covered sofa by the back door. 'He'll be sick if he eats those.'

'I'll be sick if *I* eat them,' Tolly says.

'They're hot dogs, not sausages. You like hot dogs.'

'No, I don't. They look like willies.'

'Bartholomew!'

Tolly giggles, covering his mouth with dimpled hands that have yet to lose the fat of babyhood, his brown eyes dancing with mischief. I try to hold my stern expression, but it's impossible. Tolly scrambles to his feet and launches himself at me full throttle, and we tumble back onto the sofa, laughing, as Bagpuss leaps out of the way. My little boy snuggles into my lap and I stroke his wild mop of russet curls, filled with overwhelming love for my son. Tolly, my unexpected, glorious autumn baby, squeaking in under the wire just before I turned forty.

I'd never expected to have another child after the problems I had with my first pregnancy. I'd had two miscarriages before Bella was conceived, and then my waters broke at just thirty-five weeks. After seventy-two hours of stop-start contractions and drugs and exhortations to push, to pant, to breathe, to give it one more try, I was finally rushed into theatre for the emergency C-section I should have had two days earlier. Bella was absolutely fine, a healthy six pounds two ounces; after her initial check-up, she didn't even have to go to the NICU. But I'd lost a lot of blood, and all that pushing and trying had all but torn me inside out. No more babies, the obstetrician warned. Not that it was likely to happen anyway.

I had a healthy, beautiful baby girl in my arms, and whenever I felt a lingering sadness at the rabble of children I'd never have, I only had to look into her deep blue eyes to be overwhelmed with gratitude for what I *did* have.

And then, five years ago, I skipped a period. I didn't pay it too much attention at the time; the *Post* was undergoing some major restructuring – for which read redundancies – as it attempted, like every other legacy media institution, to compete with online news sources, and what with everything else that was going on in my life, my stress levels were through the roof. But then I'd missed another cycle, and suddenly I couldn't stand the smell of eggs. My silhouette went from Olive Oyl to Jessica Rabbit overnight. I had been thrown a miraculous lifeline, just at the moment I thought I'd drown.

I'd known from the beginning the odds of a successful pregnancy were stacked against me. My age and previous history didn't bode well, and then I started spotting at ten weeks. My obstetrician insisted I give up work, and rest as much as possible. Leaving the *Post* had been a risk, even for just a few months, with so many jobs being cut and hungry young freelancers willing to work for half the pay and no benefits; but I didn't hesitate. All that mattered was my baby. And somehow I managed to keep Tolly safe. I reached my second trimester, and then my third. Everything looked good. The baby seemed healthy, all my scans and tests came back normal. I got to thirty-five weeks, then thirty-six, and thirty-seven.

At thirty-eight weeks, I was dropping Bella off at school when I collapsed in the middle of the playground. Had it not been for the quick thinking of another parent, a doctor who recognised the signs of pre-eclampsia, both Tolly and I would almost certainly have died.

There's very little I remember about the next ten days. I have a few hazy memories of the ambulance ride to hospital, of sirens and lights and Andrew, white-faced, rushing along the corridor as they wheeled me into theatre, gripping my hand so hard I thought he'd break my fingers. Tolly had been hastily delivered via Caesarean, safe and well, but they'd struggled to stabilise me as my blood pressure soared and my blood refused to clot properly. At one point, as my organs started to shut down, the doctors told my parents and Andrew to prepare for the worst. He even brought Bella in to say goodbye. I can't imagine what it must have been like for her, a twelve-year-old child, facing the loss of her mother.

Andrew's face was the first thing I saw when I regained consciousness. He was fast asleep in the chair next to me, his head pillowed on his wadded-up jacket, still holding my hand as if he had never let go. He looked drawn and grey and ten years older than when I had last seen him.

He opened his eyes as I stirred. 'Louise?'

If I had ever had any doubt that he loved me, it vanished then. I had only ever seen him cry twice before: at the death of his mother, and the birth of our daughter. 'Don't try to speak,' he'd said anxiously, leaping up and pouring me a cup of water from the jug beside my bed and holding it to my lips. 'They had to intubate you. Your throat will feel sore for a while.'

'The baby—'

'He's fine. At home with Min. She's been looking after him while I've been here with you.' He sat on the bed next to me and took my hand again, mindful of the IV line taped to the back of it. 'I thought I'd lost you,' he said thickly. 'Oh, God, Lou, don't ever do that to me again. I couldn't bear it if I lost you. I love you so much.'

The room had suddenly filled with medics, checking charts and monitors and IV bags, making adjustments and tapping away on iPads, frowning in concentration. I'd leaned back against the pillows while they'd bustled around me, smiling exhaustedly as Andrew kissed the back of my fingers. Our son was safe. Our children wouldn't have to face growing up without a mother. Our family had survived, and we'd be stronger than ever because of what we'd been through together. Everything was going to be OK.

A week later, Andrew left me.

Chapter 5

Caz

My right heel snaps as I step off the escalator at Sloane Square. I pitch forward, arms windmilling as I try to keep my balance. 'Goddammit!'

The tide of commuters shows no mercy. I hobble to the side before I'm mown down, leaning one palm against the wall and hingeing my knee behind me to check my heel. It's totally fucked. Even if there was a heel-bar nearby, which there isn't, and I had time to wait for them to fix it, which I don't, the heel hasn't come unglued, it's completely snapped in two. There's no way it can be repaired. These are my sensible M&S granny shoes, the ones I can actually *walk* in. Now I'm going to have to spend the rest of the day teetering around in the four-inch stilettos I keep at work for date nights with Andy.

I hitch my bag back onto my shoulder and stumble unevenly down the King's Road. I haven't even had my first coffee and my day has already gone to shit. First the invitation, plopping onto our doormat this morning like a giant embossed turd, and now this.

Bloody Celia Roberts. She probably jinxed me with some kind of voodoo spell over the invite involving chicken feathers and the blood of virgins.

AJ is waiting anxiously for me in reception. He falls into step with me as I swipe my card through the chrome barrier and head towards the elevators. 'Where have you been?'

Grumpily, I jab the lift button. 'Jesus. It's not even eight. Where's the fire?'

'Patrick's doing his best to contain it. You'll see when you get to the conference room.'

'AJ, I'm not in the mood for games.'

'Tina Murdoch's here.'

I look up sharply. 'You've got to be kidding me. The client meeting's not till next week.'

'Tina brought it forward.' He peers down at my shoe. 'What happened to you?'

'Don't you read *Vogue*? Uneven heels are going to be huge next season. You wouldn't believe the strings I had to pull to get these.'

'Seriously?'

I love AJ, though he's never been the brightest crayon in the box. But he seems particularly distracted this morning, and I suddenly notice his eyes are suspiciously red. 'You all right?' I ask.

'I'm fine,' he says quickly.

'AJ—'

'Wayne and I had a bit of a row. It's nothing, really. Lover's tiff. Come on, we'd better get a move on. Patrick's waiting.'

Upstairs, the office has the deserted air of the *Marie Celeste*. Everyone is already gathered in the glassed-in conference room on the other side of the atrium. Patrick spots me as I change my shoes at my desk, and gesticulates for me to come and join them. I hate open-plan offices.

AJ thrusts a file into my hands and we hustle into the conference room. When Patrick assigned me this campaign, it never occurred to me I'd end up working for Tina. Seven years ago, when she was still working for Whitefish, she almost torpedoed my career. I was her assistant brand manager on Tetrotek, a major client, and we'd been working for months on a new pitch for them. Two days before we were due to deliver it, a rival advertising agency, JMVD, presented a pitch that was almost word for word the same as our own. Assuming *we* were the plagiarists, Tetrotek defected to JMVD, and there was a searching internal investigation at Whitefish to find the source of the leak.

I'd been the one seen lunching with JMVD's Business Director twice in the preceding month; lunches Tina had personally asked me to take, and subsequently denied requesting. She deliberately set me up to take the fall to get back at me because she'd found out about me and Andy. Patrick came within a whisker of firing me, and it took me a long time to claw back my reputation and his respect.

'OK, Caz,' Patrick says, as I sit down, 'why don't you start us off with a general overview of where we are on the campaign?'

'Well, it's still early days,' I stall. I haven't even had a chance to speak to the creative team yet. I glance at Nolan Casey, our Creative Director, for help, but he's studiously looking the other way. 'Once we have a clearer idea as to what Univest are looking for on this—'

'But you're the Account Director,' Tina coos. 'Isn't it your job to tell me what I want?'

I've had enough of this. 'As you know, Univest has scored a few own goals recently,' I say crisply. 'That business with the sweatshops in India – it got a lot of media play. Then there was the scandal over the paraben-free shampoo, and the recall on the organic fabric softener—'

'Obviously, that was all before my time as Marketing Director,' Tina says testily.

'What you need to do now is re-establish trust,' I shoot back. 'JMVD's policy when they had the account was to ignore these PR disasters and focus on the quality of their brands, but I think they're wrong. What we need to do is acknowledge the elephant in the room, apologise, and move on.'

'*Apologise*?'

Patrick makes a calming motion to Tina. 'Let's hear her out.'

AJ nudges me and I open the folder he gave me, fanning a sheaf of bright graphs and pie charts onto the beech conference table. I have no idea what they're supposed to show, since I haven't yet had a chance to read them, but no one looks at them; they never do. 'You're not the only conglomerate to get caught up in a shit-storm like this. But the more you ignore it, the more the problem festers.' I tap the graphs as if it's all right in front of us. 'After Barclays apologised to its customers for the role it played in the Libor rate-rigging scandal, the problem went away. Toyota, Goldman Sachs, even Facebook – they've all used the corporate apology as a means of addressing branding issues, and they've all bounced back quickly as a result.'

'I disagree,' Tina snaps. 'If we apologise, all we'll do is bring attention to the issue and give the story legs. Our brands are blue-chip. We need to focus on their strengths and let these distractions die down.'

How did this woman end up running the marketing division of one of the biggest international companies in the country? She wouldn't recognise a market trend if it bit her on her flabby, conniving arse.

'There's no such thing as blue-chip anymore,' I say tersely. 'Your customers are dying off, and the next generation doesn't have brand loyalty to anything. Social media has changed the landscape. The era of a specific media push around a single theme is over. Brands need to be having a conversation with their customers 24/7 to win their loyalty. And the foundation of any relationship is honesty.'

I hold her gaze, daring her to contradict me. We both know I'm not talking about advertising.

'This is why I wanted Caz on this,' Patrick intervenes. 'You and I are part of a different generation, Tina. We need to think the way these kids think.'

Tina turns puce, and I think AJ's going to choke on

his caramel frappé. We spend the next hour and a half going around in circles, but Tina's on the losing side, and she knows it. Challenging her relevance to the next generation was a winning move on Patrick's part. There's a reason he's the CEO, even though, at fifty, he's an archaeological curiosity in the ad business. He knows *people*, and that's what this game is all about.

But my victory is Pyrrhic. I may have won this battle, but I'm still stuck working with Tina. She's going to fight every pitch I make tooth and nail on principle. The next six months of my life are going to be a nightmare. I can feel a headache coming on at the mere thought of it.

Patrick shows Tina back to the elevator, and I grab a couple of paracetamol from my desk drawer and swallow them dry, then retreat to the bathroom and lock myself in a stall. I love my job; I've worked hard to get to where I am. I started here five years ago knowing next to nothing about advertising, having spent the first three years of my career in PR. But I listened and learned; I put in sixteen-hour days and seven-day weeks, and didn't take a holiday for the first two years I was at the agency. Client servicing is demanding; agency heads want more billing; creatives want more time, quick approvals and minimal changes; clients demand everything *yesterday*. Despite the Tetrotek fiasco, Patrick's entrusted me with some of the company's most important clients. I refuse to let Tina Murdoch sabotage everything I've worked so hard to achieve.

I open the cubicle door, and jump when I see Tina

leaning against the washbasins waiting for me. 'What do you want?' I ask coolly.

'I want you off this account.'

I turn on the tap. 'That's not going to happen. You heard what Patrick said. He wants me on this.'

She reaches across me and turns the tap off again. 'You may have Patrick wrapped around your little finger, but you don't fool me,' she says. 'Take yourself off this account, or you'll regret it.'

I lean on the washbasin as she slams out of the bathroom, my heart thumping in my ribcage. I practise my breathing the way my therapist taught me, trying to calm myself down. I can't let her get to me. I know what I'm doing, and I'm good at what I do. I can handle this.

My pulse finally stops racing. I straighten up, and smooth my hair back from my face. AJ is waiting right outside the bathroom when I come out, and I mentally resolve to make time next week to get to the bottom of what's going on with him. He's the most loyal man I've ever met, and he deserves a little kindness. There's no way I'd survive going toe-to-toe with Tina Murdoch if I didn't have AJ to watch my back.

'So,' he says, as I head briskly back to my desk. 'Do you have a plan?'

I always have a plan.

ANGIE LARK
PART 1 OF RECORDED INTERVIEW

Date:- 28/07/2020
Duration:- 41 Minutes
Location:- Kingsbridge Police Station

Conducted by Officers from Devon &
Cornwall Police

(cont.)

POLICE   And you are Caroline Page's best friend, Ms
          Lark?

AL   I've known her since we were at primary school
          together. I'm telling you, she wouldn't lie about
          something like that.

POLICE   When was this altercation, exactly?

AL   I don't know. Three weeks ago? Maybe four. [Pause.] You must have a record of it; Caz reported it.

POLICE   And until—

AL   Not that anyone *did* anything. Caz warned you what Louise was capable of, but none of you took her seriously.

POLICE   We take all such reports very seriously, Ms Lark. But until the altercation between them last month, there hadn't been any trouble?

AL   [Laughs.] Are you kidding?

POLICE   No, Ms Lark, I am not. I don't consider murder a laughing matter.

AL   Look, Caz is no angel. She'd be the first to admit that. Technically, Andy was still married when they hooked up. So, you can imagine, Louise wasn't exactly Caz's biggest fan. But the woman behaved like a total bitch over the divorce. She wouldn't let the kids meet Caz for, like, a year. She just couldn't let Andy go. If it's over, it's over, you know?

POLICE   So how would you characterise the relationship
            between the two women?

AL   Shit, is how I would characterise it.

POLICE   Care to explain?

AL   All that stuff about Caz in the papers, none of
            it's true. I can't believe Louise has the balls to
            play the grieving widow when she's the one who
            killed him!

POLICE   If we could just stick to the facts, Ms Lark, rather
            than speculate—

AL   I've seen Louise in action. She comes across so
            nice and sensible, right? Mother of the year. But
            I'm telling you, underneath it all she's a fucking
            psycho.

POLICE   In what way?

AL   Well, for a start, she used to call Caz all hours
            of the day and night, yelling and crying down
            the phone. I mean, Caz is tough, but she's put
            up with years of it; it'd wear anyone down.

POLICE   You witnessed these calls?

AL   I was there when Caz got some of them, yeah.

45

	But Louise is smart. She never called when Andy was around.
POLICE	Did you hear what was said between them?
AL	I didn't need to. My best mate ended up in tears, and she doesn't cry easily. It wasn't just the phone calls. Louise was a bloody stalker. She wouldn't let Caz alone. Turning up at the house, at her *work*, and then claiming Caz was harassing *her*. I thought there were laws against stalking these days?
POLICE	Yes—
AL	She's got form, you know that, right?
POLICE	"She" being—?
AL	*Louise.*
POLICE	Yes, right.
AL	She got done for stalking before. Caz said some bloke had to take a restraining order out against her.
POLICE	When was this?
AL	I don't know the details. Look, don't you people

have computers or something? You can look it up.

POLICE   Ms Lark, are you all right? You seem a little upset. Would you like to take a break?

AL   Sorry. It's just . . . [Pause.] I know Caz is my friend and everything, and I would say this, but she's, like, so the opposite of a drama queen. I've been telling her for months to report Louise, but she wouldn't have it, said it'd just make things worse. But that woman hated Caz . . . [Pause.] Sorry.

POLICE   We can take a break here if you'd like.

AL   Sorry, no, I'm . . . I'll be fine.

POLICE   Roy, would you get Ms Lark some tea? For the tape, Detective Sergeant Steve Roy is leaving the room.

AL   I told Caz not to go to that damn party – I knew something bad would happen.

POLICE   Why?

AL   Things have been building up. Ever since—

POLICE (SR)   DS Steve Roy re-entering the room.

47

POLICE   Here you go. Careful, it's hot.

AL   Thanks. It's just . . . no one believed Caz and look what's happened. Louise is really plausible, but I'm telling you, there's another side to her; honestly, I think she's unhinged. I mean, that business with the cat, and all the nonsense she pulled with the school play. Who *does* that?

Six weeks before the party

Chapter 6

Min

Luke is curled up on the sofa when I come downstairs on Saturday morning, a small boy snuggled into the crook of each arm. All three are covered with Coco Pops, the empty cereal box on the floor testament to their nutritious breakfast. Akin to the unshod cobbler's child, the offspring of doctors are the least healthily nourished in the land. 'I can't believe I slept in so late,' I exclaim. 'It's after eight. You should have woken me.'

My husband cranes his neck around me so he can still see the television. 'You pulled a double shift. You needed your sleep.'

'Mummy! You're in the way.'

'What are you watching?' I ask, glancing at the screen.

'*Stranger Things*,' seven-year-old Sidney says.

'Luke! Isn't that a bit scary for them?'

'We like scary,' Archie says, burrowing further into his father's arms.

I pick up the cereal box and open the curtains,

ignoring the boys' squeals of protest as the Stygian gloom is dispelled. 'Where are the twins?'

Luke finally yields to the interruption and pauses the TV. 'It's not lunchtime yet. Where d'you think?'

Dom and Jack transitioned effortlessly from getting up at five to sleeping in till noon as soon as the clock struck teenager. The sadist in me takes great pleasure now in waking them up for school, frequently with the aid of cold water, after a decade of being rudely bounced from my bed before sunrise. 'I promised I'd go over and help your mother with the party this morning,' I say. 'Can you make sure the twins get to footie practice on time?'

'What's she need help with? The party's not for weeks.'

'She's invited Andrew and *that woman*,' I say indignantly. 'Someone has to talk sense into her!'

'Ah. So not exactly *help* then. More like interfere.'

Sidney grabs at the TV remote. 'Dad! Push play!'

'Your mother and I are talking,' Luke says, holding the remote out of Sidney's reach. 'Honestly, Min, it's up to Mum who she invites. I wouldn't get involved.'

'I know you wouldn't,' I say crossly.

Luke Roberts is the very definition of a good guy. He loves his family, works hard – doing what, I've never quite worked out, something unfathomable in IT, I think – and buys me flowers for my birthday, our anniversary, and sometimes for no reason at all. I've loved him heart and soul for more than thirty years, ever since he walked into double biology and tripped over my backpack, literally falling at my feet. But he is aggravatingly neutral about everything. *Nothing* bothers him. He never takes sides, or voices an opinion. Which is all very well, but we can't all be Switzerland, or the world would be overrun by Nazis.

I'm not saying Celia Roberts is a Nazi, of course. But she could run the Gestapo with one hand tied behind her back. God knows, she's had to be strong to survive what happened to her family; not many women could go through a tragedy like that and stay on their feet. But that's no excuse to let her get away with murder. This nonsense with Andrew has to stop. It's been *four years*. It's not healthy to keep giving Lou false hope. She insists she's over Andrew, but she isn't, not even a little bit. She hasn't even dated anyone since he left her. We all know how *intense* she can get, and I fear Celia's started something with this party that won't end well.

I leave the boys to their dystopian television programme, feed the dog, and drive over to Celia and Brian's. They've lived in the same lovely old stone property on the outskirts of Steyning for nearly forty years; Lou and Luke both grew up there. Celia's very lucky her children both live so close to her – something my own mother, up in Yorkshire on her own, never tires of reminding me.

My mother-in-law is kneeling by a flowerbed in the front garden when I arrive. She puts down her trowel and stands up when she spots me. 'Min, how lovely to see you,' she exclaims, tilting her cheek for me to kiss. 'Was I expecting you?'

'I'm sure you were,' I say dryly.

'Lemonade, darling? I made it fresh this morning. We can sit on the terrace in the back garden and enjoy the sun.'

I follow her around the side of the house. Brian waves genially in my direction, but doesn't come over. He's perfected the art of fading into the background over decades, and, like his son, hasn't offered an opinion on anything in years.

Celia pours a tall glass of fresh lemonade for each of us, and we settle into a pair of wicker chairs on the veranda, for all the world as if we're in an episode of *Downton*. My eyes water as the tart lemonade hits the back of my throat, but it's delicious, especially on such a warm day.

'You've got new tomato beds,' I say, suddenly noticing the rectangle of dark, loamy earth enclosed by old railway ties at the end of the lawn. 'How wonderful. You've wanted a raised bed for ages. When did you have it put in?'

'Andrew came over last weekend and did it,' Celia says.

'*Andrew* did it?'

Celia takes a sip of lemonade. 'You needn't look so surprised. He knows how to get his hands dirty.'

That's not what I meant, and she knows it. 'Yes, but why? What was he doing here?'

'He often comes over when he's down this way. He and Brian like to go down to the White Horse for a few beers on a Sunday afternoon. He offered to sort out the flowerbed a few weeks ago, when Brian had that bout of sciatica.'

I feel a rising tide of indignation. 'Don't you think that's a bit . . . *odd*?'

'Why? He's quite handy around the house. Did the whole thing himself in two days.'

She's being deliberately obtuse. I love my mother-in-law, but sometimes she can be *extremely* infuriating. 'I honestly don't understand you, Celia!' I exclaim. 'How can you even bear to speak to that man after what he did to Lou? Anyone would think you're on his side!'

'Min, darling, it's very sweet of you to care so much about Louise,' she says firmly, 'but I'm not sure that sort of attitude is entirely helpful. Andrew is still part of this family. We didn't stop loving him just because he stopped loving Louise. He's been very kind to Brian and me. We're extremely fond of him. And he's Tolly and Bella's father.'

I can't bear it. I just *can't*. Andrew is so charming and handsome and everyone's taken in by him, even Celia, even now, after everything he's done. If she knew what he was *really* like, she wouldn't want him and Lou to get back together. She'd stab him with her gardening fork and bury him in a bloody flowerbed.

'It's not fair!' I say angrily. 'Andrew can't just dump Lou and still keep you! There should be some . . . some *shame*! Some consequences! You can't destroy someone's life and be allowed to carry on like nothing's happened!'

Celia puts down her glass and takes my hot hands

in her cool ones, and my vision suddenly blurs. She is truly like a mother to me: I've known her more than half my life, ever since I was a teenager, and have spent far more time with her than I have with my own mother, whose chilly, detached temperament is so different from – and incompatible with – my own. Outwardly, Celia may be the epitome of the composed, stiff-upper-lip Englishwoman, but I've known her long enough to understand how fiercely passionate she is about people and causes she cares about. I know she'd do anything for Luke or Lou or me; that's the trouble. She doesn't realise she's just making everything *worse*.

'Min,' Celia says, 'I appreciate your loyalty to Louise. I do. But Andrew isn't the devil incarnate. I'm not saying what he did was right—'

'Well, at least we can agree on that!'

She looks hard at me. 'Do you think, darling, perhaps you care about this a little *too* much?'

That brings me up short. I don't want Celia getting any peculiar ideas; I am married to her son, after all. 'It's this party,' I say. 'It's bad enough having to see that woman at things like Bella's play, but inviting her to such a special, *family* time like your anniversary – it's as if you're giving them your seal of approval. You do see that,' I add earnestly, 'you do *see*, don't you, Celia?'

She releases my hands, and picks up her lemonade again. 'You catch more flies with honey than vinegar, darling.'

'What do you mean?'

'I mean, you don't need to worry,' she says serenely. 'It's all in hand.'

I recognise that expression on Celia's face; I see it on those of my four sons whenever they're plotting trouble. 'Celia,' I say suspiciously, just as her phone rings. 'What, *exactly*, are you up to?'

Chapter 7

Louise

I lean on the horn and check my watch again, even though I already know how late we're running. In the back, Tolly bounces delightedly in his car seat, clapping his hands. 'Do it again, Mummy! Do it again!'

Unbuckling my seatbelt, I open the car door and lean on the window frame to shout up at the house. 'Bella! We need to go!'

'I'm coming!' Bella yells.

It's another five minutes before she finally appears. She's wearing a pair of jeans that are more holes than denim, and a long-sleeved black T-shirt I haven't seen before, emblazoned with the slogan 'Friday is my second-favourite F-word.' Her father would have a fit if he saw her, but we don't have time for her to go back and change.

'It's twenty-eight degrees,' I restrict myself to saying mildly, as she flings herself into the front seat. 'Aren't you hot?'

'No,' she snaps.

She pulls a woollen cap from her backpack, and tucks her hair under it, until the only thing showing are a few dark wisps at the front. A thick line of kohl is smudged beneath eyes smeared with heavy grey shadow. It looks as if she's slept in her make-up beneath a bridge somewhere. Wisely, I say nothing, even though it breaks my heart to see my beautiful girl doing her best to disguise her loveliness. Her best friend, Taylor, is exactly the same, the two of them dressing as androgynously and monochromatically as possible, like extras from a dystopian movie. I suppose it's better than crop-tops and micro-minis. And it's just a phase, I remind myself with an inward sigh. She'll grow out of it.

I start the car, and the engine makes its usual clunking, grating sound before reluctantly coughing into life. And then suddenly it cuts out. I try again, but the engine grinds ominously and then dies. The third time, it doesn't even turn over.

'Mum!' Bella cries. 'I can't be late!'

'We already are,' I say crossly. 'I wasn't the one who kept us all waiting for twenty minutes.'

'I'm supposed to be there at ten! It's the dress rehearsal, they can't start without me!'

I let it go, knowing how nervous she is. She was up half the night practising her lines, and this morning she vomited up her toast five minutes after eating it. She was the same when she took her GCSEs last summer. 'I know that, darling,' I say. 'It's not like I'm doing this on purpose.'

'The car's been making weird noises for ages! You should have got it fixed!'

'I don't have the money to fix it, Bella.'

59

'Dad gives you money, doesn't he?'

'None of your business, darling,' I say nicely.

'It is if our car breaks down!'

My patience frays. 'Bella, please don't talk to me like that.' I get out of the car again. 'It's not the end of the world. We'll just call the school and let them know you'll be a bit late. These things never start on time anyway. I'll call Gree and ask her to take you,' I add, reaching into the back and unbuckling Tolly from his car seat. 'She'll be here in ten minutes.'

'I'm too old to call her Gree,' Bella mutters, storming towards the house.

I have a sudden flashback to Bella's babyhood, and a smiling apple-cheeked cherub lisping Grelia – soon shortened to Gree – because Grandma Celia was too much of a mouthful. The contrast with the spiky, resentful teenager stalking ahead of me is painful. I would have treasured those sunlit childhood years more had I known how brief they were. 'Fine,' I sigh, shooing Tolly into the hall and speed-dialling my mother. 'You can take it up with your grandmother. Hi, Mum,' I add, as my mother picks up. 'I've got a bit of an emergency. Can you do me a huge favour? The car won't start and Bella needs to get to school for her dress rehearsal and we're already late. She's in a total state. I was wondering—'

'Of course,' my mother says.

Bella glares from the foot of the stairs. 'I'm not in a state!'

I shush her with my hand. 'Oh, thank you, Mum, you're a total life-saver.'

Bella stomps upstairs to her room, no doubt to text her friends details of the latest monstrous injustice done to her. I open the back door so Tolly can go outside to play, watching him affectionately through the kitchen window, the phone crooked between my neck and shoulder as I run hot water over the dirty breakfast dishes.

'I'll bring your father with me, too,' my mother says in my ear. 'He can have a look at your car while I'm running Bella to school.'

'Are you sure Dad won't mind?'

'Of course not. He's just deadheading the roses.' I hear her call his name, with muffled instructions to get ready. 'Andrew should have given you the Range Rover, and taken the Honda himself,' she adds reproachfully. 'I can't bear to think of you driving that deathtrap with the children.'

'It's not a deathtrap, Mum,' I say softly, knowing where this is going. 'It's just a bit old. If Dad can get it going again, I'm sure we can limp on for a bit longer.'

Outside, Tolly is happily kicking a football back and forth across the lawn. It doesn't bother him in the least to play on his own. He is light to Bella's dark, sunshine to her shadow. I wave at my son, my heart expanding in my chest as he grins and waves back.

'Nicky was so proud when he bought his first car,' my mother says suddenly. 'He worked all summer to save for it. He was out on the driveway every spare moment, washing and polishing and tinkering. Wouldn't let anyone else drive it, not even your dad. Everything he earned mowing lawns and picking fruit that summer, he spent on that car.'

She pauses, but I know better than to interrupt. Trying to deflect her by reminding her that I'm not Nicky, that lightning doesn't strike twice, will only upset her. And who am I to say how she should think or feel? I've never lost a child.

'You should have seen it,' Mum says, laughing. 'Honestly, it was a sight. One door brown, and the rest green, but your brother was so proud of it, you'd think it was a Ferrari. There was a pair of blue fluffy dice hanging from the mirror. Nicky wouldn't take them off – he thought it was funny.' I can hear the smile in her voice. 'Retro, he called it.'

Tolly is lying on his tummy now, poking at something in the grass, his mop of curls glinting russet and ochre in the sun. I watch him, unable even to imagine a world without him in it.

I was almost thirteen when Nicky died. My funny, warm, invincible big brother, his life snuffed out in an instant by a drunk driver. All that energy and love and potential, gone forever. He was only eighteen. He'd recently won a place at Imperial to study physics, and had just fallen in love for the first time. He was captain of the school rugby team and the cricket team and hated mushrooms and loved woodwork and knew the words to every song Sting had ever recorded. I was his annoying baby sister, I shouldn't even have been on his radar, but somehow he always had time for me.

I know when anyone dies tragically young, everyone only sees their virtues and not their faults. But Nicky was one of those people who lit up a room. There was no bad side to him, no mean-spiritedness. He saw only the best in people, and then reflected it back at them.

His death changed our family forever. Luke lost his younger brother, and his best friend. The two of them were only sixteen months apart; for Luke, it was like losing half of himself. I think a good part of the reason he married Min, his first girlfriend, when they were both only twenty-one was because he couldn't bear to be alone. I lost my protector, the person I admired most in the world. And my parents – my parents lost their child.

His funeral took place on my thirteenth birthday, but no one even realised what day it was until afterwards, including me. My childhood ended that day. I got my first period in the middle of the wake; I remember sitting in the bathroom at home, staring at the blood in my knickers, with no idea what to do. It felt like my whole body was grieving. Mum had gone through the menopause herself and hadn't thought to get any sanitary towels in for me, so I was reduced to stuffing a flannel between my legs. For years, every month I was reminded of my brother's loss in the most brutal, bloody way.

Mum became someone to whom you couldn't say no. If she wanted the shattered remnants of her family with her for Christmas, birthdays, Mother's Day – especially for Mother's Day – we came. Luke and I never had the chance to create our own holiday traditions with our own families. Nicky's loss rippled outwards, shaping all our lives, even those of children who hadn't been born when he died.

'Do you need me to pick Bella up again after rehearsal?' Mum asks.

'No, don't worry. I'll ask one of the other mothers to drop her off afterwards – I'm sure Taylor's mother won't mind. I really appreciate this, Mum.'

'It's fine, Louise. After all, it's not like I've got anything else to do.'

A silence falls that's filled with half a lifetime of grief.

'Your dad is here with the car,' my mother says, her shadowed mood passing as quickly as it came. 'We'll be right over. Poor Bella must be going frantic.'

'Thanks again, Mum.'

'And make sure you wear something nice tonight,' she adds lightly. 'Maybe that pale blue dress Andrew always liked?'

'That's a bit fancy for a school play.'

'Oh, didn't Andrew tell you? We're all going to The Coal Shed afterwards for dinner. His treat. See you in a minute, darling.'

I stare at the phone in astonishment. How the hell did she pull that one off? Caz must be spitting feathers.

Min was right, I think suddenly. My mother *is* up to something.

Chapter 8

Caz

'You agreed to *what*?'

Andy opens the fridge and grabs an energy drink, swallowing half the bottle in a single gulp. I don't comment on the nutritional unsuitability of following a life-enhancing five-mile run with a life-diminishing hit of caffeine and sugar. I'm hardly in a position to complain about the effectiveness of the advertising campaign that brainwashed him into thinking energy drinks are healthy because his mum used to give them to him when he was sick. 'Don't worry,' he says airily. 'Celia already called the restaurant. We were lucky – they'd had last-minute cancellation, so they could fit us all in. Bloody lucky, actually, on a Saturday night.'

I snap my laptop closed. 'Andy, I thought we said we were going to have a *family* celebration.'

'This *is* family.' His hair, greyer now than when we first met, stands up in sweat-soaked spikes, but thanks to a miracle of modern technology, his expensive micro-fibre shirt and shorts are bone dry. 'Luke and Min can't make it because they'll need to get the younger boys to bed, so it'll just be Celia and Brian.'

'And Louise.'

'Well, obviously Louise.'

I'm prevented from saying something I'll regret by Kit, who runs into the kitchen, brandishing an empty Frubes tube in his fist. At least a third of the contents are now smeared all over his face and Coco pyjama top. 'I'm still hungry, Mummy. Can I have another one?'

'You've already had two,' I say.

He lolls stickily against my lap, batting eyelashes that are wasted on a boy. 'Please, Mummy. One more? I'll let you work in peace?'

Andy tips his Lucozade bottle at me. 'I told you. Blackmailers always come back for more.'

In a sudden rush of affection, I pull Kit onto my lap and snuggle him close, heedless of the yoghurt damage to my silk T-shirt. My son may not have been part of my life plan, but now that he's here, I love the very bones of him. 'No more Frubes, kid. And no more blackmail. I'm done with my work.'

'I'm just going to jump in the shower,' Andy says, standing on the back of his trainers to pull them off, and leaving them, backs still stomped down, in the middle of the kitchen floor. It's one of his less endearing habits. 'Then we'd better get going, if we want to beat the traffic.'

I seethe about dinner all the way to Brighton. Slightly to my surprise, I'd actually been looking

66

forward to taking Bella out on our own. She can be a pain in the arse, and she's stroppy and prickly and self-absorbed, but there's a vulnerability about her, a loneliness that resonates with me. I'm an only child, raised by a single parent; I know what it's like to feel isolated and lonely. Bella may have more family than she probably wants, much of the time, but despite all the negative attention she deliberately provokes, no one ever really *sees* her. She's just a problem to be managed. She's not cute like Tolly and Kit, or glossy and confident like most of the other shiny-haired cheerleaders at that over-privileged, entitled private school of hers. She pushes people away, and makes herself difficult to like. In many ways, she's her own worst enemy. We have that in common, too.

For the first couple of years after Andy and I got together, Bella wouldn't give me the time of day. Jesus, she was a piece of work. I actually caught her spitting in my coffee once. She blamed me for her parents' split, and Andy was never going to tell her the truth about what Louise did. But things have changed between us in the last few months or so. Bella is like a cat. If I ignore her, and pretend I don't care one way or another if she curls up in my lap, she'll come to me, I know it.

I've never been great with small children; I love Kit with all my heart, but spending the entire day with a three-foot-high tyrant who thinks farts are funny is my idea of hell. But teenagers, I get. Their sense the world is out to get them, that no one takes them seriously, their anger and frustration and longing to stand out while desperate to fit in – oh, yeah, they're playing my song.

I jump when Andy reaches across the car and puts his hand on my thigh. 'Is something the matter?' he asks. 'You've been really quiet.'

'I'm fine,' I say shortly. 'Just tired. Work, the usual.'

Andy puts his hand back on the steering wheel. 'I couldn't say no to Celia,' he sighs. 'The woman's nearly seventy. Who knows how many of these family celebrations she's going to see?'

Celia's strong as an ox. She still goes running every morning, and has competed in the West Sussex Over-Fifties Tough Mudder 10K every spring for years, finishing in the top ten per cent every time. I've seen her forking manure onto her bloody roses like she could do it all day. She'll outlive us all.

'You know how much family means to her,' Andy adds, when I say nothing. 'And you and Louise get on pretty well, these days, don't you? Plus, it's good for the kids to see us all together.'

'They'll see us at the play.'

'It's not the same, is it? And it's been a while since you spent time with Celia and Brian. It'll be nice to see them properly again.'

My husband is an intelligent man. He is incredibly well informed; the only son of a BBC radio engineer and a librarian, he was a surprise late baby, born when his mother was forty-four and his father well into his sixties. He grew up listening to the World Service, and reading *The Times* alongside the *Beano*. In the twenty-two years he's been a reporter with INN, he's covered everything from the September 11 attacks to the civil war in Sudan, interviewing presidents, popes, countless politicians and more showbiz celebrities than you can shake a stick at. He can name the capital city, annual rainfall and GDP of every country in the world (all 195 of them, if you include the Holy See and the State of Palestine). He speaks five languages, including Arabic and Farsi, and even knows how to sign. But sometimes he can be remarkably stupid.

Celia Roberts loathes me, and in her place, frankly, I would, too. She adores Andy; as far as she's concerned, he replaced the son she lost. She didn't want to blame him or her nutcase of a daughter for the divorce; far easier to cast me as the scheming home-wrecker, and lay it all at my door.

On the few occasions we've met, she hasn't bothered to hide what she thinks of me. If she were Andy's mother, I'd have to put on my tin helmet and suck it up. But she's his ex-mother-in-law! Andy and Louise are *divorced*. There's no earthly reason why I should ever have to see her, never mind put up with being treated like shit on the sole of her shoe.

I let it go now, not wanting to row in front of Kit, but when we get to the house in Brighton, I work off my fury airing the place out and remaking all the beds. Andy slopes off to his study. I know he's calling Louise. He has that familiar, hangdog air.

I'd planned to wear a simple pair of skinny black jeans this evening, with a silvery halter top I know

Andy loves, but suddenly think better of it. I'm going to be walking into the school auditorium with a scarlet letter on my back. The other woman, the trophy wife. I know from experience what it'll be like: the cold stares, the conversations that fall silent as I walk past, then resume when I'm not quite out of earshot. Louise is a popular parent; she knows most of the other mothers, she's served on the PTA, and even got the school newspaper up and running a couple of years ago. Being hated is exhausting. I'm never going to win friends here, but there's no need to lean into my shredded reputation.

Sifting through my wardrobe, I pull out a pale pink tweed Chanel suit I bought at cost after a photoshoot we did for *Vogue* last year. It's a bit prim and Jackie O, not very me, but I knew it'd come in handy for something like this. It's ironic: until I met Andy, I never cared what anyone thought of what I wore. I dressed for me. I've inherited my mother's high breasts and good legs, and I used to like showing them off. But since we married, I've felt self-conscious about wearing anything too revealing. I don't want to look like a bimbo on Andy's arm.

My husband pulls a face when I join him in the sitting room, where he and Kit are cosied up on the sofa watching *Peter Rabbit* for the billionth time. 'That's a bit much for a school play, isn't it?'

I look down at myself. 'You don't like it?'

'It's not my favourite look,' Andy says doubtfully.

'You look weird,' Kit agrees. 'Like an old lady.'

'Exactly the image I was going for,' I say crossly. I switch off the television, ignoring Kit's howl of protest. 'Come on. We need to get going. Louise said we had to be there early if we wanted to get good seats.'

'Wait. Haven't you forgotten something?' Andy asks. He waits a beat, and then grins. 'I'm sure we can find you some pearls somewhere—'

I thwack him with a cushion. 'Don't laugh. This is all your fault.'

He fends off the pillow, and catches my hand. 'Don't let Celia get to you,' he says, suddenly serious. He pulls me onto his lap, and tightens his arms around my waist. 'Wear what you want to wear, Caz. You don't have to dress for her or anyone else.'

'Easy for you to say.'

'Since when did you give a shit what anyone thinks?'

He's right. Celia Roberts and the self-righteous Mummy Mafia are never going to like me. Why keep pushing the boulder uphill?

I run back upstairs and change into the skinny jeans and halter top and a pair of skyscraper heels. Andy's eyes light up when I come back downstairs. 'That's more like it,' he says.

'Come along then, trophy husband,' I say, picking up my bag.

The car park at Bella's school is surprisingly full when we arrive. Louise wasn't kidding, I think, as Andy circles the lot looking for a space. It's not even six-thirty, and it already looks like it'll be standing room only inside.

But as we open the door to the auditorium, we're

blocked by a sudden flow of people leaving. I catch Andy's eye, puzzled. Perhaps there was a matinee, too. I wish I'd known; I'd much rather have gone to an earlier show so Kit didn't have to eat so late.

'Excuse me,' I say, stopping a woman in a flowery dress who looks vaguely familiar. 'Was there an early show?'

'Well, it was at four, if that's what you mean.'

'Oh. I didn't realise there were two performances.'

She looks at me as if I'm mad. 'There aren't.'

'But it doesn't start till seven—'

'It *started* at four,' she says tersely, turning on her heel to rejoin the throng of chattering parents exiting the auditorium.

I swing round to Andy, not knowing what to say.

'Are you kidding me?' Andy exclaims. 'We *missed* it?'

'Louise told me it started at seven!'

'You must have made a mistake. Jesus, Caz. Didn't you write it down?'

'I did *not* make a mistake! She told me the wrong time on purpose!'

Kit tugs my hand. 'Is it finished? Can we go to dinner now?'

'Of course she didn't tell you the wrong time on purpose,' Andy snaps. 'She's not a bloody bunny boiler. You obviously got it wrong.'

He sounds like he's giving me the benefit of the doubt, but I can tell from his expression he doesn't believe I made an honest mistake. He thinks I deliberately sabotaged Bella's evening.

Just as Louise intended.

Chapter 9

Louise

'They're cutting it a bit fine,' I mutter, craning my neck to look behind me. 'It's almost four. The play will be starting in a minute.'

'Andrew will be here,' my mother says confidently.

'Well, they'll be standing at the back, then. The place is packed.'

Mum puts her hand on Tolly's shoulder as he kneels up on his chair between us. 'Stop fidgeting, Tolly. We should have saved them some seats, Louise. There were three right next to us.'

Min leans around me to address my mother. 'No, Celia, we absolutely should *not* have saved them seats. It's bad enough Lou's going to have to sit with that woman at dinner. I'm so sorry we can't come,' she adds to me, leaning back again. 'I don't mind leaving Dom and Jack to babysit their brothers for a couple of hours now they're fifteen, but not for the whole evening. They'll kill each other or burn the place down.'

'It's fine,' I whisper.

'It's *not* fine,' Min hisses back. 'Honestly, Lou, you can't keep letting her do this to you.'

I wish Min had known my mother before Nicky's death. It wasn't just that Mum was happy, although of course she was, in the way you don't appreciate until it's in the rear-view mirror. When your children are healthy and safe, when your marriage is good and you have a roof over your head and food on the table, it allows you to be unhappy about a set of holiday photos that come back from Boots all blurry, or the chip in your brand-new kitchen counter. Mum worried about Nicky and Luke and me, of course, in the way every mother fears for their children; she warned us to wear our bicycle helmets and never to accept sweets from strangers, and insisted we call her if we were going to be late home. But her style of parenting was one of benign neglect, the same way she'd been raised. She let us have the freedom to make our own mistakes, to climb trees and break wrists, to refuse sunscreen and get burned.

Nicky's death changed who she was. She didn't wrap us in cotton wool, although that would've been a perfectly natural response. Instead she gathered us close, *closer*; she inserted herself into every aspect of our lives in a way she never had before, as protective and fiercely territorial as a tigress.

When Luke was turned down for a place studying physics at Imperial College, his first choice, without even being given an interview, Mum drove to London the next day and barged into the admissions office with his school reports in her hand, haranguing them until they agreed to see him. He was horribly embarrassed, but Mum didn't care. Embarrassment was no longer part of her vocabulary, or her experience. She cared only about getting us what she felt we deserved, advocating for us when we couldn't or wouldn't advocate for ourselves.

It's why she refuses, even now, to accept Andrew is a lost cause. She'll fight our battles for us, whether we want her to or not. She's seen too much, been through too much; all that's left for her is to make things right for her family. I can't take that away from her.

Dad grieved differently. Before Nicky's death, he and Mum parented us jointly, but afterwards, he ceded everything to Mum. I glance across at him as he fiddles with his old-fashioned camera. He still uses the same one he did for our school plays, and I wince as he tests the flash, which leaves a Hiroshima-like glow imprinted on the retinas of anyone within a ten-foot radius. On the other side of him, Luke holds up his new iPhone and hits record, checking for light levels. Peas in a pod, give or take a bit of technology. They survived Nicky's loss as I did, by fading into the background, and leaving Mum alone in the spotlight of her grief.

The lights dim, and there's a sudden hush, the rustle of programmes, and a few self-conscious coughs. The headmistress, Mrs St George, comes on stage and makes the usual remarks about how hard everyone has worked and what troupers the PTA have been, but I'm not really concentrating. Bella will be devastated if her father doesn't come. As the headmistress asks everyone to turn off their phones and people grope in their bags, I take the opportunity for one more look around the audience, trying to find him. If he's here, he must be right at the back.

Then the curtain lifts, and Antonio walks onto the stage with his Shakespearean bros. I send up a prayer that Bella doesn't get stage fright or forget her lines, and I wait anxiously for her opening scene. After all the drama getting her to her dress rehearsal this morning, her nerves are frayed to breaking point. She dropped her eyeliner when she was putting on her make-up this afternoon, and burst into tears.

But as soon as she comes out and launches confidently into her first monologue, I know she's going to be fine. I've rehearsed her lines with her so often, I can recite them backwards, and find myself murmuring along with her: '... so is the will of a living daughter curbed by the will of a dead father.'

My mother jabs me in the ribs, and I shut up.

Two and a half hours later, I have tears in my eyes as I leap to my feet along with the rest of the audience to deliver a standing ovation, clapping and cheering until my palms tingle and my throat is raw. For the duration of the play, I completely forgot that Portia was my daughter. She is beautiful, gracious, intelligent, quick-witted: Shakespeare's most appealing heroine. It's only a school play, and there were forgotten lines and fluffed cues and wooden acting – Antonio showed less range of emotion than a table leg – but Bella was an absolute revelation, and if I say that as her mother, it's only because she was so completely *other*. I have never seen her sparkle and dazzle the way she just has up on stage. The sullen, withdrawn child I live with was nowhere to be seen. In her place was a confident, brilliant woman: a drama queen, indeed. I feel as if I'm seeing my daughter for the first time.

'Wasn't she amazing?' Min cries, as we join the madding crowd heading towards the exits.

'Wonderful,' I say, straining to find Andrew. He can't have missed this. Bella was extraordinary. 'Can you see Andrew anywhere?'

'There!' Tolly cries, pulling away from me. 'Daddy!'

I struggle to hang on to my son as he forces his way through the throng, apologising profusely as I jostle shoulders and step on toes. 'Tolly, wait!'

I still can't see Andrew, though Tolly obviously has him in his sights. As we reach the double doors to the entrance vestibule, the cast comes running through the side corridor that leads backstage, still in costume, shrieking and laughing as they reunite with proud parents in the auditorium. Bella races towards us, hand in hand with her friend, Taylor, a smile splitting her face from ear to ear. She scoops Tolly up in one swift movement, swinging him around, bubbling with triumph. 'Did you see me?' she cries. 'Did you see me?'

'We could hardly miss you.' I smile. 'You were brilliant, darling. Absolutely amazing. I told you that you would be. You too, Taylor. I loved your Bassanio. You were brilliant.'

'Thank you, Mrs Page,' Taylor says. 'Oh, there's Mum! Catch you later, Bel.'

Bella can't hide her elation, and I love her for it. 'I messed up on my speech at the beginning of Act II Scene 1 but I don't think anyone noticed.'

'I can't believe it was you up there,' I say honestly. 'You were incredible, Bella. You blew us all away. It'll be the Oscars next.'

'Where's Dad?' she asks, looking past me as Celia, Min and Luke force their way through the crowd and catch up to us.

'I see him!' Tolly shouts, pointing.

Andrew and Caz are standing in the entrance hall, talking to Taylor's mother. They must have been standing right at the back for the whole performance. That can't have been comfortable in the ridiculous stilettos Caz is wearing. She looks like she's dressed for a nightclub, not a school play.

My heart swoops as Andrew turns. For a split second, I'm twenty-four again, walking into the wine bar opposite the INN TV studio, and coming face to face with the most beautiful man I'd ever encountered. Now, as then, it's as if the crowds around us fade away, and there are just two of us in the room. When we met, Andrew was in his early thirties, tall and dark-haired and dressed more formally than most men his age in a grey suit – I soon learned he was a reporter, and this was his on-camera attire – his tie pulled loose around his neck, his jacket hooked casually over his shoulder on one finger. He'd glanced around as I'd let the heavy door swing shut behind me, and I'd seen appreciation and interest in his leonine amber eyes, and his mouth had quirked into a smile. The blood had pulsed in my ears and I'd felt the fizz of butterflies in my stomach. I feel them still. I think I will until the day I die.

Andrew puts his palm on the small of Caz's back, and murmurs something in her ear, and the pain I'd thought I'd tamed flares as sharp and stinging as the day Andrew left me.

Bella puts her brother down, and Tolly barrels through a forest of legs towards his father. 'You're late!' he cries. 'You missed it *all*!'

There's a sudden silence. I glance at Andrew, assuming he'll say they were just out of sight, at the back, but he shrugs helplessly. 'We got the time wrong. I'm so sorry,' he adds, as Bella's face crumples beneath her stage make-up. 'I've been listening to people talking about how wonderful you were. The star of the show—'

She doesn't wait for him to finish. With a terrible sob, she turns and runs back into the auditorium.

Andrew starts after her, but Min blocks his way. 'I think you've done enough damage,' she says coldly.

'How could you get the time wrong, Andrew?' I cry furiously. 'I told Caz it started at four at least three times!'

'You said seven,' Caz protests.

'Don't be ridiculous,' Mum snaps. 'School plays are always in the afternoon, so siblings can come and watch without having to stay up late. You came last year, Caroline. You should know that.'

Andrew glares at his wife. 'Caz obviously made a mistake. I'll go and find Bella and apologise. I'm sure she'll understand.'

'I did *not* make a mistake,' Caz says firmly. 'I thought it was a bit odd, but Louise insisted it was in the evening this year. That's why I told you to book the table for nine-thirty.'

Andrew hesitates, and I see the sudden doubt in his eyes. Surely he can't think I'd be that petty and underhand?

But I know the answer to that one. I've cried wolf before, and now, when the wolf is at my door – in the heart of my family – no one believes me.

Chapter 10

Caz

I sit at the end of the table, playing with my salad. I should feel vindicated, but even though Louise was the one in the wrong, not me, somehow I still feel like the villain.

Andy spent forty minutes calming Bella down and persuading her to come out to dinner, but he didn't once apologise to me. Instead, in the car on the way over to the restaurant, he said Louise and I needed to 'communicate better' next time, and then refused to discuss it any further. Even after I've given him cast-iron proof she's trying to sabotage me, he still makes excuses for her.

I don't know why I expected anything else. For the last four years, Louise has had Andy twisted around her little finger. All she has to do is snap her fingers, and he comes running.

It's not just his ex-wife I have to share him with, either. He's been part of the Roberts family for seventeen years, and divorce hasn't changed that. Even when it's not our weekend for the kids, Andy's often over at their place, fixing wonky shelves in the living room or taking Brian out for a pint. He spent a whole weekend a few weeks ago putting in a new tomato bed, for God's sake. But if I object, I look like an unreasonable, jealous cow.

I know the bonds of relationships are complicated, even when two people are no longer sharing a life together. I understand when there are children in the picture, both parents need to be involved in their lives, and I've never had a problem with that. But just because I'm Andy's second wife, that doesn't mean I should always be in second place.

There's a sudden kerfuffle on the other side of the restaurant, and I glance up. The woman in the flowery dress from Bella's school has just entered with her daughter, Taylor, and the rest of her extended family, and they're all waving madly at Louise. My heart sinks. Great. Louise's travelling fan club. Just what I need.

Flowery Dress rushes over to our table, and Louise and Andy leap up for hugs and mutual congratulations. They both put a proud arm around Bella, and I sit there, completely ignored, as everyone takes photos of the three of them on their phones. Then Andrew drapes his arm around Bella and Taylor, who's clearly a bit starstruck by him, and the nonsense starts again. The husband of Flowery Dress raves about Bella's perform- ance, talking stage school and Oscars, and they all bask in a love-fest from which I'm pointedly excluded. I might as well not be here.

The only person less comfortable than me is Bella

herself. She ducks her head, tucking her hands into the long sleeves of her black top, looking like she wishes the ground could swallow her up. Being able to hide behind another persona on stage is very different from standing in the spotlight in real life. You'd think Louise and Andy would have figured that out.

I push back my chair and go over to rescue her. 'Bella, why don't you and Taylor take the boys outside for five minutes for a bit of fresh air?' I suggest.

She doesn't need to be asked twice. As they all hurtle out, I stand by the table like a fool, waiting for someone to acknowledge me.

'Rebecca, Hugo, I don't believe you've met Caroline,' Celia finally says, with a poisonous smile. 'Andrew's *second* wife.'

My husband is not Mormon or Muslim. He does not belong to a religious group where polygamy is practised. Andy was divorced, and a single man, when we tied the proverbial knot. I am his *wife*, plain and simple, no qualifying descriptor necessary.

Rebecca gives me a cold smile, but it doesn't reach her eyes, and I see her tug her husband's sleeve as he goes to shake my hand, his arm falling obediently back to his side.

When everyone finally disperses, I take my seat at the table again. Bella brings the boys back in, and I have Kit on one side of me, and Tolly on the other; Celia ensured I wasn't seated next to an adult, so I have no one to talk to all evening. When Brian leans across his grandson and tentatively offers an opinion on the likelihood of rain, Celia cuts across him, and he doesn't try again.

I'm not normally given to self-pity, and certainly didn't expect to be the centre of attention on Bella's night, but this meal is costing us – costing *me*, since Louise already swallows up all Andy's disposable income – a fortune, and they're all treating me like something the cat dragged in.

And then, miraculously, the night is unexpectedly redeemed.

As we leave, Bella hangs back from her parents and offers an awkward thank you, her dark hair falling across her face. 'I know Mum can be a bit . . . you know,' she adds, fiddling awkwardly with the strap of her watch. She's the only sixteen-year-old I know who wears an old-fashioned timepiece. 'I'm sure she didn't mean to give you the wrong time for the play.'

The whole miserable fiasco of an evening was worth it, just for this. 'I'm sure she didn't either,' I lie. 'It was just a mix-up, that's all.'

Bella shrugs. 'I guess.'

'Come on, Bella,' Louise calls sharply. 'Time to go. Your brother needs to get to bed.'

I'm taken aback: this is *our* weekend with the kids. I turn to Andy. 'Aren't Bella and Tolly coming home with us?'

He can't quite meet my eye. 'Louise thought they should go home with her, as Bella was so upset we missed the play,' he says. 'We'll have them next weekend instead.'

84

'But I booked the Escape Room for tomorrow morning,' I object. 'It's all paid for. It's too late to change it now.'

'I'm so sorry, but that's not going to work for us. Perhaps if Bella hadn't had such a *trying* evening,' Louise says acidly.

I'm literally too angry to speak. I storm out to our car, not bothering to wait for Andy and Kit. Andy has had a couple of glasses of wine, which means I'm driving, and I stare rigidly through the windscreen, watching him kiss his ex-wife and her family goodnight, Kit asleep in his arms. It's not just the waste of money that makes me so furious. I'm beyond fed up with the way Andy lets that woman dictate our lives. Why can't he *ever* stand up to her?

'You were a bit ungracious tonight,' Andy says, as he buckles Kit into his car seat and gets in.

'*Me*?'

'Sssh. You'll wake Kit.'

'How was *I* ungracious?' I demand, in a furious whisper.

'You barely spoke to anyone all night. And when Becky and Hugo Conway came over to congratulate Bella, you interrupted them.' He reaches for his seat-belt. 'I know you and Bella don't really get on, but it was *her* night. You could have made a bit more of an effort.'

I'm so incensed, I almost reverse into a lamp-post. 'We just spent nearly seven hundred pounds on a dinner where the only two people to talk to me all evening were four years old!' I retort. 'And I interrupted the Conways because you were all making Bella incredibly uncomfortable. She hates being the centre of attention—'

'Don't be ridiculous. Everyone said how brilliant she was!'

'*Onstage*, yes. Onstage, she gets to hide behind the character she's playing. And it's not true I don't get on with her. She was the only person who even bothered to thank me for dinner.'

'Shame we couldn't make it on time to her play, then,' Andy mutters.

'If you think I'm going to Celia's damn party after—'

'*I'm* going,' Andy snaps. 'You do what you like.'

We drive the rest of the way home in silence. Angie warned me years ago, when Andy and I first got engaged, that I wouldn't just be marrying him, but I didn't take her seriously. I knew I'd have to take on his kids, of course, but it never occurred to me I'd have to deal with his ex-wife's entire family.

No one ever chooses to fall in love with a married man. Five years ago, when Andy ran a red light and hit the side of my Fiat Uno, I didn't clock the wedding ring on his left hand as we exchanged insurance details and think, *Yes, this will be a nice challenge.* Of course I fancied him; he was crazy good-looking, I'd have been blind not to. But I'd never been one of those women who felt empowered by being a mistress, naively imagining themselves as a figure charged with some magical, carnal power, superior to the dull, wifely creature who did the supermarket shop and the school run.

But I knew, too, that when he called the next day and asked me out for a drink to 'apologise for the inconvenience', the invitation was far from innocent.

His marriage was already over, but I didn't know that then, and I went anyway. And by the time I left the bar in Covent Garden, I was already halfway to being in love with him. I'd heard the expression 'walking on air' before, but that night I understood for the first time what it meant. I felt as if I was floating seven inches above the ground, weightless with joy. I had no idea then what I was letting myself in for.

Second wife. Second best. Second fiddle.

My pregnancy with Kit wasn't special, even though Andy did his best to seem excited, because he'd done it all before. Our wedding was a lovely, classy, elegant affair at Kensington and Chelsea Register Office, but it wasn't the big white church wedding I'd dreamed of as a little girl, because Louise had already had that. We've never been to Venice, or South Africa, or to see the Northern Lights, because he's been to those places with her. He was unfaithful to me: he broke all our promises to each other when he and Louise slept together again, but because I was the mistress, because he was Louise's before he was mine, I accepted it and took him back.

I wasn't the reason for their break-up, but somehow I've always felt it was my fault. So I've put up with the litany of seconds instead of firsts; the guilt and the compromises, the snide remarks, and the open hostility. I've sucked it up and plastered on a smile, accepting it all as the price of loving him. I always believed that, if I gave it time, Louise would move on with her life, and Andy would be wholly, unquestionably mine.

But what I failed to understand until this moment is that it's not just Louise who's mired in the past. *Andy* is the one who can't let go.

I pull into the driveway outside our house, watching my husband as he gets out of the car, and for the first time since that night in Covent Garden, instead of floating on air, I find my feet planted firmly on the ground.

WILHEMINA JANE POLLOCK
PART 2 OF RECORDED INTERVIEW

Date:- 25/07/2020
Duration:- 34 Minutes
Location:- Kingsbridge Police Station

**Conducted by Officers from Devon &
Cornwall Police**

(cont.)

*Normal introductions were carried out. Continuation
of Interview.*

POLICE   Sorry about the interruption, Dr Pollock. Did
          someone get you some tea?

WP   Please, call me Min. I'm fine, thanks. Look, is

	this going to take much longer? I've left my four boys with my husband and I really need to get back.
POLICE	I'll try to make it quick. We've been a bit short-staffed here. I won't keep you any longer than I have—
	[Phone rings]
WP	Shit, sorry. My husband. I thought I had it on silent.
POLICE	Do you need to take that?
WP	No, it's OK.
POLICE	Dr Pollock – Min – we were talking about your sister-in-law's relationship with Mr Page. Was their divorce amicable, would you say?
WP	Of course not. [Pause.] Sorry, I didn't mean to snap. But if people can sort things out amicably, they don't get divorced, do they?
POLICE	So they didn't get on well?
WP	No, no, they get on fine now. Shit. I mean, they *got* on fine. [Pause.] Sorry. I still can't quite believe Andrew's dead. I wasn't his greatest fan, but he didn't deserve this.

POLICE   Do you need to take a moment?

WP   No, I'm OK.

POLICE   So, would it be fair to say things were difficult
         in the immediate aftermath of the divorce, but
         that Mr and Mrs Page got on well now?

WP   Too well.

POLICE   In what sense?

WP   [Pause.] Doesn't matter.

POLICE   Dr Pollock, we are investigating a murder.
         Everything matters.

WP   Just . . . [Pause.] Oh, you know. Andrew had
         Lou twisted round his little finger. I kept telling
         her she had to move on with her life, but . . .

         [Pause.]

POLICE   Your sister-in-law still had feelings for him?

WP   She'd have taken him back in a heartbeat.

POLICE   Was that a possibility, do you know? That they'd
         get back together?

WP	I don't know. But he was certainly sending mixed signals.
POLICE	What do you mean?
WP	Look, he was just . . . I don't know. It was hard on her, that's all. [Pause.] She takes things to heart. Especially after what happened at Oxford with her tutor— Well, you know about that.
POLICE	Did Mrs Page believe there might be a reconciliation between her and Mr Page?
WP	We all knew the divorce was a huge mistake. Andrew said as much.
POLICE	He told you that?
WP	Not in so many words. But he said he wished he could go back and do things differently.
POLICE	And you took it to mean he regretted his divorce?
WP	It was obvious what he meant.
POLICE	Did he say anything else?
WP	Only that he was going to sort the whole bloody mess out this weekend.

POLICE   What mess?

WP   No idea. That's just what he said. "Whole bloody
         mess." His words.

POLICE   What do you think he meant?

WP   I told you, I don't know.

POLICE   When did you have this conversation with Mr
         Page?

WP   Just after he got back from the beach last night.
         [Pause.] God. That was the last time I talked to
         him.

POLICE   How did he seem to you?

WP   I don't know. A bit upset. I suppose you heard
         what happened at dinner?

POLICE   Can I hear it from you, Dr Pollock?

WP   It was fine, at first. Louise was in a good mood,
         though how she doesn't strangle Caz— Sorry.
         Figure of speech. Anyway, right at the end of
         dinner, Caz said something stupid and upset
         everyone, and Lou walked out. Andrew went
         after her, and they had this huge row down on
         the beach. We all heard them.

POLICE   Mrs Page didn't mention that.

WP   Well, it probably wasn't anything serious. I don't want to make too much of it. I saw Andrew after, and he said they'd sorted everything out.

POLICE   Do you know what the row was about?

WP   No. [Pause.] To be honest, after everything that's gone on these last few weeks, I'm surprised it took this long for someone to end up dead.

Five weeks before the party

Chapter 11

Louise

Chris is already waiting for me at a beachfront table when I get to the Venezia, pecking away at her iPad. A large glass of white wine is sweating on the table in front of her. She pushes her oversized sunglasses on top of her head as I thread my way towards her, waving aside my apologies. 'Glad you were late, darling,' she says cheerfully, as I bend and kiss her cheek. 'Gave me time to finish my emails. And this is my second glass, if you're planning to catch up.'

'Not unless you want me arrested on the drive home.'

'Get an Uber. What's the point of having a weekend off from the kids if you don't take advantage of it?'

I sit down and stretch out my legs, tilting my face into the sunshine. The Venezia really is one of the nicest restaurants in Brighton, perfectly situated above the beach with its romantic views across the water. I should come here more often.

I should do a lot of things more often.

A waiter brings me a glass of iced water, and we order: West Country mussels in white wine sauce for me, and black truffle ravioli for Chris, who is, irritatingly, still the same svelte size six she was when we were at school together. I know she takes no pleasure in it; her daughter, Alyssa, who's in Bella's class, inherited her father's big bones and tips the scales at thirteen stone, and takes her mother's supermodel figure as a personal insult.

'So, I hear there was quite a post-performance show after the play,' Chris says, as the waiter puts a basket of bread on the table between us. 'I'm sorry I didn't hang around now.'

I reach for a granary roll. 'Bella's hardly spoken to me all week. As if it was *my* fault her father turned up three hours late.'

I'm hurt more than I care to admit by Bella's cold shoulder. I realise having your children hate you is part of the maternal job description, but until just a few months ago, Bella and I were always so close. These days, I'm lucky if she gives me the time of day. I don't know why she started pulling away from me, but it's coincided with a thawing in her relationship with Caz. Somehow, that woman is poisoning my own daughter against me.

The only good thing to come out of the miserable evening is that, for a few short hours at dinner, Andrew and I were able to take pride in our daughter together.

It's one of the things no one ever tells you about divorce. The lack of money, the custody disputes, the pain of seeing your husband with another woman; those you expect. But there are so many other small, bitter losses, too. Bella was such a wanted child; a manifestation of love who could walk around, make jokes, do cartwheels and go to university. The joy of our shared parenthood was something I took for granted, until it was snatched away from me. Of course we're both still proud of Bella, of course we still love her, but it's something we have to do separately now. I know Andrew hates that as much as I do.

Chris forks up a mouthful of ravioli. 'Are you around next week?' she asks. 'I've got tickets to Wimbledon. I was going to take Alyssa since Jeff's working, but she thinks I'm trying to make a point about exercise again.'

'I wish I could. But I'm trying to pick up some free-lance work over the summer. I can't afford to take time off.'

'I thought summers off were one of the perks of teaching?'

'I'm on contract. I don't get anything in the summer unless I pick up some extra tutoring, which is almost impossible in my subject.' I sigh. 'I know I should've set something aside to tide us over, but there just hasn't been a penny to spare.'

'Can't you go back to the *Post*? Surely they'll use you, with your track record.'

'It's not that easy. Most of my contacts have moved on. The *Post* has got rid of a lot of their permanent positions, and replaced them with freelancers.' I drop a mussel shell into the bowl by the side of my plate, and lick my fingers. 'It would be different if I was living in London, but it's a bit out of sight, out of mind. I've been pitching ideas, but it's hard to get commissions when you're not right there and the editors don't know you. I've been out of the game since Tolly was born. Four years is a long time in this business.'

'So what are you going to do?' Chris asks.

'I should be able to pick up some work here and there, enough to keep the wolf from the door. Some of the magazines will use me as holiday cover. And one of the mothers on the PTA has offered me some PR work for the school.'

'You hate PR!'

'Yeah, well. Beggars can't be choosers. There's more money in PR than journalism these days.'

'Can you just switch like that?'

'I've done it before. It's pretty much the same sort of work. You just ditch the impartiality in favour of whatever brand you're promoting.'

'Let me put out some feelers, then,' Chris says thoughtfully. 'Maybe I can put something your way.'

She insists on paying the bill when it comes, and even though it's humiliating, I let her. We've been friends for thirty years, during which time our financial fortunes have fluctuated wildly. Our friendship is about much more than money. But I still hate not being able to pay my way. I'm forty-three, and I've been working for more than two decades. I should be able to pay for my own lunch.

Two fat raindrops land on the credit card slip as Chris hands it to the waiter. We glance upwards just as the sun abruptly disappears behind a large bank of ominous grey clouds.

'Wimbledon week,' Chris sighs. 'Better get moving. The heavens are going to open any minute.'

Even as she says the words, a smattering of raindrops bounce off the esplanade, and then, in seconds, it really starts to come down. We give each other a quick hug, and Chris leaps into her Uber and I race down the street to my car, holding my straw bag over my head as an umbrella. It's as effective as it sounds, and by the time I leap into the front seat, I'm drenched.

I put my ruined bag on the passenger seat and shake out the wet folds of my dress, wincing as I catch sight of myself in the rear-view mirror. My mascara has run, and my hair is plastered unflatteringly against my skull. Not that it matters; there will be no one to see me when I get home except Bagpuss.

The rest of the weekend stretches yawningly in front of me, a void of hours I will struggle to fill. This is something else no one ever tells you about divorce: the sheer loneliness. Before I had children, I relished my own company, and often spent an entire weekend happily alone, reading a good book or researching a story. But I have adjusted the contours of my life to fit Bella and Tolly, and now their absence is a physical ache.

I join the Saturday afternoon traffic on the way into town. Bella texted to ask me to drop off her laptop at her father's house this morning; Taylor is coming over to work on a school project, and she'd left her computer at home.

Even on the fastest speed, my windscreen wipers

struggle to keep up with the teeming rain, and I peer up at the lowering clouds as I pause at an intersection, chewing my lip anxiously. My kitchen roof started leaking last winter, and although my brother did a temporary patch job to see me through until I could afford to get it fixed properly, a downpour like this is seriously going to put it to the test. I should have had it repaired in the spring, but all the estimates ran into several thousand pounds. Money I simply don't have.

Finally, there's a gap in the traffic. I lift my foot off the brake, and with depressing predictability, the engine cuts out. With a sigh, I turn off the ignition and try again. Nothing.

A car beeps behind me, and I put on my hazards, trying again to turn the engine over. Absolutely nothing happens. I'm blocking traffic; I'll have to call a garage out. God knows how much that's going to cost.

The SUV behind me sits on its horn again, and I fling open my car door and leap furiously into the pelting rain. 'Look, I've broken down!' I yell. 'Go round me, can't you!'

The driver of the SUV gets out of his car, too. 'Need a hand?'

'Andrew!'

He waves at the traffic to go past us and opens the bonnet. 'Let me see if I can get it going again.'

But even Andrew's magic touch fails to revive it this time. He closes the bonnet, wiping the rain from his eyes. 'I want you to steer it over there,' he says, pointing to a shallow forecourt to the side of the road. 'I'll push.'

Fortunately, the Honda is light. It doesn't take much effort to push it out of the way of the flow of traffic.

'Thank you,' I say, as I get out and lock the car. 'I'll have to see if I can get someone to come out and tow it. Let me give you Bella's computer, before I forget. You couldn't drop me at the bus stop, could you?'

'Don't be ridiculous. You're soaking wet. Come back to mine and get dried off.'

I hesitate. I've dropped the children off at Andrew and Caz's house in Brighton many times, but never been inside, and nor do I want to. But I'm soaked to the bone, and I can't think of a reasonable excuse not to take Andrew up on his offer.

'Come on,' Andrew urges. 'I've got a mate, Tom, he runs a garage not far from here. I'll call him and get him to tow it and see what he can do. He won't charge you. He owes me a favour.'

'If you're sure,' I say.

''Course I'm sure,' Andrew says.

Chapter 12

Caz

I leave the florist with a spring in my step and an armful of Casablanca lilies, popping my umbrella open as I dart through the rain to my car. The flowers were a bit extravagant, I know, but I couldn't resist them when I saw them on my way home from the off-licence.

It's been a really good weekend. We took all three kids to the latest Pixar movie last night, and then out for pizza, and Bella dropped the emo act and teased her brothers like a normal teenager. She got up at a reasonable hour this morning, too, and even offered to come with me to the Saturday farmers' market without being prompted by her father. She wasn't particularly chatty, but then she never is. I like the fact that she only talks when she has something to say. And when the woman weighing the tomatoes casually referred to her as my daughter, Bella didn't correct her. I *knew* I was getting somewhere with her. It's just a question of being patient.

Shifting the bouquet to my left arm, I unlock my Audi, and settle the flowers carefully into the well of the passenger seat. Andy should be back with the fish and chips by the time I get home, and I'm looking forward to a family night in, though I slightly wish Bella hadn't asked Taylor over. The girl's really got a crush on Andy, though I seem to be the only person who can see it.

'I'm home!' I sing out, as I let myself into the kitchen. 'Where is everyone?'

'In here,' Andy calls from the sitting room.

I put the lilies in the sink, and root around beneath it for a vase. 'Did they have any haddock left, or did you get cod?'

He doesn't reply, and I wander into the sitting room, the vase in my hand. Sitting on my sofa, next to my husband, and making herself thoroughly at home, is Louise.

'Louise's car broke down on her way over to drop off Bella's computer,' Andy says, looking slightly sheepish. 'I happened to be right behind her when it conked out. The engine wouldn't even turn over. Tom's towed it to his garage. Poor Louise was soaked to the skin, so I brought her home to dry off.'

'How very lucky for her,' I say, through gritted teeth.

'Wasn't it?' Louise says.

I don't believe for one second this is a coincidence. She probably sat in a side street for hours, waiting for Andy to go out, before staging her little "breakdown". I want to slap her stupid, smug face.

'You might as well stay to dinner,' Andy says to her. His arm is casually resting on the back of the sofa, and she smiles up at me from within the safe circle of his loose embrace. 'I bought more than enough fish and chips to go round. The boys never finish theirs, anyway.'

'Andy,' I say tightly. 'Could I have a word?'

I stalk into the kitchen, my body quivering with rage. How can he not see what she's doing? She hijacked last weekend, and now here she is again, inserting herself into the middle of our family time.

Andy shuts the kitchen door behind him. 'Look, I know it's not ideal, but what else could I do?'

'Oh, I don't know. Let her call the AA, like a normal person?'

'Caz, I'm not going to leave my children's mother stranded in the pouring rain by the side of the road,' he says tersely. 'We live two minutes away. We'll have a bite to eat, and she'll be off. Come on, where's the harm?'

If I create a scene, I'll just be playing into Louise's hands. I made that mistake last week, and she came out smelling of roses, while I ended up reeking of something altogether less fragrant.

'Fine,' I say. 'We can have the fish and chips while Tom looks at her car, and if he can't fix it today, we can call her an Uber.'

'Actually, I've already said she can have the Range Rover.'

'Andy! I'll need it next week to pick up the dresser for Kit's room. How long have you lent it to her for?'

He looks uncomfortable. 'The Honda's on its last legs.

What if she'd broken down with Bella and Tolly in the car?' His voice takes on a defensive note. 'We have the Audi. We leave the Range Rover sitting here for weeks at a time, and even when we're here, we hardly use it. We're in walking distance of the station, and it's impossible to park the damn thing anyway. It'll be a lot less hassle without it.'

It's not about the cars. It's the way Andy allows himself to be manipulated by Celia and Louise that drives me crazy. When it comes to the Roberts women, he has all the spine of a jellyfish.

'You've *given* her the car?' I say, unable to hide my anger. 'You don't think you should have run something like this past me first? This affects both of us! It should have been a joint decision.'

'The Range Rover was our car before you and I even met,' Andy says, a little truculently. 'I think it's up to me if I give it to Louise or not.'

'And the Audi was mine. That doesn't mean I'd donate it to the RSPCA without talking to you.'

We glare at each other. The battle over Louise has ebbed and flowed over the same domestic territory for years now. Periodically, we call a truce, and we'll have a few months of peace and quiet; and then Louise will drop a grenade between us, demanding money for Bella's braces or changing the summer holiday schedules when we've already paid for flights, and we're right back to square one.

The kitchen door opens. 'I'm sorry to interrupt,' Louise says, looking anything but.

'You're not interrupting anything,' Andy says. 'We were just about to put the fish and chips on plates. Caz, can you find the vinegar and Worcestershire?'

'I'm sorry, but I can't stay for dinner after all,' Louise says. 'I just had a really unpleasant text from Gavin, the farmer who owns the field opposite me. He says my kitchen porch is collapsing because of the rain. I can't let that happen – he's looking for any excuse to get the house condemned.'

'*Condemned*?' Andy exclaims. 'What on earth for?'

'He wants me to sell the bottom paddock to some developers so they can get access to his land to build a new estate. I've refused, and he's not happy about it. Look, I'd better go. You know how rickety that porch is – some of the beams are rotted right through. I need to get back and see what's happening.'

'I'll come with you,' Andy says.

'Oh, there's no need—'

Andy shoves the warm plastic bag full of fish and chips into my hands. 'Don't be ridiculous, Louise. I'm not leaving you to sort this out on your own, especially if you've got a vindictive farmer on the warpath. At the very least, we need to get a tarp over the porch until we can get someone out to fix it. Caz can look after the kids for an hour or two.'

'What about dinner?' I protest, as I follow them into the hall.

He looks at me like I'm feeble-minded. 'I'll have mine later.'

Bella and Taylor are already waiting by the front

door, their hair caught up under matching black beanies, rucksacks hitched over their narrow shoulders.

'You're leaving too?' I exclaim. 'What about your fish and chips?'

'I'm not hungry,' Bella says.

Tolly comes running down the stairs. 'Wait for me!'

Louise ruffles her son's hair. 'You want to come back with Mum, darling? We can snuggle up on the sofa together and watch *Coco* – d'you fancy that? Or would you rather stay here with Caz? I'm sure she'll find something for you to do.'

Tolly leans into his mother's legs. He's four years old; it's no contest. 'I want to be with you, Mummy.'

'Bella, I thought you wanted to come with me to that cool antique market tomorrow morning,' I say, trying to keep the note of pleading from my voice. 'They do some great steampunk jewellery. You'll love it.'

She shrugs, twisting her thumb ring round and round with her fingers. I don't know what Louise said to her when we were out of the room, but it was clearly enough to send her back into her shell again.

Andy opens the car door for Louise with a casual familiarity that twists the knife in my heart. 'I'll text you, Caz, let you know what's happening. I'll be back in an hour; two, tops.'

I watch Louise get into *my* car with *my* husband, feeling like I've been mugged. How does the woman do it?

He still hasn't texted three hours later, when I finally

tuck Kit into bed. I throw the uneaten fish and chips in the bin, hating the feeling of insecurity that gives me sick butterflies in my stomach. I know my feelings around Louise aren't rational, but I also know how torn Andy was, shuttling back and forth between the two of us for a year before he finally left her. We're married now, we have a son of our own, but how can I be *sure* he won't go back to her again?

I wait till ten, determined not to look needy and jealous, but finally I can't stand it anymore and text him. When he doesn't respond after twenty minutes, I text again, and then finally, at eleven o'clock, I give in and call him.

He doesn't pick up.

Chapter 13

Louise

Andrew and I haven't been alone with the children like this in more than four years. It should feel awkward, but, oddly, it just seems comfortable and familiar. I glance over my shoulder: Bella and Taylor are glued to their phones, and Tolly is drowsing against the headrest of his car seat, his eyelids already fluttering closed.

'You didn't have to drive me home,' I say, as Andrew navigates the narrow road towards Petworth. The rain is coming down even more heavily now, and I'm glad he's the one driving, not me. 'I'd have been fine getting a cab.'

'I told you, you're keeping this car,' Andrew says. 'We never use it anyway. You should have had it in the first place, instead of the Honda. We're in London most of the time and it just sits here outside the house. Anyway, the kids spend far more time with you. I don't know why we didn't think of that at the time.'

Min thought of that. My divorce lawyer thought of that. God knows, my mother made her feelings on the subject clear. But the problem with the adversarial nature of divorce is that once lawyers get involved, even the most reasonable of people dig in their heels and go ten rounds over things they don't even want. Andrew didn't like the Range Rover. He always thought it handled like a pig, and lectured me frequently on its gas-guzzling consumption. He only fought me over it because, by that stage, we were fighting over teaspoons.

I can't just blame Andrew for our clichéd descent into divorce hell. I was hurting, and grieving, and my life had been turned upside down. I fought dirty, too. I made life more difficult than it need have been when it came to the children. I'm not proud of it, but access to Tolly and Bella became my weapon of choice, as money was his. It reflects badly on both of us.

Andrew turns into our rutted lane, splashing through deep puddles that would've swamped my poor Honda. Even before we reach the house, I can see the damage to the porch. One support is bending alarmingly outwards under pressure from the gravid ceiling above it, which sags as if pregnant with some alien life form. I pray to God it's just the porch that's threatened, not the kitchen itself.

Andrew leaps out into the driving rain. 'Bella, take your brother inside,' he shouts, scooping our dozy son out of his car seat and handing him to his sister, who shields him from the deluge as best she can as she and Taylor stumble towards the house. 'Louise, do you have anything in one of the outbuildings we can use to prop up that porch column?'

'Nothing really strong enough,' I shout back, barely able to hear myself over the torrential downpour. 'Maybe one of the old horse jumps?'

We run towards the back of the property, past the vegetable garden, to what was once a paddock, long before we bought the house. I'm already soaked through to my underwear, and even though it's not cold, I'm shivering so hard my teeth are chattering. The paddock is waist-high with weeds now, but some of the old jumps and poles are still there. We heave one out of the clinging weeds, wiping off dirt and worms. The rain makes it slippery, but between us we somehow manage to heft the horse jump around the cottage and onto the porch.

It feels both strange and completely natural to be working in tandem, as if the last five years had never happened. No wonder Caz has fought so hard to prevent a situation like this. Some visceral sense must have warned her that the pull of familiarity, the habit of love that'd lasted more than a decade before her intervention, was more lethal than passion could ever be. Especially when it wasn't the death of that love, but her deceit and manipulation, that split us apart.

We look so bedraggled and pathetic by the time we get inside, we both start to laugh. 'I think you left a sweater or two upstairs,' I say, squeezing water from my hair onto the flagstones. 'Let me take a look while you go into the attic and check out the roof.'

I don't need to look. I know exactly where Andrew's clothes are. When he left so suddenly that awful night four years ago, a week after Tolly was born, he took only the clothes that suited his metropolitan, sophisticated new life with a glamorous blonde on his arm. Expensive black jeans, cashmere sweaters, designer sportswear: the clothes I'd noticed gradually creeping into his wardrobe over the preceding twelve months. He abandoned the Aran sweaters that had been part of his life with me.

I dig into the back of my cupboard now, pulling a pair of jeans and a plaid shirt from the top shelf. I pause and stroke the soft flannel for a moment. A part of me always knew that one day, he'd come back for them.

As I come back out onto the landing, Andrew emerges from the walk-in attic, brushing dust and plaster from his hands. 'It's the same spot,' he says, referring to the old leak in the roof our surveyor pointed out sixteen years ago. 'It's going to need more than a patch this time. The tiles have had it. The slate's so soft, it crumbles as soon as you touch it. That whole section needs to be replaced.' He rakes his hand through his wet hair in a gesture so familiar my heart clenches. 'I've moved the soggy insulation, which is adding weight to the ceiling you don't need. Fingers crossed it'll hold till we can get outside and sort it out.'

I hand him his dry clothes. 'Do you want a hot shower? Your lips are blue.'

'Wouldn't mind,' he admits. 'What about you?'

'Is that an invitation?'

The second the words are out of my mouth, I flush to the roots of my hair, absolutely mortified. I lost the right to say things like that to my husband when he married another woman.

But he laughs, a genuine gust of amusement, and in that single exchange the lingering politesse of strangers, which has starched our relationship for the last four years, is dispelled.

'Don't worry, your virtue is safe.' I grin. 'I'll go in the shower after you. Toss your wet clothes outside the bathroom door and I'll put them in the dryer. And don't use all the hot water.'

A few minutes later, Andrew dumps his sodden jeans and shirt on the landing. I pick them up and go downstairs, cracking the door to the sitting room. The three kids are curled up on the sofa together in front of the TV. None of them even look up. I leave them to it, pausing in the hallway for a moment to listen to the sound of the shower upstairs. I know this isn't real. A nostalgic flying visit to the past for both of us, that's all. But right now, my husband is upstairs, my children are next door, and for the first time in as long as I can remember, my world feels in balance.

I open the door of the tumble dryer in the kitchen, and automatically start checking pockets before throwing everything in. I stop abruptly when I find Andrew's phone in his jeans. There are no missed calls yet, but we've been gone for nearly two hours; it won't be long before Caz calls Andrew to heel.

I switch the phone to silent and slide it beneath a pile of tea towels. I just want to keep him here a little longer, to be a family again, if only for a few hours.

It's good for Bella and Tolly to spend some time with their father, without her around.

After pulling out a homemade shepherd's pie from the freezer – Andrew's favourite – I put it in the microwave to defrost. A few minutes later, I hear laughter next door: the sound of Tolly shrieking as he's tickled, Andrew's low, lazy laugh, and the rare joy of Bella giggling. I haven't heard her laugh like that in two years or more.

A little later, Andrew strolls barefoot into the kitchen, trailing flushed, pink-cheeked children like the Pied Piper. 'Hey, Lou. Taylor here says she's thinking about becoming a journalist,' he says, nodding towards the teenager. 'Thought you might be able to give her some pointers.'

'Sure,' I say, glancing up as I set the kitchen table for five. 'Are you interested in newspapers or magazines, Taylor?'

The girl awkwardly twists a large silver ring on her finger. 'No offence, Mrs Page, but I'm kind of more interested in TV.'

'I don't blame you,' I sigh. 'Newspapers are an endangered species. If there's any future in journalism, it's going to be online. But Andrew's the one you want to talk to if it's TV you're thinking about.'

'Dad, why don't you show her round INN?' Bella suggests. 'She could come up and stay with us in London, and you could take her into the office to meet everyone.'

'Oh, my God, that'd be super-cool!' Taylor exclaims.

'The summer holidays start soon, don't they?' Andrew

asks, locating a bottle of Pinot Grigio in the fridge and rooting around in a kitchen drawer for the corkscrew. 'Why don't you come up and spend the whole day at the studio, Taylor? See the programme put together from soup to nuts?'

'*Seriously?*'

'Might even be able to get someone on the newsdesk to take you out on a story, if it's a slow news day.'

'That would be, like, *so* awesome!'

I serve dinner for the five of us at the kitchen table. The kids are drawn to Andrew like iron filings to a magnet. Tolly chatters nonstop, while Bella cleans her plate for the first time in months. In his favourite old pullover and worn jeans, Andrew looks younger and more relaxed than I've seen him in years.

'God, that was good,' he says, pushing back his chair and hauling Tolly onto his lap. 'No one makes shepherd's pie like you.'

'Thank you.' I smile.

'I suppose I really should call Caz. It's after ten. She'll be wondering where I am.'

'I suppose you should,' I agree.

A beat falls.

'She might be asleep,' he adds. 'She hasn't called, so she's obviously not worried. Although I'm not sure where I put my phone . . .'

'There's some rhubarb crumble in the fridge,' I say.

He groans. 'You're killing me. How can I say no to your rhubarb crumble?'

I get up from the table and open the fridge, just as

117

a thunderous rumble starts. For a moment, I think it's the storm outside.

'The ceiling!' Andrew shouts suddenly.

He leaps up from the table, Tolly in his arms, and pushes the two girls towards the door. I fling myself across the room to join them, and the five of us watch from the doorway in disbelief as the ceiling finally bursts, releasing a confetti of browned pipes and splintered wood. The air is filled with choking plaster dust, and belatedly Andrew shoves us into the hall and slams the kitchen door shut. We listen with something akin to awe to what sounds like the end of the world.

Finally, it falls silent. 'Wait here,' Andrew warns the children, putting Tolly down.

Gingerly, the two of us peer around the kitchen door. The entire ceiling has come down, destroying half the kitchen. China and glass and broken timbers litter the floor. The collapse has even brought down a section of wall; rainwater is already blowing in through the gap. It looks like we've been bombed with a rocket-propelled grenade.

Andrew puts his arm around me as we survey the wreckage in shock. 'It's going to be OK,' he says.

I can't help but let out a half-sob. Never mind the financial implications, or the threat from the farmer; this kitchen has been our home for sixteen years. On the wall now pouring with water, the pencil marks charting our children's growth are being washed away. Tolly took his first steps across tiles now buried beneath a foot of rubble.

Andrew pulls me against him, just as I lift my tear-stained face. For a moment, our eyes lock. He bends his head towards me, and kisses me, and every nerve ending in my body lights up with remembered passion. We fit together. We always have.

I press the flat of my hand against his oh-so-familiar flannel shirtfront. 'Stay,' I say.

Chapter 14

Caz

He's gone all night. All night, without a phone call or text. I almost hope he's had an accident on the way home, rather than think about what he might have been doing with *her*.

The irony isn't lost on me: this must be how Louise felt when she knew he was with me. I toss and turn in my empty bed, consumed by acid jealousy. It was bad enough when Andy went back to her four years ago, after she got pregnant with Tolly. But in those days, despite Andy's promises, I'd known he wasn't entirely mine, not really. There had still been a residual guilt on my part, the sense that somehow I deserved the uncertainty and agony of wondering if he'd ever come back to me.

But it's a thousand times worse now. I'm his *wife*. We have a son together. How can he do this to me?

The same way he did it to her, I suppose.

'Go round there,' Angie demands, when I call her at midnight, unable to sleep. It's Saturday night; she's out clubbing somewhere, and I can barely hear her over the pounding music in the background. 'You're not some sad sack wifey, barefoot and pregnant in the kitchen. Go over and sort her out.'

'I can't. I've got Kit.'

'Stick him in the back of the car. He'll sleep through it.'

'I'm not dragging Andy home like a bloody fishwife,' I say crossly. 'I wouldn't give her the satisfaction.'

'Well, change the locks, then. I would.'

Easy for her to say. Angie's never really liked Andy, though she hasn't said a word against him since we got married. But she hated it in the months when he ping-ponged between us, despising a man who wasn't content with making just one woman unhappy, but rendered two miserable. Those months I spent waiting for Andy to decide between us were the worst of my life, like having my skin flayed from my body in tormented, bloody strips. When he finally walked out on Louise, hurt and bitter and angry, he swore he was done with her for good.

Despite what she thinks, I wasn't the one who screwed her out of a decent divorce settlement: that was Andy. He wanted to make her suffer. He was the one who insisted on us getting married the minute his divorce came through, too. I'd wanted to wait, to put some clear water between one marriage and the next, but he was determined. I knew even then it had less to do with loving me, and more to do with punishing Louise. He hated her so much, he didn't have room for anything else.

But hatred is exhausting, and takes too much energy to feed. And there were the children to consider. We all needed to find a civilised way to behave with each other, for their sake. Hard to believe now, but I actually felt relieved when Andy stopped referring to Louise as That Bitch, and started talking to her when she picked the children up from our house on Sunday evenings. For a brief moment, I thought we might be turning into a modern, blended family, able to get on with our own lives.

I should've known better: Andy isn't capable of just having a cordial relationship with Louise. It's all or nothing for him. Love and hate are opposite sides of the same coin. She's always been able to get under his skin, and nothing I do seems to change that. And so here we are, with Louise pulling his strings, and Andy running over to her house every time she needs a lightbulb changing. For four years, she's just been biding her time, waiting for her moment. And now here it is.

I stare up at the ceiling, my stomach churning with anxiety. I can't imagine my life without Andy in it. If he's gone back to her, I don't know how I'll put myself together again.

I must fall into a fitful sleep, because I wake with a jolt, and it's daylight. I sit up abruptly, my heart pounding, listening to the sound of movement downstairs. For a moment, I wonder if someone's broken in, and then I hear Andy's voice.

My initial relief that he's back is instantly swept away by the urge to leap out of bed and storm downstairs, demanding to know where he's been. I have to force myself to lie back down, breathing deeply until I can get my emotions in check. I can't go in swinging. He's come back, which means it's not over yet. And I can hear Bella and Tolly's voices, too; surely he wouldn't have brought them here if he was planning to go back to Louise?

My pulse slows. Perhaps I've been overreacting after all. In the clear light of day, my rabid jealousy seems less rational. It *was* pelting with rain all night; the storm was fierce enough to bring down trees. Louise lives in the middle of nowhere. Mobile reception there is spotty at best. Perhaps he didn't want to risk driving back in the middle of the night with branches down on the roads, and couldn't call to tell me. The lane might have flooded. Or—

'You awake?' Andy whispers, sticking his head around the door.

Arranging my expression into one of welcome, I swing my legs out of bed. But my measured request to know why my husband has been out all night dies on my lips as I clock the hideous lumberjack flannel shirt and dad jeans. 'What the hell are you wearing?'

He glances down at himself. 'My clothes were soaked from the rain. We put them in the tumble dryer, but then we lost power, so I had to wear some old clothes I'd left at Louise's.'

I can't bear to see him in them. It brings back too many unhappy memories. 'Let me get you something decent to wear,' I say, opening the wardrobe. 'You can't go around looking like that—'

'I'm fine,' he says impatiently. 'Look, I'm sorry I didn't call last night and let you know I was staying over. It's been a hell of a night. The whole damn kitchen ceiling collapsed, and my phone is buried somewhere beneath a foot of rubble. Thank God none of us were hurt.'

If only the house had come down on top of Louise, like the Wicked Witch of the East, leaving nothing but her ruby slippers. 'I was worried about you,' I say, without turning around.

'I know. I'm sorry. Like I said, we lost power, so I couldn't ring you on her landline. But you knew where I was, so I knew you wouldn't be worried.'

It's precisely *because* I knew where he was that I was out of my mind with anxiety. 'Did you get any sleep?'

'Bunked in with Tolly for a couple of hours, but not really. I'm shattered.'

I turn, searching his face, alert to any hint he's lying. Andy's an accomplished actor: he can affect concern or cynicism on cue, depending on the story he's reporting. Even after four years together, I'm still never sure if he's liked a meal I've made or is just being polite.

Something doesn't ring true. He's holding my eyes just a little *too* steadily. His expression looks oddly familiar—

Of course it does. It's the one he wore when he used to go back to Louise after he'd spent the night with me.

I don't have the chance to process the information that my husband has just cracked our marriage wide

124

open. Before I can respond, the woman responsible appears in my bedroom doorway like an apparition from hell.

'Sorry to bother you,' Louise says, 'but can you tell me where you keep the spare sheets?'

Date:- 01/08/2020
Duration:- 27 Minutes
Location:- Kingsbridge Police Station

Conducted by Officers from Devon &
Cornwall Police

(cont.)

POLICE   So you've known Louise Page for how long, Ms
            Murdoch?

CM   God, I don't know. Thirty years?

POLICE   And you say the job was *your* suggestion, not
            hers?

CM	Yes. To be honest, I didn't think she'd be interested once she knew the details.
POLICE	But she was?
CM	She needed the money.
POLICE	When did you have this conversation?
CM	I don't remember exactly. [Pause.] We had lunch maybe four or five weeks ago. Louise mentioned she didn't get paid over the summer, and was trying to pick up more freelance work to tide her over, and I said I might be able to help. She called me about it a week or so later.
POLICE	So it was at *her* instigation?
CM	No, like I said, she just reminded— Look, what does it matter? It's got nothing to do with what happened to Andrew. Louise wasn't the one stalking Caz; it was the other way around.
POLICE	But she moved into the current Mrs Page's house, correct? That didn't strike you as odd?
CM	It was Andrew's idea, not hers. Her kitchen ceiling came down in a storm, and she had nowhere else to go. Her parents' place isn't big enough, and she couldn't afford a hotel.

POLICE	Mr Page could have afforded one, presumably?
CM	I don't know. I suppose so.
POLICE	But instead, he suggested his ex-wife and children stay at his house?
CM	That's what Louise told me.
POLICE	Why do you think he did that?
CM	I've no idea.
POLICE	Caroline Page can't have been happy about it, surely?
CM	I don't suppose she was thrilled. But she and Andrew live in London most of the time. Louise was just borrowing the place for a couple of weeks. They weren't all going to be living together like Mormons.
POLICE	So the plan was for Mr and Mrs Page to return to London with their son, while Louise Page remained with her children at the house in Brighton until her kitchen was repaired?
CM	Yes.

POLICE   But a week or so later, she suddenly moved out.
          Do you know why that was?

CM   Louise and Caz had a row.

POLICE   This would have been the altercation when the
          police were called?

CM   No, that came later.

POLICE   Do you know what this earlier row was about?

CM   Not really. [Pause.] Look, I don't feel comfort-
          able speaking for her. You'll have to ask her
          about it.

POLICE   We will. Would it be fair to say, Mrs Murdoch—

CM   Ms.

POLICE   Sorry, *Ms* Murdoch, would it be fair to say that,
          overall, Louise and Caroline Page were not on
          good terms, particularly in the last couple of
          months?

CM   Yes.

POLICE   And yet you still thought employing Louise Page
          a good idea? Surely you were pouring petrol on
          a situation that was already extremely volatile?

CM   It had nothing to do with Andrew's death.

POLICE   Are you *sure* about that, Ms Murdoch?

Four weeks before the party

Chapter 15

Louise

It's weird and unsettling to be in the house Andrew and Caz share. There are so many items I recognise, familiar things I lived with for more than a decade before Andrew took them with him in the divorce: the Syrian carpet we bought together, a painting of Bella aged six that I had a friend do for Andrew's birthday one year, a pair of matching bronze figurines that used to be his mother's.

But so much is different, too. Andrew has switched sides of the bed; his books and reading glasses and old-fashioned alarm clock are on the right bedside table now, instead of the left. Caz is clearly a bit of a neat-freak; there are none of the notes or magnets fixed to the fridge there used to be when Andrew and I lived together, and every counter in her sparkling modern kitchen is anti-septically clear. That must drive him mad; he used to hate it if I put away the coffee machine he used every day, or tidied his piles of newspapers into a drawer. He likes things within easy reach, to be surrounded by the familiar detritus of family life. Or he did.

I reclaim several of my favourite books from the shelves in the sitting room, and go into Kit's bedroom to tuck them away in the bottom of my suitcase. I can't bring myself to sleep in Andrew and Caz's bedroom, so I'm using Kit's, even though my feet hang off the end of his bed. I put a sweater across the books, and close the case. Andrew never reads: he won't even miss them.

Ever since he and Caz married, I've been careful to avoid imagining their lives together. I didn't want their relationship given flesh and substance. But now it's unavoidable. I drift around the house when Bella and Tolly are at school, tormenting myself with the ordinary, domestic background of their marriage. There are photographs of the two of them together, or with Kit, everywhere. I wonder if they're happy together, or if it's all just for show.

'He looks miserable to me,' Min says, putting a photograph of the three of them at a ski resort back on the hall console. 'Look at his eyes,' she adds. 'You can tell he's hating every minute of it.'

He does detest being cold. 'He always refused to go skiing when we were married,' I say sourly. 'But he'll do it for *her*.'

She's already on her way up the stairs. I follow her into Caz and Andrew's bedroom, watching as she flings open the door to Caz's huge walk-in wardrobe, shamelessly prying. 'Jesus! I've never seen so many shoes. No wonder Andrew's always pleading poverty.'

'Wait till you see her sweaters.' I pull open a row of drawers. 'Look at them, all colour-coded. Cashmere, too. Not the cheap M&S kind, either, these are the real thing—'

'Louise, what are you doing in this house?' Min demands suddenly. 'It's fucked up. I've told you, I'll give you the money for a hotel.'

'I'm not taking your money.'

'Fine. Put it on your credit card. Rob a bank if you have to. But you can't stay here any longer. It's not *healthy*.'

I knew Min would take this the wrong way. 'It's not like Andrew and Caz are actually *here*,' I point out. 'The house sits empty most of the time.'

'What are you going to do when it's their weekend with the kids? Play piggy-in-the-middle?'

'Bella's going to take Tolly to London on the train, so Andrew and Caz don't need to come down to Brighton till the kitchen's finished. The three of us can stay here as long as we need to.'

I can feel judgement coming off her in waves. I understand how it looks from the outside, but it's not like that. This is just a practical solution to a logistical problem, that's all.

'So how long is this going to go on for?' Min asks, as we go back downstairs. 'You've already been here a week, and your kitchen still looked like a war zone when I stopped to pick up your post.'

'It looks worse than it is. The builder said he'd been done in a week or two.'

'Builder time?' Her expression softens. 'Look, I get it. If it were Luke, I'd want to pick the scab, too. You

135

can't bear to see their life together, and you can't bear *not* to see it either. But it isn't doing you any good, Lou. Why rip open old wounds? You need to be putting more distance between you, not less.'

She's right: I haven't been able to stop thinking about Andrew since the night of the storm. I thought I'd put this constant ache for him behind me, but after last Saturday, I feel as if I've gone right back to square one.

Min knows me too well. 'This isn't about the money, is it?' she says presciently. 'You can afford to stay at a B&B for a few weeks. What's really going on?'

I can't quite meet her eye.

'Oh, my God,' Min exclaims. 'You *slept* with him!'

'No! It was just a kiss,' I say quickly. 'We got caught up in the moment, that's all. Too much nostalgia and red wine. It won't happen again,' I add, more to myself than Min. 'You can't tell anyone. Swear to me, Min. You can't breathe a word, not even to Mum. *Especially* not to Mum.'

'Jesus, Lou. What were you *thinking*?'

I don't have an answer for her. I've replayed that kiss a thousand times in the last few days, analysing it from every conceivable angle. I'm almost certain Andrew started it, but I was the one who put my hand on his shirtfront and told him to stay. Maybe I opened the door. Perhaps he thought I *wanted* to be kissed. Something happened between us that night, we both felt it. Not that we talked about it afterwards, of course. We both pretended it hadn't even happened.

I wouldn't be human if I didn't take a tiny bit of

guilty pleasure in turning the tables on the woman who stole my husband. But it doesn't feel as good as I thought it would. Andrew's built a life and a family with Caz now; breaking them up would make me no better than she is. I've spent the last four years trying to get over Andrew. I can't put myself through the misery and torture of those months when he vacillated back and forth between us again.

After Min leaves, I sit at the kitchen table and stare into space for a long time, mulling over what she's said. There were any number of options I could've taken instead of moving into Andrew and Caz's house. We could've squeezed into my parents'; I could have braved the builder's dust, and stayed at the house and ordered takeaways for a few weeks. But I knew coming here would upset Caz, and drive a wedge between them.

I suddenly feel thoroughly ashamed of myself. I've been behaving like a spiteful teenager. I'm not that person anymore, I don't do that kind of thing. I've *changed* since Roger Lewison. I'm a mother now, a respected journalist. A university professor. As soon as the kitchen's halfway liveable, I need to move out of here.

Shoving back my chair, I push the thought of Roger from my mind and sift through the pile of post Min has left propped up on the counter. I spot an official-looking letter from Sussex University, and put down the rest of the envelopes to open it. They don't usually send out new contracts this early, and I wonder if they've changed my course schedule.

I unfold the letter and quickly scan it, and then I read it again, more slowly this time, with mounting fury. I know exactly who's behind this.

Well, if she thinks this will scare me off, she's soon going to find out it's had exactly the opposite effect. Two can play this game.

Maybe I haven't changed that much after all.

Chapter 16

Caz

You'd think it'd be the thought of my husband in another woman's bed that keeps me up at night, but it's the idea of Louise in my home that makes the hairs on the back of my neck stand up. I imagine her pawing through my clothes, opening drawers and cupboards, spitting at my photograph as she noses through my things. Andy thinks I'm ridiculous, of course. 'She'd never do that,' he said indignantly, when I objected to the arrangement, as if I was twisted for even thinking it.

I've put up with a lot over the years, God knows, but he's crossed the line this time. Inviting Louise into our *home*, for God's sake! Angie's right: any other woman would have thrown him onto the street.

An email pings into my mailbox, startling me out of my bitter contemplation. I open it, then exclaim in frustration. 'AJ! Get the creatives on the Vine account down here!'

AJ swings round in his chair. 'What's the problem?'

I tilt my computer screen towards him. 'Take a look.'

'Seems OK to me,' AJ says.

'Take a *closer* look.'

He scoots over and peers over my shoulder, then looks at me, confused. 'You said you wanted diverse. Mantiba is really cool right now, everyone's using him. Her. You know what I mean. Gender fluidity is—'

'I'm not worried about the model, AJ,' I say tightly. 'Take a look at what they're *wearing*.'

'You don't like pyjamas? Vine want their kicks to look relaxed, like you could wear them all day—'

'*Blue-and-white-striped* pyjamas,' I interrupt. 'Remind you of anything?'

'Not really,' AJ says.

'Well, maybe we might get away with it, though I think it's a little close for comfort, if it wasn't for the *star-shaped yellow Vine logo* on the top left pocket.'

The penny drops.

'Oh, my God!' AJ exclaims.

'There you go,' I say, turning the monitor back to face me.

'That looks just like—'

'I don't *think* Holocaust chic is a thing,' I say, 'but let's not put it to the test, shall we? Go and put a rocket up the joint creative arse and get them to fucking sort it out, would you? Before we end up crucified in the *Daily Mail*.'

To my dismay, AJ's eyes fill with tears. 'I'm so sorry,' he says. 'I've let you down. This is all my fault—'

'Shit, AJ. This isn't on you.' I crouch down by his desk and put my arm around him, feeling awful for making him cry. 'Come on. We caught it in time. It'll be fine. There's no need to panic.'

'Wayne and I split up,' he says suddenly. 'It's OK. It'd been on the cards for a while.'

I'm a crap friend. I should've picked up on this sooner. AJ's always been a bit fragile. He was brutally beaten up by some homophobic thugs in his second year at art school, and dropped out of college for a year. The worst of it was, his boyfriend at the time was still in the closet, and actually joined in the attack. AJ's found it hard to trust anyone since then, and it took him a long time to risk his heart again. 'Oh, AJ,' I say softly. 'I'm so sorry. I thought you two would really go the distance.'

His eyes cloud. 'So did I.'

AJ's phone rings, and he takes the call. 'Talk later,' I mouth, and he gives me a quick thumbs up.

I need some air. I haven't smoked since I was in college, but the last few days have had me back on the Marlboro Reds, though I've had to limit myself to work hours because of Kit. I grab my bag and go down to the mezzanine floor, shoving open the glass doors to the terrace overlooking the street.

I light up, and inhale the reassuring hit of nicotine and carcinogenic chemicals. AJ dropped the ball on Vine, but I should've caught the cock-up myself, and I would've done, if Louise wasn't taking up all the space on my mental hard drive. I still don't know what really happened the night Andy stayed at her place. The doubt is gnawing away at me. I'm reaping the reward of every

141

mistress: I know without question the man I love is a liar.

I should've walked away from Andy a long time ago, before we ever got married, the second I found out he'd lied to me. I know that. There's only one reason I haven't, and it's the oldest and lamest one in the book. I love him.

It doesn't take a genius to figure out why I fell for a man nearly twenty years older than me. Daddy issues, I hold my hands up, but who doesn't have issues of some sort or another? My father died when I was eleven. A record producer, he was travelling with one of his bands when the minibus came off the road. The lead singer and bass guitarist survived, and lived to re-form another day, but Dad and three other band members and the driver were all killed. It was just Mum and me after that, no brothers and sisters to take the edge off, just the two of us. Mum never remarried, or even dated again. If I'm a screw-up, I lay it at her door.

But Kit's here now, and I owe it to him to keep his family together. If Andy and Louise did have a nostalgic fuck, it doesn't have to mean the end of *us*. I can get past it. If it was just once. If it doesn't happen again.

My cigarette shakes in my hand. Despite my bravado, the thought of the two of them together is crucifying me. How could he even bear to touch her, after what she did to him? I was the one who picked up the pieces and put him back together. He may choose to forget it now, but I know just how much she hurt him.

I stub out my cigarette just as a black cab pulls up

142

in the street below. Tina Murdoch gets out, glancing up at the building, and I duck back out of sight. Christ. This is all I need.

Patrick is waiting by the lifts when I go back inside, just as Tina rises up towards us in the glassed-in elevator like the phantom of the opera. He steps forward as she alights, his hand extended, but she goes in for a one-two air-kiss, and he submits with good grace. 'Good to see you again, Tina.'

'Always a pleasure, Patrick. Hello, Caz. I thought I'd come in personally to introduce my new PR to Whitefish,' Tina says, gesturing to the woman hovering behind her. 'I'm sure you'll all make her feel welcome.'

I don't know whether to laugh or cry.

'Good to see you again, Louise,' Patrick says, giving her a warm hug. 'It's been a while.'

'You know each other?' I blurt.

Louise smiles coolly. 'We met a few years ago, when I did a piece on Patrick for the *Post*.'

'Far kinder than I deserved,' Patrick adds.

My fingernails dig so deeply into my palms, I'm certain I draw blood. 'I had no idea you did PR work, Louise.'

Her smile doesn't falter, but her eyes are like chips of granite. 'Most journalists can turn their hand to PR,' she says. 'I found myself with some spare time, and Chris – sorry, I forgot you go by Tina at work – was in a bit of a bind, so I offered to help out. We go back a long way,' she adds, clearly relishing every moment of this. 'Actually, we were at school together. You probably

143

didn't know that when she introduced you to my husband at that RSPCA fundraiser.'

I feel sick. Of course I had no idea Louise knew Tina Murdoch. Andy's mentioned Louise's best friend 'Chris' a few times, but I'd never met her and it'd never occurred to me who she really was. No wonder Tina tried to get me fired: I ran off with her best friend's husband. She probably blamed herself for introducing us in the first place. She's obviously wangled this job for Louise now to fuck with me. I am in deeper shit than I ever imagined.

'Louise will be my liaison on the Univest campaign,' Tina says, her gaze drilling into me. 'She's got my full authority to make any decisions necessary on the account.'

'I think having someone here in-house to oversee your PR strategy and take advantage of the synergy with our ad campaign will be very helpful,' Patrick says. 'It's not something we do very often, but we're a small enough company to make it work, and I've found it useful before. Look, I'm afraid I have to dash,' he adds to Louise, 'I've got a conference call with New York, but I'll catch up with you later. Tina, do you have time for a quick word in private?'

With a final, malicious glance in my direction, Tina leaves us alone. Louise ignores me completely, strolling out onto the terrace like she owns the place. It takes me a moment to recover myself, and then I storm after her, so angry I can hardly see straight. 'What the *fuck* are you doing here?'

144

'Such a lovely view,' Louise says, leaning on the railing. 'What a wonderful part of town to work. I'm so looking forward to—'

'Cut the crap. Why are you here?'

'You started this,' she hisses, dropping the act.

I'm suddenly aware people are watching us through the plate glass windows, and lower my voice. 'What are you talking about?'

'You know damn well. Sussex University had an anonymous tip about my record, and decided my services were no longer required.' Her voice hardens. 'I have children to feed, or didn't you think about that? I still have to keep a roof over our heads—'

'A roof over your head? You're living in *my* fucking house!'

'It'll be my house soon,' she says coldly. 'And I will be living there with *my* husband.'

She walks away, leaving me rooted to the spot. I've always known she hates me, but I had no idea just how much. I wonder if she's a little mad. She was locked up in a psych ward once for attacking the wife of an ex-boyfriend; that's why she's got that criminal record. It was a long time ago, but how do I know she's not going to do something crazy again?

The knot in my stomach tightens. Andy, the one person I'd normally talk about all this with, the one person who should have my back, is part of the problem. I don't think I've ever felt so isolated in my life.

Chapter 17

Min

Putting my doctor's hat on for a few minutes, I've seen patients decompensating before. They all have essentially the same symptoms: the functional deterioration of a system that had been previously working with the help of allostatic compensation – in Louise's case, a combination of counselling, CBT and time. Together, these therapies have kept her visceral fear of loss – initially triggered by the traumatic death of her brother, and affirmed by what happened with Roger Lewison at Oxford – at bay for many years. But I think a perfect storm of circumstances are causing the sudden and alarming decay of these protective structures. In layman's terms: I suspect Lou might be headed for another breakdown.

It's something I worried about when Andrew deserted her four years ago, which is why I kept such a close eye on her at the time. In retrospect, I think the demands of caring for a newborn had the counterintuitive effect of protecting her by keeping her too busy to think about anything else; too busy to think at all. But now the past is catching up with her, and I'm more alarmed than I care to admit.

I check the time on my phone, wishing the waiter hadn't seated me in the centre of the restaurant; irrational, I know, but I hate people walking behind me. He's late. I'm already regretting this, but my concern, as I tried to explain to Celia, is for Lou. Nothing else would induce me to sup with the devil, no matter how long the spoon.

Louise can rationalise her actions however she wants, and no doubt that woman of Andrew's provoked her. But speaking as her friend, now, not a doctor, I have to say that moving into her ex-husband's house isn't normal, no matter what the excuse. Taking a job where his new wife works *is not normal.*

There's a muted stir behind me, and I look round to see Andrew hastily making his way to my table, ignoring the whiplash glances of recognition from other diners. 'So sorry I'm late,' he apologises. 'Bloody Circle Line.' He puts a hand on his chair, but doesn't sit down. 'You hate sitting in the middle of a restaurant, don't you? Let me see if I can get another table.'

'Oh, there's no—'

'Excuse me,' Andrew says, politely accosting a waiter, 'but would you mind terribly if we sat in one of the booths over there, out of the way?'

'Please go ahead, sir.'

'You didn't have to do that,' I mutter, as we're swiftly ushered to a private corner of the restaurant.

'If you don't ask, you don't get.' Andrew smiles.

147

He is extremely handsome. He looks good enough on television, but in real life, he has a presence, a charisma, that's beguiling. It's something in the way he looks at you, as if he sees only you, *all* of you. Even now, I have to remind myself of who he really is.

'So, what are you doing in London?' Andrew says, not taking his eyes off me as the waiter unfolds his napkin for him and drapes it across his lap. 'Something to do with work, or are you taking a day for yourself?'

He makes the latter sound faintly risqué. With an effort, I break his gaze, and take a large swallow of water. 'This isn't a social lunch,' I say sharply. 'I know what happened the other night with Lou. I'm here to tell you that you need to stay away from her, Andrew. I'm not kidding. You're both playing with fire, and I'm not going to let her get burned again.'

To my surprise, he leans back and laughs. 'That's what I love about you, Min. As direct and frank as always.'

'You think this is *funny*?'

'Of course not,' Andrew says, his expression suddenly serious. 'It was just a kiss, Min. It wasn't planned, and it certainly didn't mean anything.'

'Does *Lou* think it doesn't mean anything?'

The waiter returns to our table and hands each of us a menu. Andrew doesn't even glance at his before placing it on the thick white linen tablecloth. 'I didn't put that well. Of course it meant something. But I'm not going to drag Louise back into my mess. I put her through enough before. It shouldn't have happened, and I'm sorry.'

148

'Sorry doesn't cut it. I want your promise that it's not going to happen again.'

'It's not just up to me, Min,' Andrew says. 'Takes two, you know.'

We both jump as there's a sudden crash of plates on the other side of the restaurant. The entire room abruptly falls silent as everyone turns to stare at the young waitress standing in the midst of a sea of spilt food and broken crockery, looking like she's about to burst into tears. Before anyone else has a chance to react, Andrew leaps out from our booth and goes over to help her. 'God, don't you hate it when this happens?' he asks, grabbing a napkin from the nearest table and putting the largest shards of crockery into it. 'At least you didn't do it live on air. You're probably too young to remember me knocking an entire row of priceless crystal off the sideboard at Highgrove . . .'

He keeps up the cheerful one-sided conversation as a phalanx of restaurant staff recover their wits and rush over to reassure the diners whose lunch is now scattered across the tiles. Within minutes, order is restored, the mess is cleaned up, and Andrew returns to our table.

'That was kind of you,' I say awkwardly. 'I think you just saved that poor girl's job.'

'It requires depth of character to be truly wicked,' Andrew says dryly. 'As Celia will no doubt agree, I have only hidden shallows.'

I sigh. 'I don't think you're wicked. Just bloody selfish.'

'Progress.' He raises a hand to attract a waiter. 'Are we allowed a glass of champagne, Doctor Pollock?'

'I don't usually drink at lunchtime—'

'Oh, Min. Live a little,' Andrew teases. 'I won't tell anyone.'

I hesitate. 'All right, then.'

I'm unnerved by how much I want to like him again. *This is the man who betrayed your best friend*, I tell myself forcefully. *The man who also made a pass at* you *when he was already in the midst of an affair with another woman.*

I've never told anyone about that night, when Andrew drove me home from their house because I'd had too much to drink on a girls' night out with Louise. When the two of us sat parked outside my house for just long enough for him to try to kiss me, and when I let him for just too long for either of us to pretend that I hadn't wanted him to.

He leans across the table. 'Min, I meant what I said. I don't want to hurt Lou any more than I have already. I honestly didn't intend that kiss to happen.'

'The road to hell is paved with—'

'I miss her,' he says simply.

It's the combination of lethal sex appeal and vulnerable little boy that makes him so irresistible. He has the charm and ego of a child. I'm torn between wanting to give him a consoling hug, and a desire to punch him on the nose. 'You *left* her,' I remind him curtly. 'You gave up the right to miss her when you walked out.'

The waiter returns with our champagne and a bowl of salted edamame beans, which he places on the table between us. We both order a Cobb salad, and wait until the man has gone before resuming our conversation. Andrew picks up one of the beans, and then puts it down again. 'I'd forgotten what it could be like when Lou and I were a team,' he says. 'That night, fixing the roof together, it reminded me. It's not that easy to turn your back on fifteen-odd years of history together. Me and Caz, we don't have any of that.'

I give him a hard look. 'Andrew, if you're saying what I think you're saying, stop right there. You had an affair and broke up your family for that woman. You're married to her now, for better or worse. You have Kit. You made your bed.'

'What if it's not the one I want to lie in?'

'These are people's *lives* you're playing with,' I say. 'Louise has only just got her life back on track after you blew it all apart. Don't reel her back in, Andrew, just because you can. Stay away from her. It's not fair on anyone.'

'I don't just miss *her*,' Andrew says, ignoring everything I've just said. 'I miss all of you. When I got that invitation to Celia's party, it just brought it all home. You were my family for more than a decade.' He gives me a sweet, lopsided smile. 'You can't blame me for wanting that back sometimes, can you?'

Bloody Celia, I think despairingly. This insane idea of hers to remind Andrew of what he's missing might just work. In which case, God help us all.

Chapter 18

Louise

I know as soon as I board the train to London I've got it all wrong. I spent ages last night dithering over what to wear; at the university I could get away with jeans, and when I'm freelancing I frequently don't make it out of my pyjamas, so it's been years since I had to dress for a real job. I wanted to make sure I looked appropriately smart for a London advertising agency. In the end, I plumped for a black skirt suit from my early days at the *Post* that still just about fits, and a pair of heels. But most of the other women on the train are wearing trousers, not skirts, paired with ballet flats or loafers and chambray shirts or wrap blouses, effortlessly pulling off the business casual look. I'm about two decades out of date.

The commute from Brighton is a killer, too. It's hot, the train is overcrowded and stuffy, and I can't find a seat. I stand in the cramped corridor outside the packed carriage along with half a dozen other commuters, leaning against the back of the toilet compartment for balance. I can feel the sweat gathering beneath my breasts and trickling down my back.

When Chris first suggested the job at Whitefish a couple of days after our lunch the other week, I refused point blank even to consider it: I told her I'd rather beg on the streets than work with Caz.

'You'll hardly ever have to see her,' Chris insisted. 'You'll only have to come up to London one day a week at most; the rest of the time you can work from home. And you'll mostly be based at my Docklands office, not at Whitefish. You'll need to liaise with the team there, of course, but you can use Caz's assistant, AJ, as your go-to guy most of the time.'

Even though she was offering me more money than I'd earned in years, and the chance to undercut Caz in the one place she thought she was safe, I'd turned it down, because I hadn't wanted to pour petrol on the flames and start an all-out war with the woman.

But then Caz got me fired. The letter from the head of the media department at Sussex was polite, but firm: I hadn't disclosed my criminal record, and they had no choice but to cancel my contract for the upcoming academic year. *The safety of our students . . . Extremely sorry, but we can't risk it, not in this day and age. Our legal department, you know how it is.*

Five minutes after I opened the envelope, I picked up the phone and called Chris. It's time Caz learned there are consequences.

Walking into the Whitefish offices now, though, I'm

suddenly beset by second thoughts about parking my tanks on her lawn like this. She certainly provoked me, but now I'm on territory where she feels most comfortable: she's got the home advantage, and I'm certain she won't hesitate to use it.

But *I* have the advantage of surprise. I almost feel sorry for her when I see her face as I step out of the lift; her jaw literally drops. I remember what it was like when the *Post* editor brought in an old college rival of mine to edit the Saturday pages that carried my column. I felt under attack in the one place I'd always considered my kingdom. This must be Caz's worst nightmare come true. Not only am I on her turf, but she's just discovered her new boss on this account is my best friend, and even worse, that I know Patrick, too. I can see all the pieces slotting into place in her head as she finally works out why 'Tina' tried to get her fired. Chris has always felt terrible about introducing Andrew to her at that charity event, but like I said at the time, it was hardly her fault my husband ran off with Caz.

My sympathy is short-lived. Chris will make Caz's life a misery in the next few months; maybe it'll make her think twice about sabotaging my life again. But I don't fool myself for one minute this is going to be easy for me, either. Caz may be on the back foot for the moment, but this glamorous, hip world belongs to girls like her, not middle-aged women like me. You just have to look at her in her skinny jeans and Superga sneakers; next to her, I feel like a throwback from the Nineties, overdressed and out of touch.

'Stop worrying,' Chris says, as we get a taxi back to her office at the Shard. 'You're going to be fine. You can do this job with one hand tied behind your back.'

Now that I've found out a bit more about what I'll be doing, I realise I'm going to like the work itself. Persuasive writing is a transferable skill, and using copy to promote a particular brand isn't really very different from working to a newspaper proprietor's political agenda. AJ is clearly Caz's man, but I think I can handle him. And if he starts to make my life too difficult, Chris has enough clout to get Patrick to move him onto a different account.

'It's not the job I'm worried about,' I tell Chris. 'It's whether I'm going to end up in a body bag. She'll probably put antifreeze in my bloody coffee.'

She laughs. 'Don't worry. A Starbucks gift card comes with the job.'

It's only on the train back down to Brighton, another insanely crowded commuter nightmare, that I allow myself to think about how Andrew might see all this. I don't want him thinking I've turned into a bunny boiler, first moving into Caz's house and now working at her office. It'll be difficult to defend myself: I've got no proof Caz is the one who tipped off Sussex University and got me fired, and if I accuse her, it'll just make things worse.

Min is right, I realise suddenly: I need to move out of Caz and Andrew's house right now, whether the kitchen's finished or not. If I do that, it'll take the edge off the fact I'm working with Chris for one of Caz's biggest clients. And Andrew owes me a little faith. I haven't landed him in it by telling Caz anything about what happened the night of the storm, and I could have done. Obviously, I'd *never* try to blackmail him emotionally; that's not the sort of person I am.

I hope he remembers loyalty is a two-way street.

Chapter 19

Caz

I watch Andy slide his arm around Louise's shoulders as they sit on the sofa, pulling her against his chest. She laughs, twisting in his arms to tilt her head up to him, and he kisses her, tucking a long strand of hair behind her ear in a tender gesture that makes my heart twist. I recognise the look in his brown eyes, which have softened to a warm amber with love.

Eavesdroppers never hear any good of themselves. The same principle applies to those who spy from the shadows. I should stop tormenting myself, but I can't look away.

Even as I watch, Louise kicks off her sandals, casually draping her bare feet across Andy's lap as she reaches for her mug. He makes a remark I can't hear, and she laughs, looking ten years younger than I've ever seen her. Then he takes one of her feet in his hand and starts to rub it as she sips her tea, but after a moment, his hands slide up her calf. He stops, taking the tea from her, and she wreathes her arms around his neck, pulling him towards her. He kisses her again, and then suddenly turns towards the camera and waves Bella away, laughing, tells her to turn the camera phone off, and the screen goes black.

I've watched the same clip a dozen times since I found it on Andy's Facebook page yesterday. I hardly ever check his page – he's my husband, I don't need to be his social media 'friend' – but then I received a notification Louise had tagged me in a post, and stupidly, I clicked on it. I should never have accepted her friend request a couple of years ago, when we were being 'civilised'. I've blocked her now, but the damage is done: I can't unsee the video.

The footage was taken about five years ago, by Bella: she starts with a selfie in which she talks to the camera about 'meeting my family', perhaps for some sort of school project. She's about ten, but I didn't do the maths and work out *why* Louise wanted me to see this particular video until the second time I watched it. And then it hit me, like a punch to the gut.

There's just the briefest glimpse, when Louise reaches for her tea, but it's unmistakable: the clear outline of a baby bump.

I've always known Andy cheated on me with Louise. He told me when we met they were legally separated, waiting for the slow wheels of divorce to turn, and even though I'd known it was a cliché, exactly the kind of thing all married men say, I believed him. He had his own flat in central London, devoid of any feminine touch, and we didn't just spend weeknights together, but most weekends, too; once, we even flew to Barbados for a week. I didn't know then that Louise was used to him travelling for work for days or weeks at a time, giving him the perfect excuse to be away.

Just a few weeks after that Barbados holiday, I saw them together, quite by chance, at Paddington station. I'd never met Louise Page, but I recognised her instantly from her byline in the *Daily Post*, a column I'd always enjoyed reading until I fell in love with her husband. She was smaller than I'd expected, and prettier than her headshot photo. And at least five months pregnant.

Of course I should have ended things with Andy then and there. But he was so distraught, so repentant. One night of nostalgia, he said, too much wine, they'd slept together out of habit rather than desire. He hadn't been sure of me, then, he said; he'd been convinced I'd find someone my own age, someone more appropriate, with less baggage. He swore it'd just happened once, and that he and Louise had both agreed it had been a mistake. But then a scan at twenty weeks had revealed some kind of shadow on the baby's heart, which can indicate Down's syndrome, and her obstetrician had booked her in for an amniocentesis test (thankfully negative) with a foetal expert in London. *That's* where he'd been taking her when I'd spotted them at the station. There was no relationship between them anymore. He was just doing the decent thing by his child.

Once again, I'd believed him. I'd allowed myself to be convinced he was a good man who'd made a mistake, and was now trying to do the best he could to clean up his mess. In fact, I loved him all the more because he *hadn't* walked away from Louise, knowing the way a man treats your predecessor is the best indicator of how he'll treat you.

And most important of all: I'd just found out I was pregnant myself. I couldn't face the thought of being a single mother, but at the same time, aborting the baby of a man I loved to distraction was out of the question. Every man was allowed to screw up once, surely? He swore I was the one he loved, and that was all that really mattered.

But this video changes everything. Louise didn't get pregnant on a nostalgic, one-night-only trip down memory lane. They were clearly still in a relationship the whole time Andy and I were together. I replay the clip yet again, freezing it as Andy tucks the strand of hair behind Louise's ear. He *loved* her. I can see it in his face, as clear as day. Perhaps he's never stopped. Did he love me, too, when he was rubbing Louise's feet on the sofa? Or was I just a diversion for him, providing sex and careless, child-free pleasure? Louise was his professional equal, but I looked up to him; worshipped him, almost. How that must have stoked his ego. God, what an idiot I was. I'm an intelligent, successful, ambitious woman, and I still fell for some of the oldest lines in the book. He would never have left Louise if she hadn't screwed up. He didn't *choose* me. Her mistake pushed him into my arms by default.

I snap the computer shut as I hear the front door open. There's no point feeling sorry for myself. I knew

Andy was a liar when I married him. The question is: now that I know our entire relationship has been built on a lie, what am I going to do about it? Do I give Louise what she's wanted from the beginning, and leave him? Or do I reconcile myself to spending the rest of my life with a man I can never quite trust?

I compose my face into something resembling normal as Bella and her friend Taylor come into the sitting room. 'Hey.' I smile. 'Was the movie good?'

Bella shrugs. 'It was OK.'

'Did you get anything to eat while you were out? Or do you want me to sort you something for lunch?'

'We went to Pret,' Taylor says. 'But thank you, Mrs Page.'

'Oh, God, please call me Caz. You make me feel ancient.'

The two of them hover awkwardly in the middle of the sitting room, throwing each other meaningful looks. They clearly want to ask me something, and I resign myself to handing over the rest of the contents of my wallet. Neither Andy nor Louise give Bella any kind of proper allowance, and refuse to let her get a Saturday job, which means she has to ask for handouts every time she wants to get herself a coffee or buy a T-shirt. She's sixteen now: it's humiliating for everyone. I'm tempted to set up an automatic transfer via a banking app myself, except I don't want to totally overstep my bounds.

Taylor nudges her friend. 'Go on. Ask her.'

I reach for my bag. 'How much d'you need?'

'It's not that,' Bella says quickly.

She twists the silver ring nervously on her hand. She and Taylor both sport identical ones; they could be twins, in their ripped black jeans and oversized black sweaters, except that while Bella looks young for her age, Taylor could easily pass for twenty-one.

'Come on,' I sigh. 'Spit it out. What d'you want?'

Bella glances towards the doorway. 'Is Dad here?'

'He's taken the boys to the Science Museum. They won't be back for ages.' I stand up, and grab my jacket from the back of my chair. 'OK, I'm taking you two out. We're going to Halva's Patisserie for a sugar hit. Then you can tell me exactly what's going on' – I grin – 'and why you don't want to tell your father.'

I double-lock the front door, and shoo the girls down the street ahead of me. The flat is just off the North End Road, in one of the many tiny side streets honey-combing Fulham, and jammed with parked cars on both sides, one of the main reasons we never brought Andy's SUV to London. Our next-door neighbour, a sweet woman in her seventies, opens her door to bring out her rubbish just as we pass her gate, and I call out to the girls to wait as I stop and take it to the street for her. 'Sounds like you've been partying, Mrs Mahoney.' I smile, as the bag clinks.

'Oh, get away with you, Caz.' Mrs Mahoney laughs. 'It's Ernie's pickle jars. You know what he's like.'

'I do indeed,' I say.

Ernie and Elise Mahoney were the first people I met when I bought my flat eight years ago. It was definitely the dodgy end of the borough at the time, and my flat was broken into three times in the first year before I finally wised up and got mortise deadlocks and an alarm installed. But since then, as people have been driven further and further out from Chelsea and Belgravia by the influx of Russian oligarchs and foreign money, it's become gentrified. The girls and I have to step out into the road twice to avoid basement excavations before we even reach the end of our street; it's a wonder some of these terraced rows of houses are still standing. Working-class people like the Mahoneys, who've been here forty years, are in the minority now.

We thread our way through the throng of people crowding the Fulham Road and join the queue in Halva's, where Bella surprises me by ordering a huge slab of cheesecake. Normally she eats like a sparrow, but Taylor has bought a massive slice of lemon cake, so perhaps she's just following suit.

'OK. Out with it,' I say, as we sit down. 'What's the deal?'

'You're only going to say no,' Bella says.

I rip open a packet of sweetener and add it to my cappuccino. 'You won't know till you ask. First of all, is it illegal? Because I'm not getting hold of weed for you, so don't even try it.'

'It's nothing to do with drugs,' she exclaims, looking shocked.

'So why don't you want your father to know?'

'He wouldn't approve. And Mum would, like, *totally* flip.'

'But I wouldn't?'

'You're much cooler than most people's parents,' Bella says. 'You're pretty sick, actually.'

'I assume that's a good thing,' I say dryly, hiding my pleasure at the compliment. 'I've got to tell you, you've certainly made me curious. Do you need an adult's permission for whatever it is? Do you want me to sign something?'

'She doesn't need anyone's permission,' Taylor says. 'Not now she's sixteen.'

'I'm going to do it anyway,' Bella adds defiantly. 'You can't stop me. It's just . . .' She looks at Taylor, then back at me. 'I'd kind of *like* you there. Just in case. If that's OK.'

I sip my cappuccino, considering, more curious than ever. I remember what it's like to be a teenager: if Bella's set on doing whatever-this-is, she's going to find a way to do it, whether or not I agree to help. And having an adult present would give her some backup in case things go wrong. I have no idea what she's planning, but on the grounds that it's better to be inside the tent pissing out, I'd rather go with her than leave her to her own devices.

Especially since it sounds like it's *really* going to upset Louise.

PATRICK SIMON THATCHER
PART 1 OF RECORDED INTERVIEW

Date:- 28/07/2020
Duration:- 27 Minutes
Location:- Whitefish Advertising Agency

Conducted by Officers from Devon & Cornwall
Police

(cont.)

POLICE   So you've worked with both women?

PT   Yes. Caz was already at Whitefish when I met
           Louise about five years ago. She interviewed me
           for a profile piece. And then of course Tina took
           her on to handle PR for Univest.

POLICE	Were you aware of their personal history?
PT	Well, I knew Caz was married to Louise's ex-husband, yes.
POLICE	Did you know Andrew Page had left his first wife for Caroline Page?
PT	Caroline – oh, you mean Caz. Yes.
POLICE	But you didn't think it might cause trouble, having Louise Page working in the same office?
PT	Louise isn't like that. She's a sensible woman. Very smart, actually.
POLICE	What about Caroline Page?
PT	Look, the divorce was years ago. As far as I knew, everyone had got past it.
POLICE	Caroline Page has worked for you for eight years, is that right?
PT	Yes.
POLICE	Can you tell me what kind of person she is?
PT	What kind of person?

POLICE   Is she reliable? Well liked?

PT   She's good at her job. She gets things done. That
          doesn't always make you popular.

POLICE   Does she have a temper?

PT   She doesn't suffer fools. Nor do I.

POLICE   I understand you gave her a verbal warning a
          couple of weeks ago. Why was that?

PT   We had a problem at work. The buck stopped
          with Caz, but that's not why she got the warning.
          There was a scene in front of a client. Not the
          kind of thing you can just let go, I'm afraid.

POLICE   Perry, do you have the—

POLICE   About two weeks ago, sir.

POLICE   Thank you. I gather she blamed Louise Page for
          the incident you're referring to, Mr Thatcher?

PT   Yes.

POLICE   Was there any truth to it?

PT   Like I said, Louise isn't like that.

167

POLICE	So you think Caroline Page made it up?
PT	I think Caz made a mistake, that's all.
POLICE	How well do you know Louise Page?
PT	[Pause.] I don't really see much of her. She only comes into the office about once a week. The rest of the time she works from home.
POLICE	Do you ever see her socially, outside work?
PT	No.
POLICE	Were you aware she has a criminal record, Mr Thatcher?
PT	[Pause.] No. [Pause.] No, I wasn't aware of that.
POLICE	She didn't disclose it when you employed her?
PT	Technically, she didn't work for me, she worked for Tina Murdoch.
POLICE	Would you say—
PT	Wait. Are you sure you haven't made a mistake? You're talking about Louise, not Caz?
POLICE	Yes, sir.

PT   I can't quite believe it. It doesn't sound like her.
            A criminal record?

POLICE   She was convicted for breaching a Restraining
            Order against a man called Roger Lewison, and
            making false allegations and perverting the
            course of justice.

PT   Are you *serious*?

POLICE   Mr Thatcher, if you had known this information,
            would you still have felt comfortable allowing
            Louise and Caroline Page work in the same
            office?

Chapter 20

Louise

I wait until Sunday, when Bella and Tolly are in London with their father, before packing up our things at Andrew and Caz's house. The kitchen at home is still only half-finished, which means we're going to have to rough it for a bit; Tolly won't mind, but Bella's not going to be happy. She likes being here at her dad's, in the centre of town; it's an easy walk to meet up with her friends, and since it's so close to school, she can sleep in half an hour later. She's going to kick up a storm when she finds out we're going back home.

I'm just sweeping an astonishing array of phone chargers into a plastic carrier bag in the kitchen when I'm startled to hear the front door open.

'Sorry to catch you unawares,' Andrew says apologetically. 'I know you weren't expecting them back till tonight. I wanted to phone ahead, but Tolly—'

'Mummy!' Tolly cries, pushing past his father and flinging himself at me. 'We're home! Are you surprised? Did we surprise you?' His arms wreathe around my neck. 'I didn't want you to miss us anymore,' he says, with just the tiniest tremor in his voice.

Tolly's only four; even one night without your mother is a lifetime at that age. Most of the time, he takes his weekends with his father and Caz in his stride, but occasionally he gets homesick, and Andrew is sensitive enough to take his lead from his son when that happens, for which I'm grateful.

'Thank you so much for coming home early,' I say, hugging him tightly. 'I was missing you terribly. I hardly slept at all, even though I knew you were having fun with Daddy.'

'I'm going to find Bagpuss,' he announces, abruptly pulling away from me, his ship already righted. If only motherhood was always this easy. 'I think he's missed me, too.'

Bagpuss! Thank God Tolly reminded me. I knew there was something I'd forgotten.

Bella almost collides with her brother as he races from the room. 'Why are our bags in the hall?' she demands. 'What's going on?'

'Dad and Caz have been very kind, letting us stay here, but we've imposed enough,' I say firmly. 'We're going back home. It's going to be a bit like camping until the kitchen's finished, but—'

'I don't want to go home,' Bella interrupts. 'I like it here. Can I stay, Dad? I'll be fine on my own, I promise. And it's closer to school, I can just get the bus—'

'You're sixteen!' I snap. 'You're not staying here on your own.'

'Dad—'

'Sorry, Bell.' Andrew shrugs. 'I'm with your mother on this one.'

'Bella,' I interject sharply. 'What's that in your mouth?'

For a moment, she looks nervous, and then she lifts her chin. 'I had my tongue pierced,' she says.

I stare at her, horrified. 'You did *what*?'

'It's my body,' Bella says defiantly. The effect is marred slightly by the slight lisp from the piercing in her mouth. 'I have the right to do what I want with it.'

'You're still a child!' Andrew cries, clearly just as appalled as me.

She glares at us, her lips clamped tightly together as if we might prise the piercing from her mouth. From the expression on Andrew's face, he's considering it. When did our sweet-natured baby turn into this sullen, truculent stranger?

'She must have got it done yesterday,' Andrew says helplessly. 'I'm so sorry, Lou. I had no idea she'd sneaked off to do it.'

'Actually,' a voice says behind us, 'she didn't "sneak off" anywhere. I took her.'

Caz joins us in the kitchen, dumping her ludicrously expensive cream Prada bag on the counter as if it's a carrier bag from Sainsbury's.

'For God's sake,' Andrew says testily. 'Why would you take my daughter to get her tongue pierced?'

'She's sixteen. It's not illegal. She was going to get it done anyway, so I thought it'd be better if I made sure she went to a reputable place with clean needles.' Caz shrugs. 'And it's not like a tattoo, it's not permanent. She can take it out at any time.'

'It's not Caz's fault,' Bella says staunchly. 'She's right, I would've done it anyway.'

A complicit glance passes between them. Bella used to loathe Caz, but suddenly the two of them are thick as thieves, and *I'm* the one on the outside.

'You had no right,' Andrew snaps at Caz. 'She's *my* child. When she's under my roof, she's my responsibility.'

I don't miss the sudden tension between the two of them. It's not just about the tongue piercing, either. I know what Andrew looks like when he's on the defensive. Caz is making a mistake: he doesn't like being in the wrong, and he'll find a way to blame her for it. If I had to guess, I'd say she's seen the video Bella posted to her dad's page last week. Bella didn't mean anything by it – the clip probably popped up in her Facebook 'throwback' feed and she just shared it to him – but I'll admit my motives weren't quite as pure when I saw it and tagged Caz. She may want to rewrite history now and tell herself Andrew never really loved me, but he *did*, and that video proves it. Everything that went wrong between us can be traced back to that woman's appearance in our lives, and she deserves to be reminded of that now and again.

Tolly suddenly bursts back into the kitchen, startling us all. 'Bagpuss has throwed up!' he cries, his eyes wide with drama. 'It's all over Daddy's bed!'

'On my blanket?' Caz exclaims. 'That's Peruvian vicuña!'

My son stops short, suddenly uncertain. 'It's OK,' I say quickly. 'It's not your fault. Caz isn't blaming you. Thank you for telling us.'

'Did you give him tuna, Mum?' Bella accuses.

I hesitate. 'Only a little bit. He loves licking out the tin.'

'Mum! You know it always makes him sick!'

'I assume that's why she gave it to him,' Caz mutters.

Andrew sighs. 'Bella, can you just go and sort it out. Get Kit and Tolly to help you.'

Bella is about to protest, but something in her father's expression tells her this is not the time. She sighs theatrically, grabs a roll of kitchen towel from the counter, and stomps off upstairs with the boys.

'Look, I'll fix the blanket,' I say, sorry-not-sorry. 'Get it dry-cleaned, or something. I'm sure it's not as bad as it sounds. Or I'll get you a new one—'

'You can't dry-clean vicuña,' Caz says sharply. 'And it's irreplaceable. I bought it when I was in Machu Picchu. What is that cat even doing in my house? You know I'm allergic. Andy *told* you not to bring him.'

I specifically asked Andrew if it was OK to bring Bagpuss, and he said it was fine. Clearly that didn't get approved further up the food chain. He catches my eye, and I read his wordless appeal not to land him in it. 'I'm sorry,' I say, falling on my sword. 'I didn't know what else to do with him. He's so old, he couldn't cope with my mother's dog, and Min's boys are so boisterous—'

Caz cuts me off. 'Whatever. It's done now. I suppose it doesn't matter, since you're leaving anyway.'

A beat late, Andrew picks up his cue. 'Look, Louise. It's not that we haven't been happy to help out. It's just, I think we all need a bit of distance going forward.' He coughs, and shifts awkwardly on his feet. 'I'm not sure taking the job at Whitefish was a good idea, to be honest. I'm all for keeping things civilised, but you've put Caz in a bit of an awkward position. It's difficult for her to do her job properly when there's such a personal relationship between the two of you.' He looks at her, and then back at me, clearly trying to remember the script she's given him. 'We all need a bit of space. Just so no feathers get ruffled. I could . . . er . . . give you the number of our handyman, so you don't have to call me. And Bella's old enough to bring Tolly to me for weekends without involving you.'

My cheeks burn with humiliation. The way he paints it, I sound desperate and needy, my nose pressed against the window of their lives: a sad, unloved ex-wife who can't move on. Why is it, no matter how successful or attractive a woman is, if a man leaves her she is defined by that rejection, an object of pity just because one weak man can't keep his trousers zipped?

I summon as much dignity as I can muster. 'I'm afraid I can't let Chris down, Andrew. Not now I've taken on the job.' I smile coolly at Caz. 'I'm sure the two of us can figure things out at work.'

'I'm sure we can,' Caz says. 'Now that we understand each other.'

Three weeks before the party

Chapter 21

Caz

Visiting my mother only ever goes one of two ways. There are the days when she can't wait to see me, excitedly leaping up from her chair the moment I walk in, bombarding me with questions before I've even got my coat off, and sharing all the gossip on our street in the weeks since I last visited. Those are the days when her condition is at its worst, when she still believes it's 2006 and I'm fifteen years old. She'll ask me about my day at school, and tease me about the boy who sits next to me in maths. She has no idea who Andy is, or that her grandson Kit even exists. If I try to remind her, she gets upset and confused. I've learned it's simpler to go along with her reality, because at least she's happy there.

Then there are the days when she knows exactly who I am. Those are the days when she refuses to greet me, and turns away when I bend to kiss her. I don't know which is worse: the bittersweet fiction of her world before the accident, or the harsh reality of a present where she's locked herself in a prison of sullen resentment and self-pity.

Today, it's the latter. She's sitting by the window, staring sourly at the car park below, when I walk in. She doesn't even acknowledge I'm here. She's in a wheelchair, although she can walk perfectly well. The accident affected her balance, but otherwise her mobility is fine. The orderlies at the care home indulge her because it makes their lives easier.

'Hi, Mum,' I say, dumping my bag on the coffee table. 'How are you doing today?'

I don't expect an answer, and I'm not surprised by one. My mother has few friends, but it's not companionship or amity she misses: it's someone to fight with. When no one gives a shit what you think, it's impossible to wound them. She ignores me because I'm the only one who'll even notice.

I go over to the small galley kitchen in the corner of her room and switch on the kettle, even though I know she'll refuse to drink anything I make on principle. 'Tea, Mum?' I say, getting out two mugs without waiting for a response. 'And I brought some chocolate digestives this time, like you asked.'

This finally elicits a reply. 'I don't like chocolate,' she announces, without turning around.

'Last time, when I brought the ordinary ones, you said you wanted chocolate.'

'You've brought milk chocolate. I said plain.'

'Sorry about that,' I say, unruffled. 'I'll bring plain next time.'

I make two cups of weak tea, exactly the way she likes it, and put one on the table next to her, then turn her wheelchair around from the window. 'What do you call this?' she sneers, peering into the mug as I take a seat. 'Look at the colour of it. So weak it's a fortnight.'

'I can make you another—'

'Don't bother. You won't stay long enough for me to drink it.'

'Would you like me to stay longer?'

My mother looks up sharply. The unspoken rules of our game mean she can't admit she wants me to stay, but if she says no, she can't complain when I leave at the end of our customary hour. Her eyes narrow as she acknowledges the point. First blood to me.

I sip my tea, regarding her steadily over the rim of my mug. 'Andy's ex-wife just got a job at Whitefish,' I say, knowing how much she'll relish my misfortune. 'She's actually working on one of my accounts.'

Mum's face lights up with sadistic glee. 'Oh, I bet that's put the cat among the pigeons!'

'Don't talk to me about cats,' I mutter, still sore about my Peruvian blanket. 'Turns out my boss on the new account is Louise's best friend. She tried to get me fired, years ago, when Andy and I first got together. It's only a matter of time before she gives it another go.'

'You made your bed,' Mum says, with evident satis-faction.

'Yes, I thought you'd be pleased.'

'Married men aren't fair game, Carol. I told you that when you met him.'

Despite myself, my hackles rise. 'Don't call me Carol.'

'Why not? It's your name.'

181

'Not anymore,' I snap.

Andy fell in love with Caroline, a Chelsea girl from her pearl earrings to the tips of her Hunter-clad toes. He has no idea where I'm really from, what I've had to do to get to where I am. Unlike Louise, I *earned* my place at the top table. I worked two jobs to put myself through university, and I didn't just study business management and marketing; I studied the confident, entitled students around me, the way they talked and spoke and ate. I learned to say napkin instead of serviette, and loo instead of toilet; like a latter-day Eliza Doolittle, I picked up my aitches and spoke as if I had a mouthful of marbles. By the time I graduated, Carol was dead, buried deep below her net curtains and royal commemorative plates. And that's the way it's going to stay.

Mum reaches for one of the despised milk chocolate biscuits, and I pretend not to notice. 'Hard man to keep on the porch, that husband of yours,' she observes. 'Just like your father. They all leave in the end.'

'Dad didn't leave. He *died*, Mum.'

She snorts. 'Tell yourself that, if it makes you feel better.'

I sigh inwardly. Even when Mum is more or less herself, she still has occasional slips into a parallel world, forgetting details and becoming confused. She often insists Dad ran off with another woman. I think it's more palatable to her than the truth: if he's alive, there's still the chance he might come back.

'Andy's not going to leave me, Mum,' I say. 'He just feels guilty about his kids, that's all.'

She smiles mockingly. 'Not worried he's going to go back to her, then?'

It's just a shot in the dark, but it finds its mark. 'No,' I say shortly.

'You think you beat her, don't you?'

'It's not a question of beating—'

'Isn't it? Seems to me that's what it's always been about.'

My mother may be mad at times, but she's never stupid. 'You're in a duel,' she says suddenly, her eyes burning into mine. 'A duel to the death. You need to take the gloves off, Carol. Take the fight to *her*. Andy's yours now. You need to remind her of that.'

I shiver. *A duel to the death.* It's nonsense, of course. She's veering back towards crazytown; I recognise the signs. But her comment unnerves me nonetheless. There's always a shadow time between Mum's periods of lucidity and fantasy, where it's almost like she has some kind of sixth sense. I've been preoccupied with Louise to the exclusion of almost everything else for weeks now. The woman has inserted herself into my life, forcing her way into my house and my workplace, but I'm the one who let her take up residence in my head.

We all maintain the fiction that Mum had an 'accident', but the truth is, she tried to kill herself four years after she lost my father. I remember her when I was little: she was beautiful and smart and *funny*, the kind of funny that made you snort milk through your nose. When he died, it was as if she died with him. I didn't realise I'd been holding my breath, waiting for something terrible like this to happen, until the day I came home from school not long after my fifteenth birthday, and found her hanging from the bannister in the hall.

I wasn't strong enough to cut her down. Instead, I propped her feet on a kitchen chair to take the weight while I called 999, trying to loosen the tie – my father's tie – from around her neck. I thought she was dead. Her face was purple, her eyes bloodshot and bugging from her head, her tongue protruding from between blue lips. I had no idea she was still alive until the paramedics got her down and started CPR.

She was in hospital for four months, the first week in a coma in intensive care, and then afterwards in a psychiatric ward. They put me in foster care; the family I stayed with were perfectly nice, but they didn't have much interest in me beyond the cheque they received for taking me in. Eventually, Mum was released, and they let me go home to her. Social services kept an eye, of course, but physically, she was fine. They put her on antidepressants, she saw a shrink once a week for a few months; everything seemed, if not normal, no worse than a thousand other dysfunctional, damaged families.

The memory lapses started about a year later. At first, I didn't really pay much attention; she'd forget small details, talk about events that had happened several years ago as if it'd been last week, that sort of thing. I was too caught up in my own life at the time to really notice. But then I came home from Bristol at the end of my first term at university, and Mum thought I was still studying for my GCSEs. After weeks of tests, the doctors were no closer to a diagnosis, but speculated she'd suffered some kind of brain damage during her suicide attempt. Either way, she couldn't live alone, so I sold the house and found her a care facility she was prepared to tolerate. At the age of eighteen, I was on my own.

Mum abruptly grips my hand, her fingernails digging into my skin. 'I see it in you,' she says. 'I see what you are.'

I try to pull away, but she's stronger than she looks. 'What do you see, Mum?' I ask wearily.

'Me,' she says. 'I see me.'

Chapter 22

Louise

I know Caz will retaliate for me moving in on her patch, and that it won't take long for her to make her next move. But what takes me by surprise is that Andrew's the one to deliver the blow.

'You're taking me back to *court*?' I demand, when I receive the letter from his solicitor and ring him at work. 'You know I'm barely getting by as it is!'

'You're earning three times the amount at Whitefish compared to what you were getting from the university,' Andrew says coldly. 'You're on a consultant contract; you're taking home more than Caz. It's only fair we look at your maintenance and child support again.'

'You don't need to take me to court! We could talk about it, and come to some—'

'Caz is very upset,' Andrew snaps. 'If you insist on hounding her like this, you can't complain when there are consequences.'

The gloves are really off now. Andrew's taking a risk, going after me like this. Not that I'm about to land him in it with Caz and tell her what really happened the night of the storm; I can't prove it, and he's an accomplished liar. But he's relying on my decency not to cause trouble between them, and there's a limit to how much punishment I can take.

If I'm going to do this job at Whitefish, I'm doing it on my terms. Hiding out at Chris's office when I go to London isn't going to work if I want to beat Caz at her own game.

'You want an office at *Whitefish*?' Chris exclaims, when I ask her to arrange it. 'I thought you didn't want to be anywhere near Caz?'

'Keep your friends close, and your enemies closer,' I mutter. 'I want to keep an eye on her, and make sure she doesn't screw things up on your account just to get back at me.'

I don't get an office, but I get a desk on the open-plan mezzanine floor, right in the hub of things. I'm a journalist: rooting out the real story behind the headlines is what I do. I soon discover Caz is smart and undoubtedly good at her job, and great with the clients, but she's a terrible manager. She puts people's backs up, she's autocratic and high-handed, and the creatives don't like working for her. It's AJ who follows behind her and cleans up her mess, smoothing troubled waters and using all his charm to ensure her directives are met on time. Without him, she'd be sunk. I can use this, I think cautiously. If I need to.

But I truly don't want it to come to that. I'm tired of this tit-for-tat nonsense. I can't afford to go to court; it'll cost thousands of pounds, and I earn just over the threshold to qualify for legal aid. If Andrew doesn't back down, I'll end up in even more debt. Taking the job at Whitefish was meant to make Caz think twice about messing with my livelihood. Instead, she's upped the ante yet again. I'm starting to wonder where this is all going to end.

I pick up the children from school, feeling angry and despondent. Tolly is his usual sunny self, but Bella doesn't even speak to me as she gets into the car. She's still sulking over that wretched tongue piercing. Andrew is the one who made her remove it, but it's me she blames. She's been even more sullen and uncommunicative this week, if that were possible.

When we get home, I pull into the driveway and wait for Bella to get out and open the garage door. 'Why can't we get an electric one?' she complains, as she does every single time I ask her to perform this chore.

'Same reason as yesterday,' I say evenly. 'Same reason as tomorrow.'

Tolly leans forward in his car seat, straining against the restraints. 'Let me! Let me!'

'You can't reach the handle, darling.'

Bella reluctantly slouches towards the garage, opening it with agonising slowness, and I tamp down a rising tide of irritation as she then stands in the middle of the drive, blocking my way, to check her mobile. When she finally moves, she drops one of her Bluetooth earbuds – a ridiculously extravagant gift from Andrew – and takes her sweet time picking it up, while I drum my fingers on the steering wheel and suppress the urge to scream.

Eventually, she gets out of the way so that I can park. I help Tolly out of the car, and go around the house. The builders are still working on the porch, their scaffolding preventing us from going in through the front, so we have to enter through the back door. I must admit, Gary Donahue's doing a good job. The front of the house no longer sags drunkenly forwards for the first time since we bought the place.

'I found this on the drive,' Bella says, rudely shoving something at me as she pushes past me into the mudroom.

It's an earring. Some sort of semi-precious blue stone: topaz, maybe, or aquamarine.

'Whose is this?' I ask, dumping my bag on the kitchen table.

'Caz's. She was wearing them the other week. Can you put it somewhere safe till I can give it back to her? I'll only lose it.'

'How did it end up in our driveway?'

Bella shrugs, putting her earbuds back in her ears. 'Probably fell out of Dad's car. Don't call me for dinner,' she adds, on her way up the stairs. 'I'm not hungry.'

'Bella—'

With a sigh, I put the earring in the soap dish on the windowsill, tempted though I am to drop it into the waste disposal, and reach beneath the sink for the cat food. I need to sort out the kids' dinner early, as I promised I'd go over to my mother's and help her and Min with arrangements for the party, which is less than three weeks away now. My heart sinks further at the thought. I really wish Mum hadn't invited Andrew and Caz. This celebration should be a family affair, and instead, I'll have to deal with Caz and her spiteful games. It seems like I'm never free of her these days.

I grill a couple of burgers on the barbecue outside, and take Tolly's into him in the sitting room. I don't normally let them eat food in front of the TV, and he responds as if I've just given him the keys to Disneyland. Bella's dinner I cover and leave on the dining table, in case she changes her mind while I'm out.

I go up to her room and pop my head around her door to let her know I'm leaving. She's curled up on her bed, facing the wall, a thick fleece blanket pulled up around her shoulders despite the fact it's July and 29 degrees outside.

'Bella?' I say softly. 'Are you awake?'

She doesn't say anything, but I can tell from her breathing she's not asleep.

'I'm just popping out to see Gree,' I say. 'Call me if there's anything you need. I'll be back before it gets dark.'

Bella doesn't stir. I lean over her and straighten the blanket, a fist squeezing my heart. For all her teenage attitude, she's still my baby, and right now, her face scrubbed of make-up, her slight form dwarfed by the heaped blankets and pillows, she looks not much older than Tolly.

As I turn away, the phone on the bedside table illuminates with an incoming text from Taylor, and I can't help but read it.

U hv to get it Im desperate.

I feel a flash of maternal concern. What can the girl possibly need that's so urgent?

Before I can dig too deeply, my own phone pings with a message from Luke. Any idea what's going on with Dad?

I put a mental pin in the text from Taylor, and reply to my brother as I go downstairs. Is there a problem? Mum didn't say anything to me.

She said he had a funny turn.

I sigh inwardly. I'm on my way over. Will keep you posted.

👍

Typical of Mum, I think crossly, as I go out to the car. If Dad were really ill, she'd have told me. Instead, she creates a drama by contacting Luke, knowing the first thing he'll do is come to me. Somehow, my brother avoids getting sucked into her games in a way I've never quite managed. He takes after Dad: quiet and self-effacing, he generally glides below Mum's radar, showing up – literally and metaphorically – just often enough to be left to his own devices the rest of the time. I've noticed he follows much the same policy with Min.

I let myself into my parents' house. 'Mum?' I call. 'You there?'

Dad ambles into the kitchen to greet me, a crumpled

copy of the *Telegraph* in his hand. 'Hello, poppet,' he says in surprise. 'Not at work?'

'Working from home today, Dad,' I say, kissing his cheek. 'You all right? Mum said you had a bit of a turn.'

'A bit of a turn, is that what she calls it?' Dad snorts. 'Didn't get her own way over having a band at the party, is what she means.'

I scrutinise him carefully. He looks the same as always: tall and thin, as gangly as a teenager, with an unruly halo of white fluff around his ears and a pair of frameless half-moon glasses permanently perched on the end of his nose. He's more than a decade older than Mum, but there's a youthful air of mischief about him that even Nicky's loss didn't manage to dim. I've always thought of him as ageless, but I realise he'll be eighty next April. He wears his years lightly, but eighty is old by anyone's standards.

'I heard that, Brian,' Mum says, coming in through the back door. She's been mowing the lawn, and her shoes are covered with grass clippings. I don't know how she has the energy in this heat. My parents have an old-fashioned push mower, too, not one of those labour-saving petrol ones. 'Hello, Louise. I like that dress on you. It suits you now you're carrying that extra weight.'

'Thank you, Mum,' I say, not rising to the bait.

She reaches up to smooth Dad's hair. 'Honestly, Brian, look at the state of you. You look like you've been dragged through a hedge backwards.'

'Fell asleep in my chair,' Dad says, unruffled.

'In the middle of the afternoon?'

'Churchill used to swear by a nap,' he says serenely, flapping out the pages of his paper and refolding it as he wanders back to his study.

'Churchill had a country to run and a war to win,' Mum calls after his retreating back. 'Well, since you're here, Louise, perhaps you can help me with the carrots,' she adds, handing me the peeler. 'I've got Luke and Min descending on me later with the boys. I could use a hand.'

I open the vegetable bin and get the carrots out. 'Luke said you told him Dad had a turn,' I say.

'He's not getting any younger. Cold water on the carrots, Louise.'

'But he's OK?'

'He's been a bit forgetful lately, that's all. Let his eggs boil dry the other day, and he keeps feeding the dog. She had four breakfasts yesterday – she thinks it's Christmas.'

I want to tell her that if she needs me to come over, she only has to ask; there's no need to manufacture a crisis. But that's not Mum's way. She has never directly asked for help, even in the immediate aftermath of Nicky's death. She finds our pressure points and uses them to get us to toe the line without seeming to lift a finger.

I pass her a peeled carrot and she dices it deftly, then scrapes it from the board into a saucepan. 'Min told me you'd moved back home at the weekend,' she says. 'You handled that all wrong, you know.'

I pause, a half-peeled carrot in my hand. 'Handled what all wrong?'

'I can see what you were doing, moving into Caz's space,' she says. 'I'm sure it unsettled her no end. But you need to be more careful. You gave her a genuine grievance to take to Andrew, and that wasn't smart.'

'It was his idea,' I protest. 'You think I *wanted* to stay in their house?'

She puts down the knife and looks straight at me. 'Well, of course you did.'

'No, I—'

'Louise, I spoke to Gary Donahue.'

That silences me.

'He said the damage to the kitchen wasn't nearly as bad as it looked. He repaired the ceiling and patched the hole in the wall the first day. The house was perfectly habitable two weeks ago. He says he spoke to you and told you that.' She turns back to the carrots and begins chopping again. 'It's not healthy, what you're doing. You need to put some distance between you and Andrew.'

My mother has refined passive aggression into an art form. Usually, I ignore it, as I did with the backhanded compliment about my dress, but the flagrant injustice of this statement is too much, even for me.

'*You* invited him to your anniversary party,' I say tersely. 'Even though I asked you not to. And what about dinner, the night of Bella's play? I had no intention of crashing it until you interfered!'

'I did it for my granddaughter,' Mum says. 'I thought

it'd be nice for her to have both her parents together on her big night.'

'It *was*. But—'

'I like Andrew, but despite what you might think, I neither want nor need the two of you to get back together,' Mum says. 'If it's what you want, I'll do anything I can to help, but the only thing I truly care about is whether or not you're happy.' She pauses. 'I need you to be happy, Louise.'

She loves me, I know that. Since we lost Nicky, she's poured everything into making Luke and me happy. But she adores Andrew; she'd do anything to get us back together. She sees my divorce as a personal failure on her part. 'Mum, I got over Andrew a long time ago,' I say evenly. 'We're not getting back together, and I'm happy with that. He's Bella and Tolly's father, that's all.'

'I'm not judging you, Louise,' she says, washing her hands. 'I don't mind if you lie to me, but don't lie to yourself.'

It's not that I'm lying, exactly. But if you tell yourself something often enough, you start to believe it.

Two weeks before the party

Chapter 23

Caz

AJ is already waiting for me at the table when I get to the Mexican cantina, a dubious-looking cocktail fringed with umbrellas and glacé cherries on the table in front of him. When AJ officially came out at a Christmas party four years ago, a grand total of zero people were surprised.

'Sorry I'm late,' I say, sliding into the booth opposite him. 'Got caught in a meeting with Nolan. What on earth are you drinking?'

'Sex in the Woods. It's like Sex on the—'

'Never mind. I don't want to know.' I turn to the waitress. 'I'll have what he's *not* having. Vodka martini, straight up, two olives.'

'You're so sweet to do this,' AJ says, nervously twirling his cocktail umbrella. 'Mum's been dying to meet you. I promise she won't stay long. She's got to get a train back to Crawley after lunch.'

The waitress returns with my drink. I pull the olives from their plastic stick, and squeeze them into my martini. 'It's fine. I'm looking forward to it.'

I'm not usually the kind of person people want to take home, but I suspect AJ doesn't have many friends he feels comfortable introducing to his mother. To be honest, I don't think he has many friends at all. Whitefish is his life. He's always the first one into the office, and the last to leave, which may be one of the reasons his relationships don't last. He started in the mailroom here straight out of school, and somehow managed to earn a place on the ad team through sheer commitment and determination. His temporary secondment as my assistant is his big chance to shine. If he does a good job, it'll be made permanent.

I recognise Mrs James the moment she comes into the restaurant. She looks exactly like AJ, right down to the pink nail polish her son is also wearing. 'You must be Caz!' she exclaims, throwing her arms around me as I half-rise awkwardly. 'AJ talks about you all the time! You didn't tell me she was so pretty,' she adds, throwing her son a mischievous look. 'Now I understand all the late hours.'

'It's lovely to meet you, Mrs James—'

'Please, call me Annie. Everybody does.'

She scoots into the booth next to AJ. 'So, is my boy working hard?' she asks. 'Staying on top of things?'

'I couldn't manage without him,' I say honestly.

She squeezes his arm. 'A girl could do a lot worse. He's a wonderful cook,' she adds. 'Taught himself. Had to, really, I have trouble boiling an egg.'

For a moment I wonder if the poor woman is under the impression I'm auditioning for the role of her daughter-in-law, but then she winks at me, and I realise she's teasing.

I listen as she and AJ banter in the familiar, comfortable way I've seen in other families, but never in my own. Even before my mother's accident, we never had that kind of relationship. When she wasn't drunk, she was curled up on the sofa in her nightdress, crying. I was always too ashamed of her to bring anyone but Angie home, and so I never accepted anyone's invitation to their house because I couldn't return it. Angie's own mother emigrated to Spain with her second husband when she was a kid, leaving Angie behind with her dad, so we never went to her place, either. It's one of the things I've always envied about Louise: her relationship with her mother.

AJ's mother extorts a promise from me to visit her in Crawley and leaves to get her train just as my phone buzzes with an incoming text from Patrick: **Get back to the office ASAP.**

'Shit,' I say. 'Patrick needs me back at the office. Can you get the bill and meet me there, AJ? I'll settle up with you later.'

The restaurant is only five minutes' walk from the office. I start back, my stomach churning. I have a bad feeling about this. I don't know what's going on, but it's not like Patrick to be so terse. I hope something hasn't gone south with Univest. Louise is just waiting for the opportunity to fuck me over. Maybe I shouldn't have riled Andy up about the child support payments, but that woman's been having it all her own way for far too long. It was just too much, seeing her sitting at a desk

201

six feet away from me. Ever since Celia invited me to her anniversary party, Louise has been out for blood. No matter what I do, she just keeps coming. I need to find a way to put an end to this, once and for all.

The second I get out of the lift, I see Louise talking to Franco, one of my clients, on the far side of the office. She glances up and catches my eye, and then Franco himself turns and sees me, his expression grim. Moments later, Patrick comes out of his office and signals to me to join them in the conference room. He doesn't look happy.

'What the fuck is going on?' I mutter, to the room at large. No one meets my eye. Something bad is going down, I can smell it.

No one even acknowledges me when I enter the conference room. I sit down as far from Louise as possible in the confines of the space, my stomach fizzing with anxiety. I've no idea what's coming, but it's not going to be good.

The Creative Director, Nolan Casey, and Finn Redford, the Art Director, join us, looking wary. Clearly neither of them have a clue what's going on either. I spot AJ crossing the office to his desk, and wave for him to come and join us, but Patrick shuts the conference room door in his face.

Patrick's gaze is cool as it rests on me. He flips open the laptop on the glass conference table, and spins it towards me without a word.

I gape at the screen in disbelief. 'What the hell?'

'You do realise what this means?' Franco demands

abruptly. A small muscle works at the side of his jaw. 'The backlash has already started on Twitter. We've called in a crisis management company, but this is going to cost us a fortune. It'll take years to rebuild our brand.'

'I don't understand,' I exclaim. 'This was never supposed to—'

'I'm afraid I'll be moving our account, Patrick,' Franco interrupts. 'Even if I wanted to stay with you, my board wouldn't allow it after this.'

'Franco, I am so sorry,' Patrick says. 'Of course we'll do whatever we can to make the transition as straightforward as possible.' His eyes are like stones as they rest on me. 'I want to know how the hell something like this happened. *Some*one had to authorise that change order and put it through.'

I stare again at the image on the computer screen. I don't blame Franco for dropping us. The repercussions from this will be huge. Our other clients will rightly be concerned; if it's not handled properly, this could destroy our agency. 'Patrick, I don't know who would have done that,' I say helplessly. 'We pulled this. It should never have gone through.'

'What do you mean, you pulled it?' Louise interjects.

'Louise, I don't mean to be rude, but this account has nothing to do with you,' I say tersely. 'To be honest, I'm not really sure why you're here.'

'Like I just told Patrick and Franco,' Louise says, her eyes never leaving my face. 'I was in the office when the change order was phoned through. I heard who did it. It was *you*.'

NOLAN CASEY
PART 1 OF RECORDED INTERVIEW

Date:- 28/07/2020
Duration:- 32 Minutes
Location:- Whitefish Advertising Agency, King's Road, London

Conducted by Officers from Devon & Cornwall Police

(cont.)

POLICE   So the change order didn't come from you, as the Creative Director?

NC   Of course not. AJ told us to pull it, so I spoke to the team and had it binned.

POLICE   But the ad ran anyway?

NC   I don't know how it— I spoke to Bette and she
           said it was gone. She was the main, the creative
           on the Vine account. She saw, I mean, once Caz
           pointed it out, we all agreed. That yellow logo,
           on striped pyjamas? We'd have been— Well,
           you saw what happened.

POLICE   So the campaign was officially shelved?

NC   Yes. We were working on a totally new angle.
           Finn had this brainwave. She was, like, going
           to—

POLICE   Sorry to interrupt, Mr Casey. But I just want to
           be clear. How did it end up in the press if it had
           been cancelled?

NC   It didn't 'end up' in the press. Look, there's a
           process. There are proofs, copy approval; you
           have to book ad space, all the rest of it. It's not
           like you can hit send and the next thing you
           know the ad's all over the number 44 bus.

POLICE   So what happened?

NC   Well, someone must have put the change order
           through.

POLICE	Who would have the authority to do that?
NC	Only Caz or Patrick. But obviously Patrick didn't do it, and Caz says she didn't, so . . .
POLICE	Do you believe her?
NC	[Inaudible.]
POLICE	For the tape, Mr Casey shrugged.
NC	Caz *says* she didn't do it. She was, well, she was very— She accused Louise of doing it.
POLICE	Why did she think that?
NC	Well, they don't exactly get on.
POLICE	According to Mr Thatcher, the two women had a cordial relationship.
NC	[Inaudible].
POLICE	Sorry?
NC	Patrick sees what he wants to see.
POLICE	You disagree?
NC	It was weird, the whole thing. The first day she

	arrived, she and Caz got into it out on the terrace. We all saw them.
POLICE	Is it possible Caz simply made a mistake, and put the change order through after all?
NC	[Pause.] I suppose.
POLICE	But you don't think so?
NC	Caz doesn't make mistakes like that. She can be a bit difficult to work with, but she's super-organised. She and Louise had, like, this *blood feud*. Caz started going on about some kind of conspiracy between Louise and Tina. She totally freaked out.
POLICE	How do you mean, freaked out?
NC	She started yelling and shouting at Louise, saying Caz had pretended to be her and put in the change order. She had a total meltdown; the whole office heard them. In the end, Patrick came out and told her to go home.
POLICE	Mr Thatcher blamed Caz?
NC	The whole thing was a PR nightmare from start to finish. Vine had to issue a public apology, we lost them as clients, and several others threatened

to walk. Whitefish is a small agency – we can't afford this kind of fuck-up. Patrick was furious with Caz. He nearly fired her, except no one could actually prove what'd happened.

POLICE   When was this?

NC   A couple of weeks ago? Like, two?

POLICE   So, hold on, Perry, can you get me, thank you. That would be, ah, ten days or so before the incident outside the Pages' house when the police were called?

NC   Yeah, maybe. Yes.

POLICE   Presumably that's what the altercation was about?

NC   The fight at Caz's house?

POLICE   Yes.

NC   Oh, that wasn't about the Vine campaign. It was *way* worse than that.

Chapter 24

Louise

With every mile the train from London puts between us, I feel safer. I should *never* have taken the job at Whitefish. Min warned me, but I didn't listen. She wasn't worried about what Caz would do; she was concerned about what it'd do to *me*. And she was right: going head-to-head with Caz has unleashed a darkness in me I thought I'd overcome years ago. I let myself get sucked back into a vendetta with her, retaliating every time she struck a blow, when instead I should've risen above it. But it's not too late. I can't undo the bad blood between us, but I'm going to call Chris tomorrow and tell her I can't work at Whitefish anymore. It may mean I have to tighten my belt a bit until I can get some more freelance work, but it'll be better than this constant state of warfare.

Even I was shocked by Caz's violent outburst this afternoon. I've never seen anyone that angry. I've always known what she's capable of, but it's the first time I've seen her lose control in public like that. And judging from Patrick's appalled reaction, it was the first time he'd seen that side of her, too.

At least he doesn't think I'd jeopardise the livelihood of hundreds of people over a stupid quarrel with my ex-husband's new wife. I'd hate to lose his good opinion, especially now, when I'm going to need a reference.

When I finally get home, it's after seven. Mum picked up the children from school for me, and then left Bella to babysit. I kick off my heels and go into the sitting room. Tolly is fast asleep on the sofa, the remains of a pizza crust on a plate next to him telling me they have at least eaten. I shake him gently awake, and pull him onto my lap. 'You should've been in bed an hour ago,' I whisper.

'You said I could stay up till you got home,' he mumbles.

I sigh. 'Yes, I did. OK, you, up we get,' I add. 'Did Bella feed Bagpuss?'

He rubs his eyes, too sleepy to answer. I put him down and get the box of kibble from its temporary home in the downstairs loo. I fill the cat's bowl. I can't wait till the kitchen is finished and we can stop living like squatters. 'Have you seen Bagpuss?' I ask Tolly, when the cat doesn't appear. Arthritic though he is, he usually materialises out of thin air as soon as he hears the sound of his kibble hitting his dish.

Awake now, Tolly starts crawling around the sitting room, peering under the sofa and behind doors, calling the cat's name. 'You'd better check he hasn't got shut in a bedroom or something,' I tell him, when Bagpuss still doesn't appear. 'He was in the airing cupboard all night the other day—'

210

I'm interrupted by a blood-curdling scream from upstairs. 'Muuuum!'

Visions of broken limbs and twisted ankles fill my maternal vision. I race towards the stairs, my heart pounding, just as Bella rushes down them, the cat cradled against her chest.

Fear sharpens my tone. 'Are you hurt?'

'*Bagpuss*!'

The poor cat is having trouble breathing. His eyes roll sickeningly back in his head, and he suddenly starts to convulse, his body going rigid in Bella's arms. I have no idea what's wrong with him, or how to help him.

'We need to get him to the vet,' I say urgently. 'Into the car, both of you.'

I don't need to ask them twice. The vet is only a couple of miles away, on the outskirts of Pulborough; they're open till eight, and if we hurry, we should be there in less than ten minutes. We pile into the car, Bella in the front seat with the cat still in her arms. I only realise I'm still in bare feet when I put my foot down once we're on the main road.

'Drive faster, Mum!' Bella cries, as I tear along the twisty lane as fast as I dare.

'I'm doing my best,' I say helplessly. 'It won't help Bagpuss if we drive into a tractor coming the other way.'

'What's wrong with him?' Tolly asks.

'I don't know, darling. He's pretty old. Maybe he's having some sort of seizure or a stroke.'

'It's not a stroke,' Bella says, her voice clogged with

tears. 'He's been poisoned. He looks like the rats in the barn after Dad put down that stuff.'

Bagpuss's breaths are coming in tight little pants, and I realise we don't have much time. He suddenly starts to vomit, and with surprising calm, Bella grabs an old towel we keep in the back for spills, and mops it up, murmuring soothingly to the cat all the while.

I catch a glimpse of something bright green in the towel as she wipes his mouth, and my heart sinks. He must have eaten deadly nightshade or some other toxic plant or flower. His eyesight isn't what it was, and if his sense of smell is also fading, then he's obviously at risk of eating something poisonous by mistake. I should never have let him outside. My poor, darling Bagpuss. It'll break all our hearts if something happens to him. We've had him since Bella was a baby; to lose him now, in such a way, would be devastating.

I screech to a halt outside the vets' surgery, and Bella rushes straight in with Bagpuss while I unbuckle Tolly and help him out of the car. Tamzin Kennedy has been our vet for years; she's known Bagpuss since he was a kitten. She looks stricken to see him like this. 'How long has he been unconscious?' she asks, gently easing him from Bella's arms and onto the examination table.

'I just got home from work fifteen, maybe twenty minutes ago,' I say. 'Bella found him like this in the bathroom upstairs a few minutes later.'

'He threw up this bright green stuff,' Bella says tearfully. She hands Tamzin the old towel covered in cat vomit, and I'm impressed by her quick thinking at bringing it in. 'It smells weird. Kind of sweet.'

Tamzin sniffs it. 'Antifreeze,' she says grimly. 'I'd recognise it anywhere.'

'*Antifreeze*?'

'It's not just used to stop engines freezing,' Tamzin says, ripping open a sterile packet containing a needle and syringe. 'It's also used in hydraulic brake fluids. Cats usually come into contact with it when it leaks from a car's engine onto the ground. It tastes sweet at first, and by the time the foul aftertaste hits, it's too late. It doesn't take much to make them very sick.'

'Is he going to die?' Tolly asks, his eyes wide with fear.

'Not if I can help it, sweetheart. Jamie!' she cries, calling to the young veterinary assistant in the back of the surgery. 'I need you to go and get me some vodka from the off-licence down the road. Fast as you can. The more expensive, the better. Grab some money from the petty cash box. Run!'

'Vodka?' I exclaim.

'Trick I learned when I was working in Australia. If we can get pure alcohol into his blood, it'll metabolise that instead of the antifreeze, and vodka's the purest form we can get right now.'

'Won't it make him sick?' Bella asks apprehensively.

'It'll give him a bit of a hangover, maybe, but that's all,' Tamzin says. 'If his body is metabolising the vodka, it allows the antifreeze time to pass in a less toxic form. Give his kidneys and liver a break.'

213

I frown in confusion. 'I don't understand how he could have come into contact with antifreeze. I always park in the garage, so even if the car was leaking, Bagpuss couldn't have got to anything on the ground.'

'It could've been in something else you might never think of,' Tamzin says, gently stroking Bagpuss's head. 'A lot of snow globes use it. Something like that could have smashed, and he'd have licked it up – there's a reason cats have nine lives. They need them.'

'Or someone did it on purpose,' Bella interjects.

'Who'd do that?' I protest.

Tamzin sighs. 'You read about it all the time. There are a lot of very sick people around.'

'It's that insane farmer,' Bella says. 'The one who wants you to sell the paddock. It's just the kind of thing he'd do.'

Jamie reappears, panting. 'Purest Russian vodka,' he says, brandishing the bottle. 'Will this be enough?'

'Let's hope so,' Tamzin says.

We all crowd around anxiously as she dilutes the vodka, and sets up a drip for Bagpuss. His eyes open briefly and he looks at us with sudden lucidity. I see the weariness and pain there, and feel a flash of guilt that we're putting our own feelings before his own. 'Is this fair to him?' I murmur quietly to Tamzin.

'I've given him some pain relief,' she says. 'I promise you, I won't let him suffer.'

Tolly lays his head on the table next to Bagpuss, tenderly stroking his ears, and my heart twists with anguish. 'Is he going to be OK now?'

'I'm afraid all we can do is wait,' the vet says, gently ruffling Tolly's hair. 'You all did everything you could getting him to me so quickly. And well done, Bella, for bringing in the towel. We'll get his blood tested, but I'm pretty certain it's ethylene glycol poisoning – antifreeze.'

I have to steel myself not to cry, as I watch my two children wrap their arms protectively around their beloved cat. Despite Tamzin's best efforts, I know the chances he'll make it are slim.

I can't fathom how anyone could deliberately inflict such suffering on an innocent animal. But if some sick person is deliberately going around poisoning cats with antifreeze, why on earth would they go to so much trouble as to come out here? We live at the end of a remote lane; the only person anywhere near us is Gavin, the farmer opposite me, and I don't believe even he would be so wicked as to kill our cat. It doesn't make any sense.

And then I suddenly remember the topaz-coloured earring sitting in my soap dish at home.

ELISE MAHONEY
PART 1 OF RECORDED INTERVIEW

Date:- 29/07/2020
Duration:- 36 Minutes
Location:- 17 Felden Road, London SW6

Conducted by Officers from Devon & Cornwall Police

(cont.)

POLICE   So you live next door but one to Mr and Mrs
         Page, is that correct?

EM   Should I have said something before? I should,
         shouldn't I? It's just . . . I didn't want to get
         anyone in trouble.

POLICE	No worries, Mrs Mahoney, that's totally fine. We—
EM	It's just so awful. We couldn't believe it when we saw it on the news. He was such a lovely man, always stopped and said hello if he saw you in the street. People don't do that these days, do they? Not in London, anyway. Everyone's always in such a rush. But Mr Page always stopped for a chat.
POLICE	There's no way you could have known what'd happen, Mrs Mahoney.
EM	Was it the wife? It's always the husband or wife, isn't it?
POLICE	Perhaps we could start by—
EM	Those poor children, losing their dad like that. It's just so sad.
POLICE	Mrs Mahoney, if we could go over the events of the night of the tenth of July. You were at home here with your husband?
EM	The tenth of July?
POLICE	The night of the altercation.

EM
Oh, I'm so sorry, I've got a terrible memory for dates. But I'm great with numbers – you ask me a phone number, I can tell you, like a walking Yellow Pages, Ernie says. Never needs to go on that Google thing, he just has to ask me: Elise, you got the number for the dentist? And I can reel it off. But—

POLICE
So sorry to interrupt, Mrs Mahoney. I just want to clarify, you told one of my officers on the phone you were at home that evening with your husband, and you witnessed the argument between Caroline Page and Louise Page?

EM
I know it probably doesn't matter, but I just thought I should let you know, when I heard what happened to Mr Page.

POLICE
No, I'm really glad you called us; it helps us to build a picture of what happened in the days leading up. Can you remember what time it was when you heard shouting?

EM
Well, we'd just turned off the TV, else we might not have heard it. We used to stay up for News at Ten, till they started moving it about. We used to set our watches by News at Ten. Alastair Burnet and Sandy Gall. You're probably too young to remember them, aren't you?

POLICE   Sorry.

EM   And Trevor McDonald. We liked him. Such an
           educated man.

POLICE   So it was after News at Ten? About ten-thirty,
           then?

EM   Oh, no. We don't watch it anymore, I told you,
           they kept moving it. News at ten-thirty, news at
           nine, news at eleven. To-ing and froing. News
           at *when*, we called it. We tried the BBC news,
           but it's too much for us, all that bad news before
           you go to bed. Gives Ernie nightmares. So we
           don't anymore.

POLICE   Don't what?

EM   Watch the news.

POLICE   I see. I'm sorry, you've lost me here.

EM   Oh, yes, sorry, Ernie says I go on. We usually
           go up, that's what you mean, we go up to bed
           about eleven, I'd say. I don't sleep if we go to
           bed any earlier.

POLICE   And that's when you heard shouting?

EM   It was that other woman, mainly, Mr Page's first

wife. Louise, is it? I've seen her here a few times before, dropping off the children. Shouting the place down, she was. But then Mrs Page, the young Mrs Page, got upset too, understandable, really, started shouting back. The two of them were going at it hammer and tongs. We didn't know what to do. Ernie said, she's on her own, we should go round there – the young Mrs Page, that is – but we didn't want to interfere, you know. And then the other one, she starts saying all these terrible things, making threats.

POLICE   What sort of threats?

EM   [Pause.] It was all a bit horrible, actually.

POLICE   I realise this is upsetting, Mrs Mahoney, but anything you can tell us might be helpful.

EM   Well, we'd gone outside, just, you know, to see if we could do anything. And we saw Mrs Page, Louise Page, get something out of the car—

POLICE   Did you see what it was?

EM   No, it was wrapped in one of those black bin liners. She sort of shoved it at the young Mrs Page, right in her face. She said, let's see how you feel when it's someone you love.

POLICE	'Let's see how you feel when it's someone you love?' That's what she said?
EM	Something like that, words to that effect, yes. And that's when the young Mrs Page ran back inside, and then not long after, the police came.
POLICE	We have a report of the incident from Caroline Page, but she didn't mention any specific threats.
EM	She was very upset. Maybe she didn't remember exactly. It just stuck in my mind. Such a terrible thing to say. Ernie and I lost our son fourteen years ago in a motorbike accident. I wouldn't wish it on anyone, not my worst enemy, losing someone you love.
POLICE	I'm so sorry for your loss.
EM	Thank you.
POLICE	[Pause.] So you took it to be a threat, then, what Louise Page said?
EM	Well, I didn't think she'd actually *do* anything at the time. But then poor Mr Page was killed, and I thought, it's come true. That lovely girl just lost someone she loved, didn't she?

Chapter 25

Caz

I press my back against the front door, as if it might splinter inward at any second. I only just got it shut in time; another moment, and Louise would've been in the house.

Panic sweeps through me as I fumble with the security chain, my spine prickling. I wouldn't put it past her literally to stab me in the back. I've never seen her like this before. It's as if she's possessed. I know her history, I know what she's capable of, but until this moment, I never really understood it.

The letter box flaps, and I see the tips of her fingers groping the air. 'You fucking murderous bitch!' Louise shrieks. 'Come back out and face me!'

I reach for the phone in my back pocket. The police should be here any minute, but I'm terrified she's going to get into the house before then. Louise knew Andy wouldn't be here, of course; he presents the late bulletin these days, and doesn't get off-air until eleven p.m. 'Go home, Louise,' I say shakily. 'I didn't touch your cat. I haven't been anywhere near him!'

'Liar!'

'I've called the police,' I cry. 'Go home, or they'll arrest you!'

'Like I give a shit!' she yells. 'You'll be the one going to jail, when they find out what you've done!'

Kit suddenly appears at the top of the stairs, rubbing sleep from his eyes. 'Mummy, what's the big noise?'

'Ssssh, it's OK,' I say, forcing a weak smile. 'Go back to bed, darling. It's just some silly people in the street. Mummy will be up in a minute to tuck you in.'

'Can I have a drink of water?'

'I'll bring one up. Go on, back to bed with you now.'

The pounding suddenly stops. I run into the sitting room and peer through the curtain, trying to see what she's doing now. There's no way in through the rear of the house; these terraced properties are all back-to-back with other homes. But I can't stop her pouring petrol or something through the letter box. I bolt back to the stairs, and sit a couple of steps from the bottom, guarding my son. *Let's see how you feel when it's someone you love.* What if she tries to hurt Kit? She's crazy enough to do it.

I press the knuckles of my hand into my mouth so he doesn't hear me crying. This has been the worst day of my life. A final warning from Patrick, pending an investigation into the Vine debacle, and now this. How can Louise seriously think I'd kill her cat, just to get at her? I know she hates me, but what kind of person does she think I am?

The house is eerily quiet. I tense, waiting for the

223

sound of breaking glass, for Louise to smash her way in. How long is it going to take for the police to get here? It feels like hours since I called them. Louise's shouting probably woke the entire street. Someone else must have rung the police as well as me. It can't take them much longer, surely?

The doorbell rings, and I nearly jump out of my skin. 'It's the police,' a man's voice calls. 'Is everything all right in there?'

They do a full search of the area when I tell them what's happened. But Louise is nowhere to be seen. Her car has gone, and if it weren't for the empty black plastic bin liner caught on the railing outside our house, I could almost believe I'd imagined the whole thing.

I can tell the two officers are wondering the same themselves. They're both men, one in his mid-thirties, the other about ten years older, and I'm sure they think I'm just hysterical. But I can still see Louise thrusting the dead cat at me, its head lolling sickeningly out of the bin liner. I can still hear the sickening thump as it hit the doorstep when she flung it at me. Bile rises in my throat again as I describe it.

They take notes, but even if they do believe me, there's nothing they can do. I didn't really expect anything else, though at least their appearance seems to have driven her away. And the incident is on the record. If she keeps it up, the officers say, I can pursue her for stalking and harassment. They don't add, though I see it written on their faces: *For all the good it'll do you.*

I'm still trembling when Andy arrives home close to midnight, just as the police are leaving. 'What on earth's happened?' he exclaims, shocked to see the two officers. 'Is everything all right? Is Kit OK?'

'We had a report of a disturbance,' the older policeman says heavily. 'Your wife was very distressed. She says your ex-wife turned up on the doorstep with a dead cat.'

To my astonishment, Andy laughs. '*That's* why you're here? I thought something terrible had happened!'

'Andy!'

He ignores me, speaking over my head to the two officers. 'I'm so sorry. It's all a misunderstanding. I've already spoken to my wife. Our family pet just died, and she was very upset. She brought him here so I could say goodbye to him. I'm afraid Caz got the wrong end of the stick and overreacted.'

'Your *ex*-wife,' I snap, before I can stop myself.

I see the officers exchange a look with Andy. They don't quite eye-roll, but it's close.

'You weren't here!' I protest. 'She was going crazy, threatening me—'

The older policeman's expression changes. 'What do you mean, threatening you, madam?'

'She said, "Let's see how you feel when it's someone you love." It was the way she *said* it, Andy, like she really meant it. It gave me chills. And then she threw the dead cat at me. It was horrible!'

'She was *upset*,' Andy says tersely.

'She drove sixty miles in the middle of the night with

a dead cat on the passenger seat!' I exclaim. 'Andy, that's not normal behaviour, no matter how upset she is. She was ranting and raving in the street for an hour like she was having a psychotic episode!'

'Look, I'm sorry we wasted your time,' Andy says tightly to the two men. 'This is clearly part of an ongoing domestic dispute, and we should never have troubled you. I do apologise.'

'No need,' the older policeman says. 'Better safe than sorry.'

They return to their vehicle, and I hear laughter on the air. I doubt they'll even file a report. Once again, Louise has got away with it.

'What were you *thinking*, calling the police?' Andy demands, as soon as the front door shuts. 'She loved that cat almost as much as the kids did. So did I, come to that. She wanted to let me say goodbye to him, and you call the *police* on her!'

'You weren't here,' I say furiously. 'She was pounding on the door like a lunatic! She really scared me, Andy!'

He pours himself a hefty measure of Scotch from the cabinet in the sitting room. 'You're blowing this way out of proportion. What do you think she was threatening to do? Hurt Kit? Hurt *me*?'

Put like that, it does sound ridiculous. But I saw her face when she threw the cat at me. I wouldn't put it past her to do anything, strike at anyone, to get at me.

'This thing between you two has gone far enough,' Andy says brusquely. 'I should never have let you talk me into taking her back to court. I'm calling the lawyer in the morning to tell him to back off. Lou was out of order taking the job at Whitefish, and I've told her that, but accusing her of assaulting you with a dead cat and calling the *police*?' His expression is stony and unforgiving. 'You and Louise need to bury the hatchet, and preferably not in each other's backs.'

'Andy—'

'Enough, Caz. I've had a long day. I really don't want to hear it.'

He throws himself onto the sofa, leaning his head back against the cushions and closing his eyes, terminating the conversation. There's no point trying to get him to understand. He knows what Louise is capable of, but he simply refuses to see it.

I'm suddenly filled with cold, hard fury. He's so goddamn *weak*. I always thought he had such a strong personality, but as I look at him now, I recognise he is no more than a skilled chameleon, reflecting the image of the beholder, perfectly designed for the shallow medium of television. All men to all people, and none of it real.

How can I have lived with this man for more than four years, and not seen it? He should be holding the line with me against Louise, and instead, he refuses to choose sides because he still wants her to love him, whether or not he loves her. He seems suddenly insubstantial and two-dimensional, no more than a cypher for the battle playing out between Louise and me.

My mother was right; Andy is almost incidental now. Whether we like it or not, Louise and I are locked in mortal combat, tied to each other by something that goes far deeper than our connection to Andy. A duel to the death, my mother called it. I'm beginning to think she's right.

Chapter 26

Louise

I'm a journalist. Finding people is what I do.

I peer through the rain-spotted windscreen at the rundown red-brick building across the road. Most people aren't difficult to track down, once you start digging. These days, it's almost impossible not to leave a virtual trail unless you make a serious effort to go off-grid. Social media, public records: it's all there, just a click away. And what you can't find online is usually easy to ferret out with a few phone calls. I never go through a press office – they're always far too wary – but if you talk to the real gatekeepers, the administrators and secretaries and switchboard operators, it's amazing how far good manners can take you. Sometimes I have to stretch the truth a little, mainly through omission; people make assumptions, and I don't bother to correct them. But I don't even have to tell a little white lie to find Caz's mother. The staffing manager at her care home gives me all the information I need over the phone, without even asking who I am.

I collect my bag from the passenger seat and get out

of the car. I'm done with sitting at home waiting to see where Caz is going to strike next. If I'd fought fire with fire earlier, maybe Bagpuss wouldn't be dead now.

Killing a cat isn't the revenge of a jealous woman. Taking my daughter to get her tongue pierced, having me fired – those were spiteful and unpleasant, but the kind of thing many women might do, given sufficient provocation. What Caz did to Bagpuss is psychopathic. I'm terrified of what she might do next, to the children or me. I need to know exactly what it is I'm dealing with. I don't expect a smoking gun, but I've been a reporter for a long time. I *know* there is something more to Caz's story, something in her background I need to find out.

What frightens me most is the hold Caz seems to have on Bella. I thought my daughter wouldn't want to have anything to do with her after Bagpuss, but she simply refuses to believe Caz was involved. Perhaps I went about it the wrong way, racing up to London to confront Caz last week, but I was too angry and upset to think strategically.

'Of *course* it was her!' I shouted, when Bella accused *me* of being the crazy one. 'Who else would have done it?'

'Literally *any*one!' Bella cried. 'That loony farmer, kids, who knows! Caz isn't some kind of psycho! She'd never do anything like that!'

I slammed the topaz-coloured earring onto the kitchen table between us. '*You* were the one who found this lying in the drive right by the garage,' I snapped. 'Tell me how it got there, since Caz has never been to our house!'

'I told you! The stupid earring probably just fell out of the car!' Bella exclaimed. 'She's been driving it the last four years, remember?'

The only thing that sustained me during the long dark nights of grief and misery after Andrew left was the knowledge that I still had the best of him: that Caz might steal my husband, but she could never take my motherhood, my children, from me. Listening to my daughter take her side against me hurts more than anything I've known since Nicky's death.

The rain intensifies as I lock my car now and cross the road towards the care home. At first glance, it's easy to assume Caz comes from money, with her English rose complexion and perfect Home Counties accent. But I always knew there was something off about her: even the younger royals adopt a glottal stop these days. Andrew clearly bought into her act. He's a terrible snob: a working-class boy from a Manchester council estate who made good but has never quite trusted his success; he's always had a thing for posh girls. My family's cash had run out by the time I was born, but my parents still have the odd silver chafing dish knocking about the place, and Andrew used to dine out on the fact my godfather's a baronet. I'm willing to bet good money he has no idea his current mother-in-law lives in a council care home in Dagenham.

I push open the door into the lobby, and am instantly assailed by an institutional smell of marker pens and boiled cabbage. It's the weekend, and there's no one behind the cheap Formica reception desk, which is littered with several half-drunk mugs of cold coffee, as if abruptly abandoned mid-shift. I lean over it, looking for a buzzer to summon someone. The blocky computer crammed onto the end of the desk hails from the last century, and a stack of cardboard manila patient files are propped carelessly to one side. The entire place oozes neglect and lack of funds, and I'm still front of house. God knows what the rest of the home is like if this is the face they present to the world.

A woman suddenly appears from a small office on the far side of the lobby, wiping mayonnaise from her lips. A prawn sandwich, judging by the small crustaceans clinging to the substantial shelf of her bright blue sweatshirt. 'Can I help you?' she asks suspiciously.

'I'm here to see Ruth Clarke,' I say.

'Friend or family?'

I hesitate. 'It's personal,' I prevaricate.

'Room 243,' the woman says, already bored. 'Second floor. You'll have to take the stairs – the lift's not working.'

The stairwell smells of urine and cigarettes, and the cheap, scarred orange linoleum clearly hasn't been replaced since the property was built in the Sixties. What the hell is Caz doing, dumping her mother in a place like this? She and Andrew have enough resources for them to afford something better. There's a story here; I can *smell* it.

The door to 243 is wide open, like every other room I've passed. The residents are subjected to bed baths and catheter changes in full view of anyone happening to walk past. I knock pointedly on Ruth Clarke's door before entering, but the woman in the wheelchair by the window doesn't even look up.

'Mrs Clarke?' I say. 'Do you mind if I come in?'

For a moment, I think she hasn't heard me. Then she looks over her bony shoulder, and I suddenly see how Caz will look in thirty years' time. The woman has the same fine features and high cheekbones, which are scaffolding for crepey skin grown grey from lack of sunlight. She has the same deep-set blue eyes as her daughter, too, though her hair is stringy and pulled back into an unflattering knot at the nape of her neck. But she is still beautiful, in her way.

'Who're you?' she snaps.

'I was married to your daughter's husband,' I say baldly.

Her gaze sharpens suddenly. She nods to herself a couple of times, then abruptly swings her wheelchair away from the window. 'What do you want with me?'

'I'd like to talk to you, if you can spare a few minutes.'

'It's not like I've got anywhere else to be,' she says acidly.

I glance around the room as I sit down in the only chair available, opposite her. There are no personal photographs anywhere: no pictures of Ruth holding Caz as a baby, or Ruth herself on her wedding day. The room is as bland and sterile as if she'd just moved in this morning, though I know she washed up here more than seven years ago. It doesn't take a trained psychologist to see that leaving your mother to rot in a loveless cell like this is not the sign of a healthy relationship.

'So what d'you want to know?' Ruth asks.

'All of it,' I say.

Chapter 27

Caz

Andy leans across the kitchen counter to kiss Kit, holding his tie to the side so it doesn't dip into his cereal. I try not to notice that just a few weeks ago, he'd have come around the island and kissed me too. 'Don't forget, the kids will be here this weekend,' he says, straightening up. 'You need to clear all that shit out of Bella's room. You can't just use her bed as a dumping ground.'

I want to point out that until a week ago, that room was my study. But now that the kids are coming up to London for their weekends, Andy has decreed that Bella needs her own space, so that she can have friends stay over.

It's not all bad. Giving up my office has earned me lots of Brownie points with Bella, which will drive Louise crazy.

'By the way,' Andy calls, as he opens the front door. 'We're going down to Devon next week on Friday morning, now, not Saturday, so you'll need to take the day off work. Celia's invited us to a family dinner at the hotel on Friday night, and it makes sense to be there the day before the party, so we're not in a rush.'

I chase him down the hall. 'We're not still going to the party?' I demand incredulously. 'After what Louise did?'

'Of course we're still going,' he says shortly. 'Nothing's changed. I'm not ruining Celia's big day because you and Louise had a bit of a tiff.'

'A bit of a *tiff*?'

'Caz, I don't know what's going on between you two, but you need to sort it out. This weekend will be a chance for you both to put it behind you and make peace.' He glances in the hall mirror, and straightens his tie. 'I have to go, or I'll be late for the morning briefing. We can discuss this later.'

'She turned up at our house with a *dead cat*!' I exclaim, catching his arm. 'I'm not letting our son within a half-mile radius of her!'

He shakes me off. 'I'm going to the party, and so is Kit. It's up to you if you want to stay home and sulk.' His expression hardens. 'And he's my son too, remember.'

'Andy—'

He's gone. I go back into the house, my entire body trembling. I feel sick and slightly dizzy. I don't know what's happening to us. Andy has never spoken to me the way he did just now, dismissing me as if I don't matter. I've never seen him look at me like that, distant and unreachable. In all the years we've been together, there has always been fire and heat and *feeling* between us, even when we've fought. But for the past week, ever since the police came round, he's been clipped and cold and surgically angry, almost precise in his dislike. I wonder if this is what he was like with Louise, in the dying days of their marriage.

Four years ago, when Andy finally left her, I thought I'd beaten her. But my victory was Pyrrhic from the start. Andy didn't leave Louise *for* me. I won him by default. He turned up on my doorstep, incandescent with rage and misery, not because he'd finally realised he couldn't live without me, but because he'd discovered Louise had cheated on him.

It's been a cancer at the heart of our relationship, slow-growing but always there. He didn't choose me. *He never chooses me.*

I sink onto the bottom stair, the same place I sat last week to protect our son from his ex-wife's lunacy, and bury my face in my hands. Most couples start their relationships in a cocoon of intimacy, but for Andy and me, that precious, irrecoverable time was marred by constant running battles with Louise. Somehow, we survived and made it into clear waters. She's never gone away, a permanent thorn in my side, and Andy and I have often rowed about her, but she's never driven a wedge between us like this. A month ago, I wouldn't have thought it possible we'd end up here, more bitterly divided than we've ever been. We're teetering on the brink of something from which I'm not sure we'll be able to return.

Somehow, I pull myself together, and finish getting ready for work. I drop Kit at his nursery, and head towards the tube, grabbing a latte to go and trying to clear my head so I can concentrate on the day ahead of me. Patrick has stemmed the haemorrhage of clients after the Vine debacle, but I'm well aware I have a lot of ground to make up. I can't afford another missed step now.

My phone pings with an incoming text from AJ as I climb the stairs to the platform at Parsons Green. Patrick wants to see me first thing.

I step out of the way of the tide of commuters, and put my coffee cup on the ground between my feet so I can text him back. Did he say why?

No. But Sheila will be there.

Shit. There's only one reason Patrick would have someone from Human Resources sit in on a meeting. He's going to give AJ a bollocking, and he's covering his arse so AJ can't play the homophobic card if things suddenly go south. Don't panic. I'll be there as soon as I can. Keep me posted.

I hope to God Patrick's not going to take AJ off the Univest account, because that'll leave me super-exposed with Tina Murdoch. But he's been punishing everyone involved in the Vine fuck-up, taking us off prestige accounts and cutting back on travel perks. AJ's only my *acting* deputy. Until Vine, he was on course to have the promotion made permanent, but Patrick can always throw him back in the pool with the other PAs.

I squeeze my way onto the tube, trying not to spill my latte as the crowd presses in behind me. AJ is more than my right hand: he's my eyes and ears at Whitefish.

He's neurotic and occasionally daft, but he's also intensely loyal, hard-working and that rarest of creatures: a gossip who knows when to keep his mouth shut. Losing him from the Univest account would leave me both short-staffed and politically vulnerable. He's virtually the only person in my life I wholly trust. In many ways, he's a better friend to me than Andy himself.

I change at Earl's Court, and my mobile lights up with a flurry of emails as I come above ground. I scroll quickly through them as I walk down the platform. Four messages from Tina, a couple of cc'd emails from Patrick and Sheila – an ominous sign – and another from Nolan, plus a terse reminder from Andy to pick Bella and Tolly up from the station tomorrow. And it's not even eight-thirty in the morning yet.

I suddenly stop in my tracks in the middle of the platform. Louise is screwing up my relationships both at work and at home, but there's only one I can really do anything about.

I want to make things right with Andy. He'll be tired when he gets home tonight, and because it's easier than drilling down into what's really going on between us, we'll paper over the cracks and act as if this morning didn't happen. Andy isn't perfect, God knows; he can be narcissistic and shallow, he's ridiculously weak around Louise, and he's consistently rude to me. But he's Kit's father. And like the little girl in the nursery rhyme, when he's good, he's very, very good, even though when he's bad, he's horrid. I refuse to admit

239

defeat. I know I can get us back to where we were, if I can just get us through this rough patch. I don't want to spend another week the way I've spent this last one, sleeping with a stone-faced stranger who turns his back to me before I've even got into bed. I want to put this whole thing behind us, and if that means apologising to Louise, I guess I'll just have to suck it up.

Shoving my phone back in my bag, I step back into the flow of commuters and hustle down the steps towards the Piccadilly Line. If I go over to INN now, I can catch him before his daily news briefing at ten.

Half an hour later, I walk into INN's reception atrium. In four years, I've been here just once; there was some unpleasant publicity about me in the papers when Andy left Louise, who was well liked by his colleagues at INN, and one taste of their hostility was enough for me. The atrium is bright and airy, with acres of chrome and glass. Vast photographs of the network's main presenters, including Andy, hang on invisible wires from the double-height ceiling like flags at the UN. Maybe I should stop hiding and make my presence felt a bit more. I don't have to apologise for being Andy's wife. I need to stop behaving as if I do.

'I'm here for Andrew Page,' I tell the girl behind the reception desk. 'I'm his wife.'

She turns to her computer. 'Just a moment, Mrs Page, and I'll tell him you're here.'

My phone buzzes, and I glance at the screen and see AJ's number. Damn. He must have finished his meeting with Patrick, but I can't talk to him now. I decline the call, feeling slightly guilty. One of the reasons Andy and I are fighting is because I've spent too much time and energy thinking about work instead of him. I need to put my marriage first if I want to save it.

'Mrs Page? I'm afraid Mr Page isn't picking up his phone. Would you like me to put you through to his secretary?'

'That'd be great, thanks.'

She points to a phone on the reception desk, and I pick it up. 'Hi, Jessica,' I say. 'Is Andy around?'

'He's out today,' his secretary says, sounding surprised.

As a presenter, it's rare, but not unheard of, for Andy to go out in the field. Maybe he's presenting from a remote location, or doing a big interview. 'What time will he be back, do you know?'

'Is he expecting you?' Jessica says.

'No, I was just passing. Is he out on a story?'

'Not that I know of.'

She's deliberately evasive. The hairs rise on the back of my neck. 'Do you know when he'll be back in the office?' I ask.

'Actually, he's not in at all today,' she says reluctantly. 'He's booked a personal day. Declan's standing in for tonight's bulletin.'

For a moment, I wonder if I've got my wires crossed. And then I remember Andy's sharp tone when he told me he'd be late for the morning briefing.

Chapter 28

Min

I change out of my hospital scrubs and grab a Snickers bar from the vending machine as I head to the car park. The graveyard shift is never fun, but sometimes you can at least get a few hours' sleep in the on-call room. Either that, or a multiple car pile-up or chemical explosion will get the adrenalin pumping and make you forget you haven't slept for twenty-two hours. But last night was the worst of both worlds: a steady stream of minor sprains and mysterious rashes that kept me busy but should really be the province of the local GP. We have enough hypochondriacs during the day, but there's a certain group of worried well who love nothing more than presenting at the ED at four in the morning convinced they've got Ebola. I wouldn't mind if, just once in a blue moon, one of them did.

I buckle my seatbelt and turn on Radio Four. It's almost noon; I could grab a couple of hours' kip before it's time to pick Archie and Sidney up from school, but it hardly seems worth it. And anyway, I'm far too anxious about Louise to sleep.

On a sudden impulse, I unbuckle my seatbelt again, and grab my bag from the front seat. What I need is a brisk walk and some sea air. It only takes me a few minutes to make my way from the Royal Sussex down to the seafront, which is surprisingly quiet, given it's the middle of summer. When I reach the promenade, I realise why: there's a bracingly cold breeze blowing in off the sea, and despite the sunshine, it feels more like October than July. Which is a good thing, because I need to clear my head so I can think.

Pebbles tumble and crunch beneath my feet as I go down onto the beach. I have no idea what to do about Lou. I was concerned when she moved into Andrew's house and took that job at his wife's office, but this whole business with Bagpuss is in a different league of crazy. One I wish with all my heart I didn't recognise.

As an ED doctor, I've come across Munchausen's syndrome a few times over the years. It's one of the most difficult mental illnesses to diagnose, partly because people deliberately fake or exaggerate their symptoms, but mainly because you have to rule everything else out first. Even worse is when the patient is making someone *else* sick, generally a young child in their care, but occasionally an elderly relative. It's terrible, of course, but they don't usually do it to achieve a concrete benefit, like money; they want the sympathy and special attention given to the families of those who are truly sick. People with the condition aren't wicked; they're mentally *ill*.

Perhaps it's a stretch to include a cat in the diagnosis,

but Lou certainly has all the sympathy and attention she could possibly want now, especially from Andrew. And it wouldn't be the first time she's gone down this dark path.

A wave splashes across my feet, making me jump, and I turn and crunch along the beach, hunching my shoulders against the unseasonably chill wind. I desperately don't want to believe Lou would do anything as awful as poison her own cat, I can hardly even bear to think about it, but I'm terribly afraid that's what she's done. None of us wanted to believe it last time either, when that whole business with Roger Lewison and his wife blew up, and yet it turned out to be true. If there's even a chance it's happening again, surely it's better to speak up now, before things get even more out of hand? It was poor old Bagpuss last week, but what if – God forbid – it's Tolly or Bella next time?

No. She'd *never* do anything to hurt those children. Lou is my friend, and I love her. If I raise the alarm now, I could set something in motion that's impossible to stop. And I might be totally wrong about this. Perhaps it *was* just a vindictive farmer who killed Bagpuss, as Bella suggested. Or even that jealous woman of Andrew's. I need to talk to Lou, get a better read of where her head is, before I do or say anything.

With sudden resolution, I head back up to the promenade. I should have more faith in Lou. If she says that woman poisoned Bagpuss, I should take it on trust that she's right. We all should. Celia needs to stop playing games with that damned party invitation and make it clear we all stand foursquare behind Lou.

As I reach the Parade, the sun goes in. I quicken my steps back to the hospital car park as the first fat rain-drops splatter the pavement, and then suddenly spot Andrew and Bella coming out of The Ginger Dog about a hundred feet ahead of me. How odd. It's Friday: Bella should be in school, not having lunch at a pub in Brighton with her father. She's in uniform, so it's obviously not a day off, either. I'm still quite a long way off, and they both have their backs towards me, so neither of them notice me as Andrew puts his arm solicitously around his daughter, pulling her against him and stroking her hair.

There's something about the scene that strikes me as not quite right. I can't put my finger on it, but I feel a distinct sense of unease as they disappear around the corner. Something is happening within this family, something dangerous and fracturing. And instinct tells me we're running out of time to stop it.

One week before the party

Chapter 29

Louise

Money is missing from my account. I haven't just made a mistake, or miscalculated how much I've spent on petrol and groceries over the last month. Three hundred pounds was withdrawn in cash with my debit card last Thursday, and since the card is safely back in my wallet, the only person who could've done it is Bella.

It's not the first time she's 'borrowed' money from me. Usually, it's just five or ten pounds here or there, to buy herself a coffee from Starbucks when she's out with her friends, or a new – invariably black – T-shirt at Primark. But she's never taken anything like this much before. She's put me into overdraft, and precipitated the text alert from my bank; but I'm less concerned with the hole she's blown in my finances than the reason she needs so much money. I check back through my past transactions on my banking app, consumed with worry. Is it drugs? That would certainly explain her moods. She's sixteen; I suppose it's inevitable she'd try them sometime. But three hundred pounds? That's an awful lot of weed.

I glance up as my brother, Luke, sticks his head into my parents' hallway. 'Are you coming?' he asks. 'Lunch is on the table.'

'Sorry. Be right there.'

I scroll rapidly through the rest of my transactions. No other unexplained withdrawals, so that's something, I suppose. I know parents are always the last to know about things like this, but I really can't see Bella doing drugs. She's fanatical about 'clean living' and won't even take paracetamol if she has a headache. We had hell to pay when she had to have a tetanus booster a few years ago. But if not drugs, why does she need the money?

'Louise!' my mother calls.

I hurry into my parents' dining room just as Dad bears the Sunday roast in from the kitchen with all the pride of a man who hunted and speared it himself. Mum clears a space in the centre of the table as he lays down the platter. 'Shall I do the honours?' Dad asks rhetorically, as he always does.

He carves perfect pink slices of roast pork as Mum passes a steaming tureen of Brussels sprouts around the table. Luke and Min's two youngest boys, Sidney and Archie, graphically mime vomiting until Min reaches across the table and tartly smacks each of their hands with the back of her fork.

'Is it true your cat died?' five-year-old Archie asks me suddenly.

'Of course it's *true*,' Sidney says scornfully, with all the authority of his seven years. He lowers his voice dramatically. 'He was *poisoned*.'

250

Archie tugs my sleeve. '*Was* he poisoned, Lula?'

I've always refused to be called 'Aunt Louise': it makes me sound like an Edwardian spinster. 'I'm afraid so, Archie. He ate something he shouldn't have.'

Archie looks at his plate. Min has spooned the despised vegetables onto it while he wasn't looking. 'Was it because of sprouts?' he asks dejectedly.

After lunch, Dad goes into the sitting room to read his paper, and Luke takes the boys outside to kick a ball around. Min and I shoo Mum out of the kitchen so we can tackle the washing-up, but instead of putting her feet up as we exhort her to do, she goes out to work in the garden. She could no more sit still for five minutes than the sun could choose to rise in the West.

We watch her walk past the kitchen window with her gardening trug over her arm, heading towards the new tomato beds. 'You know Andrew put those in for her,' Min says.

I know exactly where this is going. 'Min, please don't start.'

It's like trying to stop a runaway train. 'This isn't healthy for anyone,' she says. 'You've got to talk to Celia, and get her to see sense. She might listen, if it comes from you.' She scrubs the roasting pan with more vigour than strictly necessary. 'You and Andrew need to properly separate yourselves. Your lives are way too tangled these days. I'm sure Celia invited him to the party with the best of intentions, but things have changed, even she must see that.'

'I'm not so sure about her intentions,' I mutter.

251

'She stirred up a bloody hornet's nest with that invitation,' Min says crossly. 'That's where all this nonsense started.'

'I'm not arguing.'

She puts the roasting pan on the drainer, and turns to me, bubbles dripping from her soapy hands onto the floor. 'Lou, I'm worried about you. This horrid business with Bagpuss—'

'Min, you know how much I value your advice,' I interrupt.

She sighs. 'Yes, but you never take it.'

She means well, I know that. Whatever concern she has for me, it comes from a place of love. And unlike everyone else, including my mother, she doesn't have a hidden agenda. I wish I could confide in her, and tell her what I learned from my visit to Caz's mother. But even admitting I tracked the old woman down and went to see her will just fuel Min's conviction that I'm obsessed. I know she's already wondering about Bagpuss. I don't blame her: with my history, I'd do the same.

'Min, dear,' my mother says, letting herself in the back door and making us both jump. 'Would you like to go out and join Luke and the boys? I can help Louise finish up in the kitchen.'

Min recognises an imperative interrogative when she hears one: it may sound like a question, but it's actually a command. She mouths a quick '*Talk* to her!' at me, and disappears outside.

Mum puts her basket of tomatoes on the counter

and snaps on her rubber gloves, groping around in the soapy dishwater. 'You're handling Andrew all wrong, Louise,' she says bluntly, rinsing a serving bowl under the tap. 'I've told you before. Rushing off to London like a lunatic—'

'Yes, I know,' I say testily. 'I shouldn't have done that, but I was upset.'

'He needs to be gently reminded what he gave up when he walked away from you, not bludgeoned over the head with it,' Mum says. 'You know how much family means to him. He didn't just walk out on you when he left, he walked out on all of us, and he's regretted it ever since.'

I pick up the crockery and start to dry it. I don't want to have this conversation, but there's no stopping my mother when she's got the bit between her teeth. She's right about one thing: family *has* always been important to Andrew. His parents both died quite young, when he was in his mid-twenties, and he's an only child. Until we married, he had no relatives to speak of, other than some distant cousins in Salford where he grew up. He needed my extended family every bit as much as we needed him to fill the gaping hole left by Nicky.

'Mum, he doesn't regret leaving me,' I sigh. 'He could've tried to come back, but in four years he's never shown the slightest desire to.'

'He loves you, Louise. Yes, perhaps he thinks he loves her, too,' she adds impatiently, heading off my objections. 'And I don't doubt he loves Kit. But marriage is about more than love, and as you get older, you realise that. Andrew needs to be part of something bigger.' She hands me another serving platter to dry. 'It's why people like him go into television. They need the audience, the mass adoration. They need to feel like they *belong*. I'm trying to help you, Louise, but you're not making it easy.'

'Help me what?'

'Get what you want.' She turns to face me, her hands still in the sink. 'Andrew. He *is* what you still want, isn't he?'

For a brief moment, my foolish heart dares to hope. A sunlit reel plays on romcom fast-forward in my head: Andrew and me waking up in bed together, laughing with the children over the breakfast table, strolling hand in hand on the beach with the wind whipping our hair as seagulls circle overhead . . .

My head aches. 'That's not an option, Mum.'

'Of course it is.' She reaches for the gravy boat and empties its sludgy contents into the bin. 'All he needs is a reason to come back. But you have to stop chasing after him. He has to come to you.'

'I'm not chasing after—'

'Moving into his house?' Mum cuts across me. 'Taking a job where his wife works?'

I flush. 'I've already told Chris I'm quitting Univest and Whitefish. I'm trying to be the adult here.'

'And what about the cat?'

'The police aren't going to do anything. They say none of it can be proved, so—'

'Caz didn't poison your cat, and you know it,' Mum says.

'I know it's hard to believe, but—'

'Louise Roberts, you can lie to the police, you can lie to Andrew, you can even lie to yourself. But don't *ever* think you can lie to me.'

A beat falls.

I clear my throat. 'That was a long time ago, Mum.'

'I'm not blind, Louise. I can see what's happening. I warned you last time, but you didn't listen.' She turns back to the sink, literally washing her hands of me. 'You're going to regret this. If you make the same mistake with Andrew as you did with Roger Lewison, it'll end exactly the same way.'

It's not fair for her to throw that back in my face. I was only nineteen, young and in love for the first time. Who doesn't make mistakes then?

Roger Lewison was my tutor at Oxford. He was also married; something he neglected to tell me at the time.

Two months into our affair, his wife found out about us, and Roger was finally forced to come clean. He said she'd threatened to tell the college if he didn't end our relationship; he'd have lost his job, and I might have been sent down. But I was so in love with him, I simply couldn't accept it was over. I thought if I could just make his wife realise how much we loved each other, she wouldn't want to stand in our way. She'd set him free, I reasoned, once she knew it was hopeless. No woman wants a man to stay with her out of pity. It was all terribly sad for her, of course, but Roger and I were meant to be together. We were *soulmates*.

So I tried to talk to her, to explain, but she wouldn't give me a chance. She hung up the phone when I called, and refused to speak to me. I sent one or two handwritten letters, but she ignored them, too. I starting hanging around her office – she was a psychology tutor at another college – but she still wouldn't see me, and eventually had the college porter ban me from the quad.

In the end, she didn't leave me any choice. I just wanted to *talk* to her. Roger had an evening lecture every Wednesday, so I knew how to time it so he wouldn't be home. Jennifer let me in; she hadn't expected me to turn up on her doorstep, and I took advantage of her confusion to talk my way inside. She'd been preparing supper: she was wearing an old-fashioned white-and-navy striped apron, and had a dusting of flour on her cheek. She also had a paring knife in her right hand.

It was the sight of her in her apron, the domesticity of it: this woman, Roger's *wife*, cooking him dinner, waiting for him to come home. My memories from that night are confused, a blur of frightening, violent images. I remember her lunging at me, a sudden, sharp pain in the left of my lower abdomen. Jennifer told the police I grabbed the knife from her hand and deliberately stabbed myself in the stomach. I tried to explain *she* was the one who'd attacked *me*, but it was her word against mine, and she was an eminent professor at an Oxford college, and I was an infatuated student who'd been having an affair with her husband and had forced my way into her home. Jennifer Lewison took out a restraining order against me; I was lucky not to be expelled from the university.

It took me several years of counselling to be able to admit what had really happened. The therapist showed me I'd wanted Roger's sympathy, for him to see me as a damsel in distress, so that he'd come to my rescue. In my confused, lovesick teenage mind, the counsellor said, I'd sought to make literal my sense of myself as the victim, and show Jennifer as the aggressor I believed her to be. As far as I was concerned, I wasn't lying; I genuinely believed Jennifer had attacked me.

But that was nearly twenty-five years ago. I'm forty-three now, a successful journalist, a wife and mother. I know the difference between fantasy and reality. And I'm *not* making this up.

'I didn't poison Bagpuss,' I say firmly. 'Caz is the one who's lied. And I can prove it.'

I wasn't going to tell Mum I tracked Caz's mother down, for the same reason I haven't told Min, but I need her to understand now how dangerous Caz is. 'She's lied about everything, Mum,' I say urgently. 'Who she is, where she comes from. And that's not the worst of it. You've no idea the kind of person she really is. She's not who she seems.'

Mum looks hard at me. 'Who is?' she says.

Date:- 28/07/2020
Duration:- 31 Minutes
Location:- Livingstone College, Oxford

Conducted by Officers from Devon & Cornwall
Police

(cont.)

POLICE   So you and Mr Lewison are divorced, then?

JD   He's Professor Lewison. And yes.

POLICE   May I ask why?

JD   Is that relevant?

POLICE	That's what we're trying to establish, Mrs Lewison – or is it Professor?
JD	Doctor, actually. And I reverted to my maiden name, Davitt, after the divorce.
POLICE	Dr Davitt, your ex-husband formed a sexual relationship somewhere around November 1995 with one of his students, Miss Roberts, is that right?
JD	Technically speaking, she wasn't one of his students. He was her academic advisor. But yes. They were fucking.
POLICE	And do you know how long they were – how long the relationship continued?
JD	I wouldn't call it a relationship. It happened maybe three or four times.
POLICE	Did you know about it?
JD	Not until Roger tried to end it.
POLICE	Why did he do that, do you know?
JD	I imagine he got bored. Fidelity isn't his strongest suit. It certainly wasn't because I'd found out, though I gather that's what he told his girlfriend.

POLICE	Your husband broke it off with Miss Roberts sometime in January 1996?
JD	Yes.
POLICE	And then what happened?
JD	The girl rang me. She told me they were having an affair, she said they were in love, and begged me to, quotes, let him go. Roger had told her I'd threatened to go to the college and expose him if he didn't go back to me. [Pause.] He's not a very nice man.
POLICE	This was the first you knew of the affair?
JD	I'd suspected Roger had been unfaithful before, but it was the first time I knew for sure.
POLICE	So what did you do?
JD	I told Roger the affair had to stop, or I'd leave him. It was humiliating. She was one of his students.
POLICE	And did he stop it?
JD	He said he'd tried, but she wouldn't listen. She kept ringing the house, though after the first time I didn't answer her calls. Then she started

sending letters. They went on for pages and pages, dozens and dozens of them. She must have been writing two or three a day.

POLICE   Did you keep them?

JD   No, of course not.

POLICE   What did she say in the letters?

JD   The usual. [Pause.] She and Roger were soul-mates, they were meant to be together, soap-opera stuff. She even turned up at my college rooms, and the porter had to ask her to leave.

POLICE   Did you notify the police?

JD   At that stage, she hadn't done anything illegal. She was infatuated with him, obviously, but I didn't think she was a danger to anyone. I assumed it'd burn itself out, given time. [Pause.] Tell me, how many times have you gone to a bar or a gym because you were mad about a girl who went there? Or joined a club she belonged to so you could chat her up?

POLICE   [Laughs.] I spent two months learning how to salsa because my wife taught the class.

JD   We've all done it. There's a very fine line

261

between the normal behaviour, if you can call it that, of someone in love, and criminal stalking. I wasn't about to call the police because a nineteen-year-old girl with her whole life in front of her had had her heart broken by a man who wouldn't know the truth if it punched him on the nose.

POLICE   So the first time you met Louise Roberts in person was when she came to your house, the night of 4 February 1996?

JD   Yes.

POLICE   Can you tell me what happened?

JD   I'm sure you've seen the police report.

POLICE   Your story and hers conflict, as you know. I'd rather hear it directly from you.

JD   I was in the middle of cooking dinner. Roger had a late tutorial, but as soon as I answered the door I knew who she was.

POLICE   Did you let her in?

JD   She took me by surprise. She just came in, and I didn't stop her.

POLICE   Did you have a conversation?

JD   Not really. She said something about setting him free, or whatever, the same kind of thing she'd written in her letters. And then she just grabbed the knife out of my hand—

POLICE   You were holding a knife?

JD   I'd been getting dinner ready. I was paring apples for a new recipe, a sweet-and-sour sauce – God, it's funny the things you remember.

POLICE   What did she do after she seized the knife?

JD   It all happened so fast. She grabbed it and just stabbed herself in the stomach. I mean, hard, not just a superficial cut. There was blood everywhere.

POLICE   What did you do?

JD   Well, for a moment I was in shock, and then I grabbed my apron and tried to stop the bleeding, and called 999.

POLICE   At the time, she claimed *you* were the one who stabbed her.

JD   If you know that, you must also know her version

263

of events did not stand up to scrutiny, and I was later granted a restraining order against her. If I recall correctly, she spent some time at an in-patient facility.

POLICE   So she lied?

JD   It's not that simple. As I'm sure you know, memory is a very unreliable narrator, Detective. We all think memories are stored in our brains just as they are in computers. Once registered, the data are put away for safe-keeping and eventual recall. The facts don't change. But the truth is, every time we remember something, we are reconstructing the event, reassembling it from traces throughout the brain. We also suppress memories that are painful or damaging to self-esteem. Our memories reshape themselves to accommodate the new situations we find ourselves facing. Memory is flexible.

POLICE   I'm not sure I follow.

JD   Put simply, Louise Roberts was so plausible because she believed everything she said. It's how she remembered it actually happened. She'd have passed a lie-detector test, trust me.

POLICE   Are you saying she didn't know the difference between truth and fiction?

JD   In a manner of speaking.

POLICE   You're a psychologist, aren't you? Did you think she was mad?

JD   I think she was in love. Which is a kind of madness, don't you think?

Five days before the party

Chapter 30

Caz

I know it's a Hail Mary pass, but if I don't ask, I'll never forgive myself. Patrick's a shrewd operator with an eye on the bottom line, but he's a decent man. If I'd been here last Friday, instead of chasing Andy, maybe I could've spoken up for AJ and stopped this happening in the first place.

'If anyone's to blame over Vine, it's me,' I say, before I've even sat down. 'Please, Patrick. I'm the Account Director. *I'm* the one you should be firing, if you have to fire someone.'

To my consternation, my throat suddenly feels tight. Patrick stares at me for a long moment, then wordlessly reaches into his desk and produces a box of tissues. I snatch one and blow into it, willing myself not to cry. I hate women who cry at work. I can hear my mother's acid voice, whenever my lip trembled as a child: *That's right, put it in the crier's hands. Think that'll bring your father back?*

'I'm truly sorry about AJ,' Patrick says, as I ball up the tissue and stare fixedly at my lap. 'This wasn't a decision I made lightly. But you and I both know he's been on borrowed time for a while. You've covered for him more than once. Things are tight financially at the moment; we lost a lot of business over Vine. AJ doesn't put in the hours, and cuts corners. He's dead weight we can't afford to carry.'

Patrick is wrong: AJ *does* put in the hours, but not where it counts. I'm the one at fault for that: it's my messes AJ wastes his time cleaning up. I know I'm not popular with the creatives; I don't have the patience to sweet-talk them into doing jobs they're *paid* to do. AJ's wonderful at making the design team happy, but office politics has never been his thing. I can't let him take the fall for me. He'll never speak up for himself: he's a Labrador puppy in a world of Rottweilers.

'Patrick, I really need AJ on Univest,' I plead. 'I'm backed up with work as it is. I can't afford to lose him. And I know Tina likes him, too. We could shuffle some responsibilities around, make him exclusive on the Univest account—'

'This *comes* from Univest,' Patrick says.

The penny suddenly drops. Univest equals Tina, and Tina equals Louise.

I stop fighting, knowing the battle is lost. Patrick's never going to risk upsetting Tina, and she and Louise are tighter than two coats of paint. I feel like I've just had my legs cut from under me. AJ has been at Whitefish my entire career. I can't imagine working there without him. I don't think I've ever hated Louise more than I do at this minute.

I leave Patrick's office and flee to the bathroom, locking myself into a stall so I can cry in peace. It's not just losing AJ. It's everything. Patrick doesn't trust me anymore, or he'd have brought me in on AJ's firing last week. My job is on the line, and right now I'm not even sure I want to work here any longer. And then there's Andy. I still have no idea where he really was last Friday. When he got home and I asked him how 'work' had gone, he looked me in the eye and lied to my face about being stuck in the studio all day. But I'd tracked his mobile: I already knew he'd spent the day in Brighton. With *her*.

Andy would flip if he knew I'd installed stealth spyware on his phone, but I'm not a fool. Leopards don't change their spots.

My mobile buzzes, startling me. I take a deep breath, clearing my voice of tears, and then laugh in disbelief when I see the name on the screen. The sheer chutzpah of the woman is breathtaking. If Louise was within reach, I'd shove the phone down her throat until she choked on it.

It vibrates seconds later with an incoming text. **Where's Andrew?**

I ignore her. A second text hits my inbox. **At ED with Bella. He's not at work. Not answering his phone.**

That brings me up short. The Emergency Department? I love that kid, though she doesn't always make it easy. **Is she OK?** I type back. **What happened?**

OOO

I stare at the three cycling grey bubbles, waiting for

271

an answer. But then the dots suddenly vanish, and Louise doesn't reply after all. I resend my text, and when she still doesn't respond, I call her. Her phone goes straight to voicemail. I try Andy, but he's not picking up either.

Which ED? I text Louise, my anxiety mounting. Is Bella OK?

Nothing. If this is one of her sick games—

Louise has many faults, but surely even she wouldn't invent an emergency involving her child just to fuck with me. She probably had to turn off her phone inside the hospital. Oh, God, if anything's happened to Bella, it'll break Andy's heart. It'll break *my* heart. I can't just sit here and wait for Louise to ring back.

I'll have to go down there. They must be at the Royal Sussex Hospital in Brighton; it's the nearest one to Bella's school.

I let myself out of the bathroom stall and quickly touch up my make-up. I don't bother to tell anyone I'm leaving the office. Frankly, I don't care if Patrick fires me. Without AJ, I'm not staying at Whitefish a day longer than I have to. I have enough experience now to find another job at one of the bigger agencies. Maybe even finagle something for AJ there and take him with me.

I repeatedly try to reach both Louise and Andy on the train from Victoria to Brighton. His secretary tells me he's not at work again today, and this time I can't even bring myself to care where he is. Clearly not with Louise, at least, or she wouldn't have bothered to contact me. His phone's switched off, so I can't track him. I lean my head against the cool glass of the train window, and close my eyes. I'm so *tired* of all the lying. I don't know what it is I'm fighting for anymore.

Louise still hasn't replied to my texts an hour later. I get an Uber from the station to the hospital, and rush into the ED, frantic for information. The receptionist gives me a tired smile, clearly used to desperate relatives seeking news, and turns to her computer without comment when I give her Bella's name, calmly tapping her keyboard as I grip the edge of the counter with whitened knuckles. 'Is she OK?' I demand.

'I'm afraid I can't tell you that,' the woman says sympathetically. 'Are you family?'

'Yes. Well, I'm married to her dad.'

Her expression cools. 'So, not *actual* family, then?'

I suppress the urge to punch the woman on the nose. 'She's my daughter,' I say tersely.

'If you could take a seat, someone will be out to see you shortly.'

I eye the double doors to the right of the reception desk. I'm tempted to make a run for it and find Bella myself, but I tamp down my anxiety and frustration, and return to the waiting area. I go over to the vending machine, jabbing in the numbers for a strong black coffee. I realise I haven't eaten all day, and add a mini-pack of Digestives.

As I reach into the vending bin, I suddenly catch sight of Bella sitting in a small bay just along the corridor to my left. Her head is heavily bandaged, but she's

273

upright and scrolling through her phone. As far as I can see, she's alone.

I abandon my coffee and biscuits and rush over. 'Bella!' I exclaim. 'Are you all right? What happened? I've been worried sick!'

She looks up, startled. 'What are you doing here?'

'Your mother texted me. She was trying to reach your dad.' I glance around. 'Where is she?'

'She went to get the car. The doctor said we can go home, but I'm not supposed to walk anywhere for a bit, and she parked miles away.'

I perch on the hard plastic chair beside her bed. 'What happened?'

'It's nothing. A rounder's ball hit me in the head. Don't worry, I wasn't playing,' Bella adds, with a flash of dry humour. 'I had a free period, and I didn't feel like studying, so I went to watch. I was just unlucky, that's all.'

'Did you get knocked out?'

'Yeah. You know, it's true, you actually do see stars. I threw up, too, so the school called an ambulance. And Mum.' She grimaces. 'She totally freaked out. She's been ringing everyone. I'm really sorry you came all the way here for nothing.'

'She's your mum. It's her job to freak out. And I didn't come for nothing. I came to see you were OK.' I squeeze her hand. 'The same thing happened to me when I was at college. Cricket ball. You're going to have a bit of a headache for a few days, but just take it easy, and you'll be fine.'

274

'If Mum doesn't drive me crazy first.'

'Did she get hold of your dad?' I ask, trying to keep my tone casual.

'I don't think so. He's at work, right? He never picks up when he's doing interviews and stuff.'

A male nurse joins us and pulls a privacy curtain across the bay, smiling at Bella. 'Mind if I do a quick check of your blood pressure before you go?'

He wraps a cuff around her upper arm, the sleeve of her shirt riding up as he takes her pulse. Bella quickly tugs it back down; but not quite quickly enough. It takes an effort of will to keep the shock from showing on my face.

'Yep, all good,' the nurse says, unfastening the cuff. 'No more stopping balls with your head, OK?'

Bella nods weakly. As soon as he's gone, I reach for her arm, but she snatches it away. 'Bella,' I say softly. 'What's going on?'

'It's nothing,' she mutters.

I hesitate for a long moment. And then I hitch up my skirt, high enough for her to see the top of my thighs. 'It's *not* nothing,' I say.

She stares at the criss-cross hatching of pale scars on my legs. They're almost invisible now, but I know they're there. I always know they're there.

It's been years since I cut myself, but the pull is still strong. I can still remember the exquisite way it used to sting right before it bled, and the sudden release of all the pent-up fear and rage and pain from my body, all the emotion I was powerless to express. Looking back

275

now, I can't think of a single day of my childhood when I didn't feel sad. I used to lie on the floor of my bedroom, barely able to breathe, so angry and miserable I would cry for hours, hating myself for something I couldn't control, that wasn't my fault. I was depressed, but at the time, I thought my brain was broken. The only way I could cope with the pain was to shut down emotionally, to crush all my feelings and become numb.

But I was a young girl, and no matter how dead I felt inside, the yearning for life was like water, forcing its way through barren rock. Despite myself, I desperately wanted to *feel* again. There was a time when the cutting was the only way I knew I was alive. When I cut, at least I felt *some*thing.

When my mother found out about it she hit me and screamed. I started to cut myself around my ribs and on my side to hide the marks. I couldn't stop. I thought I was meant to be the girl who killed herself, so I didn't care about the scars. I couldn't imagine I had a future.

Angie was the only one who knew, apart from my mother. *He did this to you*, she said bitterly. *You're not going to let him win, are you?*

I knew she was right, but it didn't make any difference. It was only when my mother tried to hang herself that my rage was finally directed at someone other than myself. She had no *right* to take her own life. She'd known what had been happening behind my closed bedroom door, and she'd done nothing to help. Why should she get the easy way out, when I was the one in pain?

At college, I sought counselling, and it helped. It took time, and often it felt as if I was taking one step forward, only to end up two steps back. I avoided friendships and intimate relationships, I cut my mother out of my life, and eventually, I stopped wanting to harm myself. And then I found Andy, and for the first time, I knew what it felt like to be happy.

Except now I wonder: was it the old self-hatred that led me to fall in love with a man who's always, *always*, made me feel second best? Was that all I felt I deserved?

Whatever has driven Bella to do this, I can't bear her to feel such pain. The anger I thought I'd tamed long ago flares back into life, but this time, it has a new target. 'I'm not going to ask why,' I tell her. 'But you need to talk to someone about this.'

'No,' she says, alarmed. 'You can't tell anyone!'

'Bella—'

'Please, Caz. They'll send me to a shrink. I'll stop, I promise. I'm trying.'

I know better than anyone how hard it is to stop what Bella is doing. Even if you manage to control the cutting, that doesn't mean you stop self-harming. There are so many ways to sabotage yourself. Drink. Drugs.

Toxic relationships.

But I also know that Bella needs someone to listen to her. Right now, neither of her parents are looking in her direction. I've been where she is. She needs someone she can trust, not someone else telling her what to do.

'Next time you feel like cutting, you call me,' I say,

gripping her hands in mine and forcing her to look at me. 'Day or night. You call me, OK?'

'OK.'

I hug her, hard. I don't know what – or who – is driving this beautiful, intelligent, funny child to hurt herself like this, but I'm going to find out. And then I'm going to stop it, whatever it takes.

Chapter 31

Louise

I'm fetching the car from the hospital car park when Min calls me. 'I can't talk now,' I say, crooking the phone between my neck and shoulder as I scrabble through my bag for my car keys. 'They're discharging Bella, so I'm just about to drive her home.'

'What did the doctor say?'

'All the tests came back clear. There's no swelling or bleeding on the brain, thank God.'

'Thank God,' Min echoes.

We're both silent for a moment, remembering Nicky. My brother had been fine at first, after his accident; a bit banged up, certainly, several broken ribs and a lot of bruising, and a rather nasty cut on his forehead where he'd hit the windscreen, but the doctor had assured my mother it was nothing time couldn't heal.

Except Nicky hadn't had time, of course. The pathologist concluded he'd suffered from something called second-impact syndrome, when the brain swells rapidly, and catastrophically, after a person suffers a second concussion before symptoms of an earlier one have subsided. We had no way of knowing it until the inquest, but three weeks earlier, Nicky had been tackled to the ground during a rugby game. It was such a minor injury, he'd jumped right up and carried on playing; he hadn't even mentioned it when he'd got home. But that rugby tackle had somehow left his brain vulnerable, and the car crash then unleashed a series of metabolic events in his head that had doomed him even as the nurse had written up his discharge papers.

I don't care what the doctor says now: I'm not letting Bella out of my sight.

'Look,' Min says, 'I'll leave you to it. I just wanted to chat with you about something.' Can you give me a call when it all settles down?'

'Sure. Is something wrong?'

'No, no, nothing like that. It can wait.'

I promise to call her later, then drive back to the ED, and text Bella that I'm outside. A few moments later, my daughter emerges into the hot July sunshine, her head swathed in bandages. Leaving the engine running, I get out and go around to the passenger door to help her into the car.

Caz beats me to it.

It's the first time I've seen her since the night I drove to London and confronted her about Bagpuss. I dig my fingernails into my palms, fighting the urge to scratch her eyes out. 'What are you doing here?'

Bella deliberately puts herself between us. 'She came to see if I was OK. It was really *nice* of her,' she adds firmly.

'I got your text, Louise,' Caz tells me. 'I was worried when I didn't hear back from you. I had to come down and make sure Bella was OK.'

'How thoughtful of you,' I say acidly. 'But there was no need. Everything's fine.'

'Obviously I didn't know that, since you didn't reply.'

I'm aware of Bella next to me, the tension in her shoulders. She will never know how much it costs me to be civil to this woman. 'No phones allowed in the hospital, I'm afraid,' I say, forcing a tight smile. 'I had to switch it off. Sorry you had a wasted journey.'

'What about Dad?' Bella asks her. 'Is he coming here too?'

Caz hesitates just a fraction too long. 'He's at work. It'll depend on what time he finishes.'

Her tone is light, deceptively casual, but I hear it: that giveaway note in her voice, the combination of doubt and fear and denial. It's subtle: only a woman who has wondered where her husband is, and with whom, would notice it. 'He's not working,' I contradict swiftly. 'I called INN this morning. They said he'd taken the day off today.'

'He's out in the field.'

'Not according to his secretary. Jessica always knows where he is. And she said specifically he'd cancelled a shoot they'd set up for this afternoon so he could take a personal day. Didn't he tell you?'

'I don't keep tabs on him,' Caz says tightly.

I smile. 'Perhaps you should.'

She smiles back, her eyes cold. '*I've* never needed to.'

Bella abruptly gets into the car. 'You shouldn't leave the engine running, Mum,' she says, buckling her seatbelt. 'It's really bad for the environment.'

On the way home from the hospital, I stop briefly at my mother's to pick up Tolly, but I don't stay and chat as I usually would. Apart from my anxiety to get Bella home, I'm still too angry with Mum after our fight yesterday. No doubt I'll get over it, but invoking Roger's name was a low blow. The episode with Jennifer Lewison wasn't my finest hour, certainly, but it all happened a long time ago now. The situation with Caz is wholly different. I'm *not* fabricating what she's doing to my family. Why won't anyone believe me?

Bella eats a large bowl of tomato soup without complaint for dinner, so my worry about her eases a little. I send her up to her bedroom to rest, and bathe Tolly and put him to bed, then pour myself a large glass of cheap Tesco plonk, and go outside. The late evening sunshine casts long shadows as I curl up in the wicker basket chair at the bottom of the garden, cradling my wineglass. I love this house; it's my home, the only one the children have ever known. But I'm honestly not sure how much longer we can afford to live here. Our finances were pretty ropey even with the job at Whitefish; without it, we're in serious trouble. I don't want to acknowledge it, but a large part of this ridiculous vendetta with Caz is my fault. I shouldn't have retaliated the way I did. But I still don't understand what set it all off. For four years, we've muddled along in a wary Cold War without either of us reaching for

282

the nuclear button. What's brought us to crisis point now?

I dig a bare foot into the dry grass, and rock the chair back and forth as the roseate sky deepens to indigo. I can't help a tiny spark of sympathy for Caz. Andrew only ended up in her arms because I drove him away. If I hadn't screwed up, he'd never have left me. Maybe the seeds for what's happening now were sown then, when she realised she would never know the security of being his first choice.

My wine is a little warm, but I drink it anyway. What I did to Andrew was no worse than what he'd done to me. The difference was, he couldn't forgive me for it.

I found out about his affair in the most banal of ways. He'd left a phone, a *second* phone, in his jacket pocket when he went out jogging one Sunday morning, and I'd found it when it rang. I wasn't stupid; I'd known immediately what it was, and what it meant. Andrew always had to have the latest, all-singing, all-dancing technology; this phone, his second, secret phone, was a cheap pay-as-you-go with just one number in the call log. If that hadn't given the game away, the photos in the camera roll would have done.

Much as I'd wanted to confront him the second he got back from his run, to scream and cry and change the locks, a deep, atavistic instinct had told me to play the long game. This *Caz*, whoever she was, this pretty blonde snuggling against him in her pink Puffa jacket and tight jeans in the selfies on his phone, wasn't his *wife*. I'd had the advantage of Bella, of more than a decade of marriage and entwined lives and friends and family. *I* was still the one he loved, I'd been certain of that.

Somehow, I held it together and said nothing. Looking back now, I don't know how I managed it; I think it drove me a little mad. For months, I waited and prayed the affair would burn itself out, and in the meantime, I endured. If Andrew slipped away to make a 'work call', I'd pretend I had no idea he was calling his mistress. I allowed him to think he'd got away with it when he disappeared for six days on assignment to 'Glasgow' and came back with a tan. I let him make love to me every week, as he'd always done, and tried not to ask myself if he did it like *this*, with *her*.

He didn't leave me. But he didn't give her up, either. And the months of waiting almost killed me. I couldn't sleep; I could hardly eat. I felt as if I was being eaten away by acid from the inside out. I was vulnerable, distraught; hardly in my right mind. And I made a mistake.

I startle now as I hear the sound of a car on gravel. Spinning the basket chair around so I can see the driveway, I spot Andrew climbing out of a taxi, almost as if my memories have summoned him. He knows Nicky's history; he'll have been almost as worried about Bella as me. He must have come straight here from the station.

He reaches back into the cab for a battered holdall I recognise from every foreign assignment he ever went on. Slipping my bare feet back into my sandals, I leave the chair swinging and hasten around the side of the house.

The red tail-lights of the taxi illuminate Andrew's face as he stands in the middle of the drive, his expression weary and defeated. As soon as I reach him, he drops the bag at our feet and clings to me like a drowning man.

I pull back anxiously and search his face. 'What is it, Andrew? Has something happened?'

'Oh, Lou,' he says thickly. 'I've been such a bloody fool.'

Chapter 32

Caz

I'm on my way to the station to get the train back up to London when Andy finally responds to my hail of texts. **On my way.**

I stare at the screen, waiting for more, but that's it. **No need,** I type back. **Bella's fine. I'll be back in London in an hour.**

He doesn't respond. The Uber driver pulls up in front of the station, and I'm about to pay him and get out of the car when I get another text, this time from Lily, our next-door neighbour in Fulham. Andy has dropped Kit off with her for the night; she's checking in to see if we need her to collect him from kindergarten tomorrow too. Why on earth didn't Andy bring our son down with him? It's not like it matters if Kit misses a day of nursery.

There's no point going back into London if Andy's already left. I lean forward between the front seats and tell the Uber driver to take me to our house here instead, anxious and angry. I should be worrying more about what Andy's up to, but I can't stop thinking about those ugly scars on Bella's arms. I know cutting is almost a rite of passage at some expensive girls' schools these days, but what could possibly be causing that lovely, smart, funny girl to do such terrible harm to herself? I pray to God what happened to me isn't happening to her—

No. No! Andy would *never* do that.

I let myself into the empty house, shivering as if someone's just walked over my grave. I promised Bella I wouldn't say anything, but what if this escalates? Most girls who self-harm aren't suicidal. They're looking for release from emotions they can't handle, escape from feelings of worthlessness and self-loathing; cutting brings relief from the intense emotional pain. But what about the few who *are*? I couldn't live with myself if Bella did something terrible and I could have prevented it.

It's not just that she's cutting herself, either. The girl looks *ill*. She's pale and drawn, and she's lost weight in recent weeks. Something's sucking the life from her and driving her to hurt herself.

Frustrated and scared, I open a bottle of Pinot Grigio, one of the few items in the near-empty fridge, and pour myself a generous glass, pacing anxiously through the empty house. I honestly think Bella is in real trouble, and I don't know what to do. I'm twenty-nine years old; I've no idea how to deal with an angst-ridden teenager coping with divorce and peer pressure and God knows what else. The fact that I was a damaged kid myself doesn't qualify me to offer expert help.

I'm going to have to tell Andy what Bella's doing to herself, I realise suddenly. It's the only responsible thing to do. Bella will hate me for a while, and I don't blame her, but in the end, she'll understand why I had to do it. I want to be her friend, yes, but my role here is to be her *parent*.

Dammit, where the hell *is* Andy? He said he was leaving hours ago. He should be here by now.

I check the spyware app on my phone, and Andy's locator dot immediately appears: he's on the Brighton-bound train from Victoria, currently just outside Crawley, less than half an hour away. It's already six o'clock, so he'll probably just want to come here and drop off his bag, then go straight over to Louise's to check on Bella. I knock back a large gulp of wine. Like he needs an excuse to see her.

On impulse, I go into the study and log into Andy's email account, scrolling swiftly through the messages. They're nearly all related to work, other than a few charity solicitations and a couple of emails from a CNN editor who's been wooing him to jump ship. Nothing to set off any alarms; but Andy's not stupid. When we were seeing each other behind Louise's back, he bought a separate pay-as-you-go mobile, just in case she ever checked his iPhone. He knows better than to leave a virtual trail of incriminating emails.

I pull up his browser history, still not really sure what I'm looking for. All I find are news sites and a few innocuous links to pages for fishing and outdoor sports. I stop on one web address I don't recognise, and quickly click away again when an underage chatroom comes up. Andy's been working on a documentary about teenage sex trafficking, but those aren't images I want stuck in my head. Instead, I keep scrolling, going back through the last three weeks of his browser history, but there's nothing remotely untoward. So why do I suddenly feel so uneasy?

Those teenage chatrooms. But it's just for *work*. Andy isn't like my father. What happened to me is *not* happening to Bella. I know the signs. I'd have realised.

With a sigh of exasperation, I shut down his computer, and make space on the desk for my own laptop. *Enough.* I'm going to drive myself mad.

For the next half-hour or so, I use work as an escape from the storm of worry in my head, replying to emails and signing off on a few outstanding briefs awaiting my approval. Several clients have already heard on the bush telegraph that AJ is leaving, and are anxiously checking in to see who'll be handling them from now on. AJ has always been so good at managing their needs and expectations. I know Univest is important to Patrick, but why he's allowed Tina Murdoch to dictate terms and sabotage us like this is beyond me.

My stomach rumbles, and I realise I still haven't eaten all day. I go into the kitchen, scavenging some dried macaroni and a tin of tomatoes from the cupboard, keeping an eye on the progress of Andy's little red dot as I quickly knock up some spaghetti pomodoro. He arrives in Brighton just as the pan comes to the boil, but instead of heading towards me, the flashing locator starts moving along the road towards Petworth.

I suppress a surge of anger. He's obviously getting a taxi straight over to Louise's, instead of coming here first. He knows Bella's concussion wasn't serious. The least he could've done was pay me the courtesy of checking in before rushing off to his other family.

What time will you be home? I text furiously.

ooo

The three circling dots again. It's several minutes before he actually replies, which means he's composed his answer several times, then erased and edited it, before finally settling on this: Trains delayed, security scare. May not get in till late. Don't wait up.

The water hisses as it boils over, and I snatch it from the stove, cursing as I burn my fingers on the hot handle. He's lying. Why? He's already here, heading in a taxi to Louise, so why not just tell me that?

My brain beats like a bird trapped against a closed window. He doesn't want me to know he's already on his way to see Louise, because then I'll expect him home sooner rather than later. And he evidently plans to stay longer than a check on his daughter requires.

Before I have a chance to frame a response, my phone buzzes again. I snatch it up, thinking it's Andy, but the text is from AJ. Sorry to leave you in the lurch.

Don't be daft, I text back. We'll sort this out, I promise.

He doesn't respond. I call him, and it rings a few times, then cuts to his voicemail message. I end the call, and hit redial. The third time, he finally picks up.

'AJ, where are you?' I ask anxiously. 'I can come back to London if you need me—'

'No, it's OK,' AJ says. 'I'll be fine.'

His voice sounds as if it's coming from far away, and I have to press the phone hard to my ear to make out what he's saying. 'You don't sound fine,' I say uneasily.

'You've been a great boss, Caz. A great friend.'

A tight knot of fear settles in my stomach. 'AJ, where are you?' I ask again.

'Honestly, it's OK. You'll be fine without me.'

He's not talking about leaving Whitefish. This is something darker. I've seen despair before: I know what it looks like, what it sounds like, and I hear it now. 'I know this feels like the end of the world, but things *will* get better,' I say urgently. 'We all love you, AJ. There's light out there, even if you can't see it right now.'

There's a long silence. 'I'm going to miss this place,' he says finally. 'It was my life.'

This place. Abruptly I realise where he is. The clock chiming in the background, the wind whipping away his words. He's on the terrace atop the Whitefish building.

I run into the hallway and pick up the landline, dialling 999 with rigid fingers as I keep talking to AJ on my mobile. 'I know you think it's hopeless, but I've been where you are, AJ, and there *is* hope,' I say. 'There's always hope.'

'Not for me,' AJ says, but I hear a note of hesitation in his voice.

I hold my mobile against my chest as I tell the emergency dispatcher to get someone to the Whitefish building in London as soon as possible, then put my mobile to my ear again. I keep up a stream of chatter, not knowing if I'm making any sense, but I can hear AJ's breathing, so I know he's still listening.

I don't know how long it is before I hear the noise of sirens in the distance, and then a few minutes later, there are voices in the background. The paramedics must have arrived. The knot in my stomach finally eases, and I realise just how frightened I've been. In the space of a few weeks, AJ has lost Wayne, and now a job that meant everything to him. I have no idea how close he just came to doing something irrevocable, but if he had, there would have been only one person to blame. God, I hate that woman.

'I have to go,' AJ says. 'I'll call you later.'

I sink into a kitchen chair and press the heels of my palms into my eyes, my whole body trembling. First Bella, and now AJ. This is one of the worst days I can remember, and I've had to cope with everything alone. I wish Andy was here to tell me it's all going to be OK, but thanks to Louise, I have no one to turn to. I keep picturing AJ standing on the edge of the terrace, staring down at the street below, nerving himself to jump. I swallow hard, trying not to vomit.

I text Andy again, but I'm not surprised when he doesn't reply. Bitterness sours my blood. Louise thinks she's winning, taking back what was hers, smashing my life like a wrecking ball. Well, I hope she enjoys tonight. I hope she still thinks it's worth it, once she sees the consequences.

I didn't want to go nuclear, but she's given me no choice.

I have one card left to play.

Date:- 27/07/2020
Duration:- 24 Minutes
Location:- Starr Farm Senior Care Centre,
Parsloes Ave, Dagenham

Conducted by Officers from Devon & Cornwall
Police

(cont.)

RC   Her dad isn't dead.

POLICE   But Mrs Page said—

RC   It's what she always says. Easier than admitting he walked out on her. She don't like the truth;

she changes the facts to fit. Far as I know, Ted Clarke's alive and well, ruining some other poor bitch's life. Dorking, last I heard.

POLICE   Make a note, Rich. We'll need to talk to him.

POLICE   Sir.

RC   So what d'you want from me?

POLICE   When did you last see your daughter, Mrs Clarke?

RC   I don't know. A couple of weeks ago? She comes when she comes. What am I, her mother?

POLICE   Sir, are you sure [inaudible].

POLICE   The doctor said she was fit for interview, Rich.

RC   I'm pulling your leg, son. I'm old, not senile.

POLICE   When you last saw your daughter, Mrs Clarke, how did she seem to you?

RC   She brought the wrong biscuits.

POLICE   Did she discuss her husband at all?

295

RC   She didn't tell me she planned to stick a knife
            in his neck, if that's what you mean.

POLICE   You think your daughter killed her husband?

RC   Do you?

POLICE   [Pause.] Let me put it another way. Did she give
            any indication they were having problems when
            she visited?

RC   She married a cheater. Cheetahs don't change
            their spots.

POLICE   Do you mean leopards?

POLICE   It's a pun, Rich. Are you saying Andrew Page
            was having an affair?

RC   How would I know? I've never even met him.
            She didn't invite me to the wedding. How's that
            for honouring thy mother? Tried to kill me, then
            put me in here to rot. If I weren't dead from the
            neck up when I arrived, I am now.

POLICE   What do you mean, tried to kill you? Who did?

RC   My loving daughter, who d'you think?

POLICE   Sir [inaudible].

RC	I know what it says in my records. I never tried to top myself. She weren't trying to cut me down when my neighbour found her neither, she was trying to string me up. But Carol is very convincing when she wants to be. You've got no idea what she's really capable of.
POLICE	Carol? You mean your daughter, Caroline Page?
RC	Changed her name when she left home. But take away the fancy suits and la-di-dah accent, she's still Carol.
POLICE	Sorry, but are you saying your own daughter tried to *kill* you?
RC	I don't expect you to believe me.
POLICE	Can you prove any of this?
RC	Think I'd be sitting here if I could?
POLICE	Sir, I [inaudible].
RC	You were the ones came to see me, remember? You think I'm unreliable? We all tell our own truths, son. You think anyone else is telling you the *facts*?
POLICE	Thank you, Mrs Clarke, you've been very

helpful. If we need anything else, someone will be in touch. Rich, you can turn that off now—

RC   His wife came to see me last week.

POLICE   [Pause.] I'm sorry, Mrs Clarke. What did you say?

RC   Louise Page. She was here.

POLICE   What did she want?

RC   Same as you. She wanted to know about Carol. Difference is, *she* took me seriously.

Chapter 33

Louise

The taxi disappears down the lane, and Andrew picks up his holdall and follows me around the side of the house and in through the half-finished kitchen. I'm about to put on the kettle to make some tea when I think better of it, and fetch a bottle of Glenlivet 18-year-old single malt from the sideboard in the dining room. I pour a rich, thick finger of the amber liquid into a heavy crystal glass, and take it in to Andrew. The last time I touched either this bottle or the best crystal was almost five years ago, the Christmas before he left.

Andrew knocks back the Scotch in a single gulp, and holds his empty glass out to me. I go back to the sideboard to top it up, my concern mounting. I've never seen him drink like this.

I don't normally bother with alcohol myself during the week, but I have a feeling I'm going to need it tonight. I pour myself a large glass of white wine and take both drinks through to the sitting room. 'What's happened?' I ask, setting Andrew's tumbler on the coffee table in front of him. 'What did you mean outside, when you said you've been a fool?'

He buries his face in his hands. 'Oh, God. I don't know where to start.'

'Try the beginning.'

I sit down next to him, but for a long time, he doesn't speak. His shoulders heave silently, and I realise with shock that he's crying. I can count on the fingers of one hand the times I've seen him sob before.

My arms ache to reach out and comfort him, but I don't feel I have the right. 'Andrew, whatever it is, we can sort it out,' I say.

He raises a despairing face to me. 'Lou, I don't think we can.'

What can he have done that's so terrible? Is it something to do with work? I run through scenarios in my mind, wondering what could have reduced him to such despair. He's made mistakes before, run with a story without checking every fact, made a bad call that put him and his crew at risk, but instinctively I know this is something more personal. News crews work in close quarters on the road, producers and reporters doubling up in hotel rooms, travelling together for days at a time. Adrenalin and alcohol are a heady combination. And this is the #MeToo era. Has he crossed the line? Is someone accusing him of harassment, or even sexual assault?

There's a footfall on the stairs, and Bella appears in the doorway. She starts in surprise when she sees her father. 'What're you doing here?'

'Hear you've been in the wars,' Andrew says, getting up to give her a hug. No one but me would see the desperate misery behind his smile. 'That's quite the egg you've got there. How's the ball looking?'

'Ha, ha.' She tucks her hands into the long sleeves of her grey T-shirt, and I realise I can see the outline of her ribs and collarbone beneath the flimsy fabric. She's got so *thin*.

'You all right, Dad?' Bella asks. 'You look a bit weird.'

He does look terrible: red-eyed, and drawn and grey beneath his summer tan. He's putting on a good show for Bella, but his hand shakes when he reaches for his glass again, and consummate actor though he is, I don't know how long he can keep up the performance. 'My daughter spent the day in casualty,' he says. 'One day, you'll understand how that feels.'

'Back upstairs now,' I tell Bella. 'You're supposed to be resting.'

'Would you like me to come and tuck you in?' Andrew asks.

Bella looks alarmed. 'She's sixteen,' I say gently. 'She doesn't need tucking in. Go on up, Bella. Dad'll say goodnight later, before he goes.'

Bella returns to her room, and I pour myself another glass of wine, deeply troubled by whatever's going on with Andrew. The protective shock from Bella's accident is starting to wear off, too, leaving me exhausted and emotionally drained. Today has brought back so many unhappy memories. I can't wait for Bella to fall asleep, so I can sit by her bed and just watch her breathe.

301

'She seems OK,' Andrew says, as I return.

'She's awfully thin. I didn't really notice it till I saw her in the hospital bed today. She's lost a lot of weight in the past few months. Do you think we should be worried?'

'Everyone looks ill in a hospital bed.'

'You read so much about eating disorders these days—'

'She looks fine to me,' he says testily. 'She's always been skinny, you know that. But if you're worried, take her to see someone.'

'I don't want to put ideas in her head.'

He sighs. 'Then don't.'

He slumps back onto the sofa, staring moodily into his glass. I wait for him finally to tell me what's troubling him, but he's lost in his own dark thoughts. His phone buzzes a couple of times with incoming texts – Caz, presumably – but he ignores them.

'Andrew,' I begin tentatively. 'Do you want—'

He looks up suddenly. 'Let's not do this,' he says, and there's a note of desperation in his voice. 'Can we just spend a nice evening together, watch some crap TV, and not talk about anything?'

'If that's what you want. Would you like something to eat? I can throw something together—'

'Not for me,' he says. 'Unless you're hungry?'

'I'm fine. I ate earlier with the kids.'

He doesn't mention Caz, and I don't ask. Despite my anxiety, I can't help a quiet sense of pleasure that it's me he's turned to in his moment of crisis, not Caz. She may be his wife now, she may even love him, I suppose, but my bond with Andrew is deeper and older and more profound. Whatever's happened, whatever he's done, I'm in his corner, and he knows that, or he wouldn't be here.

I've been such a bloody fool, Andrew said. For the first time, I dare to hope he meant: *For leaving you.*

He reaches for the remote, and turns on the television, settling on a chilly Scandinavian thriller I've seen before, and refills his glass a third time. I get another for myself, too. It's lucky Andrew didn't drive here; he'll clearly be getting a taxi home.

Pressed together on the settee, I'm acutely conscious of the heat of his body against mine, the sweet, whisky-infused scent of his skin. The sofa is the same one we bought seventeen years ago, when I was pregnant with Bella, its chintz fabric now so faded and stained with spills and sunshine and felt-tip pen it's almost impossible to discern the original pattern. I should've replaced it years ago, but it's the sofa where I breastfed my babies, where one of them was quite possibly conceived, and I can't bear to part with it. Its springs have long since given out, and were it not for the two sturdy Quality Street tins beneath either end, holding up the cushions, our bottoms would sag onto the floor. As it is, we roll to the centre together as if on a cheap mattress. Andrew puts his arm around me, holding the pair of us upright, just as he always did. It feels as if he never left.

'Why are you so good to me?' he murmurs suddenly,

into my hair. 'After everything I've done to you. I don't deserve it.'

It's a question I've asked myself at least a thousand times in the past four years. *The heart wants what it wants.* 'No, you don't,' I agree, trying to ignore the sudden pulse between my legs.

'We had so much going for us, and we still managed to screw it up,' he says, slurring slightly. 'How did we end up here?'

'Andrew—'

He silences me with a kiss.

For a split second, I'm too stunned to respond. But my body knows what I need better than I do, and the muscle memory of my heart is too ingrained for me to hesitate more than a moment. There are four years of pent-up yearning in the kiss I return, four years of waiting and wanting and pain and longing. Every neuron in my body comes alive, and I realise that I have been dormant, living in suspended animation, since the day he left.

Abruptly, Andrew breaks away. I brace myself for the garbled apology: *too much Scotch, getting late, should never have.* But he's paused only to lever himself from the Venus flytrap of a sofa, and then he holds out a hand to me.

I take it.

I take it, and I let him lead me upstairs, even though I know what we're about to do is wrong on so many levels. I take it because I've had a whole bottle of wine, because it's late and he has come to *me*, because I'm tired of fighting how I feel, of pretending to myself that I've put the past behind me and moved on. I take his hand and follow him into our bedroom and let him undress me because I love him, and because in my head and my heart he is my husband, has always been *my* husband, no matter who he's married to.

We are strangers who know every inch of each other's skin. It comes as easily to us as it always did, but now it's enhanced by the thrill of discovering each other all over again. I'd forgotten how much I like sex, the extraordinary capability of my own body to give me pleasure.

Afterwards, we lie in each other's arms, my head nestled against his chest. Andrew has fallen straight asleep, as always. I listen to his heartbeat, pressing my palm gently against his skin. For so long, I've fantasised about this moment. Now it's here, I can't quite take it in.

I extricate myself from his embrace without waking him, propping myself up on my elbow as I watch him sleep. I don't know why he's come back to me now, after all this time, but I'm not going to question it. This is what I've wanted since the day he left: for him to come to his senses, realise what a fool he's been, and come back to me. He didn't exactly say that in so many words, but then we didn't waste much time talking. It's obvious what he meant. He's here. That's all that matters.

So why this strange sense of . . . *anticlimax*?

It wasn't the sex. *That* was satisfying on both a physical and emotional level. And yet I feel oddly flat, the way you do on Boxing Day after all the anticipation and excitement of Christmas. Wonderful as it was, of course it couldn't live up to the weight of four years of expectation. Nothing ever does.

I wish I could let him sleep, but I can't risk Tolly bouncing in at five a.m. and finding his father in my bed. We need to break this carefully to the children, once we've worked out the logistics of Andrew moving back in. I know how close Bella's got to Caz. I don't want to alienate her any further. This is going to take a bit of finessing as far as she's concerned.

I nudge Andrew, smiling as he opens his eyes. 'I hate to wake you, but the kids can't find you here.'

He glances at his watch and sits up abruptly. 'Shit. Is that the time?'

'The spare room's all made up. You can—'

'I need to get back to Caz. She'll be wondering where the hell I am.'

I watch in silence as he yanks on his trousers and sifts through the tangle of clothes on the floor for his socks. I'd assumed, because of the holdall with which he'd arrived, he'd already told Caz he was leaving her. A faint sense of unease steals over me. He must be going back to break the news to her now. He wouldn't let me down again.

He finds his socks and sits next to me to put them on. Tucking a strand of hair behind my ear, he looks deep into my eyes. 'You are incredible,' he murmurs. 'I can't tell you how much I needed that.'

I digest that for a moment. Sex is different for men,

306

of course. It's the way they communicate. How they show love. They don't need to actually *say* it.

'What are you going to tell Caz?' I ask tentatively.

'She knows I came over to check on Bella. I'll just tell her I had too much to drink, slept it off for a couple of hours on the sofa. She won't like it, but I'll smooth things over somehow.'

Smooth things over? You don't smooth things over when you're leaving your wife. You do it when you don't want to be found out.

A cold stone settles in the pit of my stomach. 'Andrew,' I say slowly. 'Andrew, when you said you'd been a fool, what *exactly* did you mean?'

Four days before the party

Chapter 34

Caz

I pace the empty house in the dark, waiting for Andy to come home, too agitated to sleep or even distract myself with mindless television. Midnight comes and goes, and his locator dot steadily pulses from Louise's house. It hasn't moved in hours. I picture Andy glancing at his phone when it buzzes with my texts, dismissing the notification without even bothering to open it, or maybe showing it to Louise, the two of them laughing at me as I wait pathetically for him to return. Or is his phone unattended in his jacket pocket, flung over the back of a kitchen chair or strewn on the bedroom floor? Is he fucking her, right now?

With a shout of frustration, I fling the phone across the room and collapse sobbing onto the sofa. He's never stopped loving her; I've always known it. My mother was right: you can't build a solid house on shifting sands. He's *weak*. It's the reason we're together in the first place.

The story Andy believes, the story I've told and retold so often I've almost come to believe it myself, is that we met by chance. A fender-bender at the junction of Clerkenwell Road and Hatton Garden: *we literally met by accident*, Andy always says, when he tells the story, *the happiest accident of my life*. He doesn't remember that we'd already met, fleetingly, six weeks earlier when Tina introduced us at the RSPCA charity auction. We barely exchanged three words that night, but for me it was enough. It wasn't hard to find out Andy's routine, and to be in the right place at the right time: he presented the evening bulletin at INN every night, and took the same route to work at the same time each day. All I did was create an opportunity.

But I didn't force him to start an affair with me. You can't steal someone's husband; they're not lipsticks to be pocketed when the store manager's back is turned. If Andy's marriage had been happy, we'd have exchanged insurance details, and that would've been the end of it. He wouldn't have called me the next day, and asked me out for a drink. He wouldn't have leaned across the pub table and tucked my hair behind my ears and told me I was lovely.

Andy led me on, I think furiously. He made me think he was falling in love with me, he encouraged me, *he* came to *me* when he found out Louise had cheated on him. He didn't have to, but he did. He *married* me. He doesn't get to change his mind now. This isn't the playground. There aren't any take-backs here.

Eventually I must fall into some kind of half-sleep on the sofa, because I don't hear Andy come in, and startle when he touches my shoulder. 'Why are you sleeping down here?' he whispers.

I struggle upright. 'What time is it?'

'Almost three. Sorry I'm so late.' He kicks off his shoes and thumps onto the sofa beside me. 'I lost track of time. Louise and I had a couple of drinks after Bella went to bed. More than a couple, actually. She's going to feel it tomorrow.' He yawns. 'Were you waiting up for me?'

'You didn't answer your phone,' I say tightly. 'Or reply to any of my texts.'

He gets up abruptly and goes over to the drinks cabinet, pouring himself a Scotch. 'I told you not to wait up,' he says, his back towards me. 'My train was delayed because of—'

'A security scare. I got your text.'

I can almost hear the wheels turning in his head as he tries to work out what I know, how much trouble he may be in. He must realise it would have been easy enough for me to check his story. 'I don't know why you're making such a big thing of this,' he says finally, settling in an armchair on the other side of the room. Putting distance between us. 'You knew where I was.'

'Until three in the morning?'

'You want me to text you every time I take a shit now?'

It's a measure of how uncomfortable he is with this conversation that's he's so uncharacteristically coarse. 'It would've been nice to know you'd got to Brighton safely,' I snap. 'Given there was a *security scare*.'

313

'Look, what is this?' he says irritably. 'It's been a long day at work, I've been worried sick about my daughter, and it's late. The last thing I need when I finally get home is the third degree from you.'

I'm tired of the verbal fencing. Tired of his lies. 'There was no security scare,' I say coldly. 'Your train wasn't delayed. Why don't *you* tell *me* what "this" is?'

He opens his mouth to bluster, and then I see him rethink it. He knocks back his Scotch. 'I spent the evening with my children,' he says defiantly. 'I was worried about Bella, OK? I just didn't want to get into it with you. You always make such a fucking drama out of it whenever I see Louise.' His tone turns aggressive. 'I wouldn't need to lie if you didn't make it all so bloody difficult.'

'That ship has sailed,' I say tersely. 'You've made it *very* plain where you stand on the subject of Louise. She just has to snap her fingers, and you go running.'

'Louise is the mother of my children,' he says coldly. 'Like it or not, she's part of my life. You knew that when you married me.' His expression is hostile. 'She's got far more reason to have an issue with *you* than you do with her, but she doesn't give me this much grief.'

'Saint Louise,' I say bitterly. 'I'm beginning to wonder why you ever left her.'

'Yeah, well. You're not the only one.'

A sudden silence falls between us. We stare at each other across a widening gulf, either unable or unwilling to bridge it. 'I'm sorry,' Andy mutters finally. 'I didn't mean that.'

I know I should let it go. It's late, and we're both tired. This isn't the kind of conversation to have at three in the morning, but I can't stop picking at the scab. 'Where were you today, Andy?'

'You know where I was,' Andy snaps. 'I just told you.'

'I mean *today*, when you were supposed to have been at work.'

He's suddenly very still. 'I *was* at work.'

'No, you weren't. And you weren't at work on Friday either—'

'Have you been checking up on me?'

'Do I need to?'

'Jesus, Caz. You *know* I wasn't with Louise today, or I wouldn't have had to rush down from London when our daughter ended up in hospital!'

'So who *were* you with?' I persist. 'Your secretary said you were taking a personal day. How *personal* was it, Andy?'

He slams his glass on the coffee table. 'Would you give it a rest!' he shouts. 'I'm investigating some very sensitive subjects – I don't tell Jessica everything I'm doing!' He rubs his hand through his hair, clearly trying to get his anger under control. When he speaks again, his tone is much calmer. 'Look. Some of my sources are very gun-shy, OK? Occasionally I go off-book to talk to them. Can we please stop this now? There's nothing going on, with Louise or anyone else, I swear to you on my life.'

I want to believe him. I hate him for turning me into

315

the kind of woman I've always despised, jealous and mistrustful, going through pockets and checking emails. I'm so confused. Everything is smoke and mirrors, and I don't know what's real anymore. Maybe I'm just paranoid, I think desperately. I've let Louise get under my skin. I need to regroup and think this through when I'm less tired. I'm too drained to fight anymore. 'I'm going up to bed,' I say, without waiting for him to follow.

I strip off my clothes and crawl into bed, but I'm too wired to sleep. The door opens a short while later, and I hear Andy undress in the dark. I lie motionless, rigid with misery, as the bed sinks beneath his weight. He presses his body against the length of mine, his arm heavy as he drapes it across my waist. 'I'm so sorry,' he whispers, propping himself up on his free elbow. 'I don't want to argue with you. I didn't mean what I said. It was the Scotch talking.'

I'm still savagely angry with him, and yet the heat of his body pressed against my back makes my pulse roar in my ears, even as I fight to hold on to my rage.

He runs his hand over my hip, his voice low and hypnotic. 'You're right, I shouldn't have lied to you. I just know how upset you get about Louise. I'm not trying to make excuses – I was wrong, and I'm sorry.' His breath is warm on my neck. 'She was a little crazy tonight, that's why I stuck around. I'd forgotten how obsessive she can get. She seems to think you poisoned poor Bagpuss. I'm beginning to think she's as unstable as you've said. Who knows what craziness she'll come up with next.' His fingers slip into the wetness between my thighs, and I don't stop him. 'She's living in fantasy land. She'll think we're getting back together next—'

I pull away from him abruptly. He's fucked her. Until thirty seconds ago, I wasn't sure, but I know Andy too well, I recognise the way his devious mind works. That little speech was laying the groundwork for his defence if she ever comes to me and admits he slept with her. *She's crazy. Look at all the insane things she said about* you. *She's obviously delusional. You can't believe a word she says.*

Andy puts a tentative hand on my shoulder, but when I jerk away again, he sighs theatrically, and rolls away from me. 'I'm just going to have a quick shower,' he says. 'I won't be long.'

I press the knuckles of my hand into my mouth. Salty tears spill onto my fingers, and I squeeze my eyes shut, swallowing my sobs through sheer effort of will. Angie was right. My mother was right. All the naysayers and doubters who told me leopards don't change their spots were right. What else did I expect? What kind of man walks out on his baby son when he's a week old, no matter what his mother has done?

The kind of man who cheats, and lies, and fools you into thinking he is capable of loving anyone but himself.

Andy is a treacherous, devious son-of-a-bitch, but he's *my* son-of-a-bitch. I have no intention of giving him up. Love him, hate him, it doesn't matter. They're different sides of the same coin anyway.

Chapter 35

Louise

I love you, Andrew said. I always have, he said.

I make a face at myself in the bathroom mirror, mimicking Andrew's voice beneath my breath. *You've no idea how much I've missed you. This has been great. I've had a really nice time.*

Stepping into the shower, I turn it to the coldest setting, and hold my face in the icy spray, furious with myself. How did I let myself fall for his bullshit yet again? Fool me once, shame on you. Fool me twice, shame on me. Andrew came to me for advice over his affair with another woman. *That's* what he meant when he said he'd been a fool, not that he regretted leaving me. I've got to hand it to Andrew. It takes real skill to cheat on two wives at once.

The cold shower does little to cool my temper, but at least it dispels my hangover. Furiously, I towel my hair, and march back into my bedroom to get dressed. I'm sure Andrew didn't come over here expecting to get laid, but it must have been a nice little bonus. He didn't exactly have to sweet-talk me into bed. The thought of him smugly reclining in the back of his taxi, totting up the notches on his bedpost as he goes home to his wife, makes me want to bloody kill him.

Last time he left me to go back to Caz, he broke my heart. I probe my feelings now, tentatively testing them as if prodding an aching tooth. I should be devastated that he's betrayed me yet again, and yet once more I feel oddly flat and unemotional. Irritated, certainly. Disappointed, even; but in the way a parent might feel about a child who's let themselves down, rather than as a lover who's been cruelly deceived. I can't quite believe it, but I don't think I care very much *what* Andrew does, or with whom. I think . . . I think I'm *over* him.

The realisation is exhilarating. My feet are wonderfully light as I go downstairs to make Tolly's breakfast. Maybe last night wasn't such a mistake after all. It took being slapped in the face one more time for me to finally realise I stopped loving Andrew a long time ago. I just didn't know it till now. Perhaps this is what people call closure.

To my surprise I find Bella already up and dressed, leaning against the half-built kitchen cabinets and eating a bowl of Tolly's Coco Pops. 'What are you doing up?'

'School,' she says, as if talking to a simpleton.

I try to get a better look at the huge purple bruise that's bloomed overnight on her forehead. 'You don't have a headache?'

She ducks out of reach, the cereal bowl still in her hand. '*You're* the one who should have the headache, after all that wine,' she says. 'What time did Dad leave?'

'Late,' I say vaguely. 'You could stay home today, darling. No one would mind.'

'I'm *fine*.'

She certainly seems all right, I think, watching her spoon chocolate milk into her mouth. In fact, it's the first time I've seen her eat such a good breakfast in months. Maybe I've been overreacting about her weight and her moods. She's a teenager. It's to be expected she'll have ups and downs.

It suddenly occurs to me I still haven't tackled her about the money she took from my account. I meant to discuss it after she got home from her weekend with her father, but it was late when he dropped the kids off on Sunday, and then of course we had all the drama of our trip to casualty yesterday. I'll talk to her about it tonight, when we're not in a rush. Whatever the explanation, she has to understand she can't just steal money from me like that. Even if we could afford it, which we most certainly can't, it would still be wrong, and she knows that. I thought I was doing a better job of raising her than this.

We leave the house early for once, since I haven't had to drag Bella out of bed. Instead of haring down the lane in our usual fashion, I'm actually able to drive at a normal speed, well within the legal limit. Which is why I'm surprised when I see a police car pull out of a concealed track behind me, its blue lights flashing. For a moment, I think he just wants to get past me, but then his siren wails briefly and I realise with shock that he's stopping me.

Bella looks up from her phone. 'What's going on?'

'I don't know,' I say. 'I wasn't speeding. Maybe one of my brake lights is out?'

I can't help feeling nervous as he approaches, even though I haven't done anything wrong. It's like when you go through the green channel at the airport: I never know whether to smile at the customs officials, or stare fixedly ahead and refuse to make eye contact.

The policeman looks about the same age as Bella. I wind down the window. 'Can I help you, officer?'

'Is this your car, madam?'

'Yes, of course.'

'Is it registered to you?'

I hesitate. 'I'm not sure, actually. It's my ex-husband's car, and I don't know if he's put it in my name yet. But I'm insured to drive it,' I say quickly. 'It's all above board.'

'Would you mind stepping out of the vehicle, madam?'

'I can call my husband, he'll tell you—'

'Please step out of the car.'

Flustered, I scrabble for the door handle, accidentally locking myself in. Bella sighs and hits the unlock button in the centre console. 'What's wrong?' I ask, following the officer around to the rear of my car. 'Is it my tail-lights, or something?'

'Have you been drinking, madam?'

'*What*?'

'You crossed into the oncoming lane twice while I was watching, and—'

'There's only one lane,' I say defensively. 'It's impossible *not* to go onto the other side.'

'I have reasonable cause to suspect you have consumed alcohol,' the officer says pleasantly. 'I'm going to ask you to consent to a breath test. Do you consent?'

'*Alcohol*?' I exclaim. 'It's eight o'clock in the morning!'

'I must caution you that it is an offence to refuse to supply a breath sample—'

He reaches ominously for his two-way radio, and I quickly backtrack. 'Yes, fine, I consent. Of course I haven't been drinking! I haven't even had breakfast!'

Bella opens the passenger door and leans out. 'Mum, what's going on?'

'Get back in the car, Bella.'

'Mum—'

'Get back in the car!'

'If you could come and join me in my vehicle,' the officer says. 'Please have a seat there, in the front.'

I climb into the police car, my heart pounding. I've never been in a police vehicle before; I've never even been pulled over. I feel embarrassed and humiliated, like I'm some kind of criminal. Thank goodness we're still in the lane, and no one I know is likely to see me. The whole thing is ridiculous. I can't imagine why he stopped a mum on the school run at eight a.m. They must have some kind of silly quota to meet before the end of the month.

The young policeman produces the breathalyser, and the school prefect in me purses her lips, determined to do it perfectly. I follow his instructions as he holds the device steady in front of me, and breathe into the tube until the machine beeps. We both wait awkwardly for it to analyse the sample I've just given. It's going to be negative, obviously. The only thing I've had to drink all morning is two cups of Tetley.

The breathalyser beeps again, and the officer reads it. His expression doesn't change. 'OK, so it's a fail 42,' he says. 'The legal limit's 35. You've failed a breath test, so you're under arrest under suspicion of driving while over the proscribed limit—'

'It can't be,' I cut in. 'It must be a mistake. Can I do it again? I swear, I haven't had a single drink this morning other than a cup of tea.'

'We'll carry out another test at the station, madam.'

'But you don't understand,' I insist. 'I really haven't had anything to drink, not even cough syrup! I must have done it wrong, or—'

'Did you have a drink last night, madam?'

I suddenly feel sick, remembering the entire bottle of wine I got through with Andrew. 'Yes, but that was eight hours ago,' I say faintly. 'I'm not *drunk*.'

'Alcohol remains in the bloodstream longer than you think,' he says nicely. 'Now, I'll be driving you to Brighton police station. I'm going to ask your children to accompany us. If there's someone who can pick them up from the station, that'll be fine.'

'There's no need to bring the children with us. My mother can come and get them right now, she only lives ten minutes—'

'I'm afraid I do require you to come to the station

with me straight away. Your mother can collect the children from there.'

I've never been more ashamed in my life as I watch the police officer walk to my car and ask my children to accompany their mother to the police station. Tolly's eyes are out on stalks, his cheeks pink with excitement as the officer transfers his car seat to the back of the police vehicle and buckles him in, but Bella doesn't even look at me as she climbs wordlessly into the back of the car.

I don't blame the officer. He's just doing his job; actually, now that the process is over, he seems to unbend a little, chatting amiably to Tolly, who is fizzing with questions. My son will tell everyone he's been in a police car, I realise. His teachers. His father. There's going to be no hiding this.

Bella leans forward between the front seats. 'Why were you waiting in the lane?'

'Please sit back, miss.'

She ignores his request. 'It's just, like, a weird place to be parked. It doesn't lead anywhere, except Barlow's farm. Nobody goes down the lane but us. Why would you even be there?'

I suddenly understand what my daughter is driving at. 'Were you *waiting* for me?'

He looks uncomfortable. 'We are acting on information received, yes, madam.'

'It's that bastard farmer, the one who wants to sell off his fields to those developers,' Bella exclaims. 'I bet he did it, because you refused to let them put their access road across the bottom of our paddock. It's just the kind of shitty thing he'd do.'

'Language,' I say weakly.

'It's him,' she says grimly. 'I know it's him.'

It's not the farmer. It's Caz. She's done this because Andrew stayed last night; he must've told her we had a few drinks. I'm quite certain he hasn't mentioned what happened between us, but as far as she's concerned, it's all-out war anyway. I should have known, the minute the police car pulled me over.

We arrive at the station, and I follow the arresting officer through to a room at the rear, leaving Bella and Tolly in reception with the on-duty officer at the desk. I feel sick to my stomach. Caz may have tipped off the police, but her ploy only worked because I failed that breath test. I'm the one in the wrong. My brother died because some middle-aged, middle-class idiot thought he could have one for the road and get away with it. Never mind facing the children, or Andrew, or my mother: I don't know if I'll ever be able to look myself in the mirror again.

I wait in a daze as the officer tests the intoximeter, and then asks me to blow in it again, twice, to ensure an accurate reading. I don't need to be told how much trouble I'm in. How am I supposed to get the children to and from school if I lose my licence? How am I supposed to work?

'You've passed the intoximeter,' the officer says unexpectedly. '*Just*. Your lowest measurement was 34. You won't be charged on this occasion, madam.'

I gawp at him. 'I *passed*?'

'Your current sample puts you below the legal drink drive limit. However,' he adds, as sternly as his youth and innate niceness will allow, 'I would strongly recommend that in future, you don't drive after a heavy night's drinking. Driving while impaired can have very serious consequences, even if you are legally below the limit.'

'Oh, thank you,' I gasp. 'Thank you *so* much.'

'No need to thank me. You've been extremely lucky this time, Mrs Page.'

I'm not going to be arrested. I wasn't drunk, or criminally irresponsible. 'I'm so sorry,' I say breathlessly. 'I had no idea I could still be over the limit. It won't happen again, I swear.'

'You're free to go. Will you require transport back to your vehicle?'

I can't face the shame of getting back into the police car. I'd rather walk. 'No, it's OK. I'll call my mother now, and see if she can pick us up.' I glance around the reception area, where I left Bella and Tolly. 'Do you know where my children are?'

'Their father collected them a few moments ago,' the officer behind the desk says. 'It's all right, madam, we verified his identity. If you're quick, they'll still be outside.'

Andrew is fitting Tolly's car seat into the rear of Caz's Audi, struggling to get the seatbelt through its slots. 'What's going on?' I exclaim.

He finally clicks the buckle into place, and straightens

up. 'Bella texted and asked me for a lift to school,' he says shortly. 'They didn't know how long you were going to be.'

Caz leans across the front seat. 'How could you be so irresponsible?' she demands through the open window. 'What if something had happened to them while you were drunk behind the wheel?'

'I *wasn't* drunk,' I snap. I lean into the back of the car. 'Bella, Tolly, out you get. I've sorted everything out, it's all fine. Come on, Bella,' I add, as she just sits there. 'We need to get going, you're late enough as it is.'

'You haven't got a car, Mum,' she mutters.

'We'll take them to school,' Andrew says. 'We can sort everything else out later.'

I'm about to refuse, but Bella looks at me in silent appeal, and I realise how desperate she is for me not to make a scene. 'OK,' I say reluctantly. 'You take them. I'll pick them up this afternoon.'

'*I'll* pick them up,' Caz snaps.

'Look, why don't you take a day or two for yourself?' Andrew adds. 'Get yourself sorted out. The kids can stay here in Brighton with Caz. We were taking Friday off anyway, for your mother's party, so it's not a problem. We can talk again then.'

'Get myself sorted out?' I repeat. 'What's that supposed to mean?'

He doesn't meet my eye. 'Maybe it'd be better if Tolly and Bella spent some time with us. Just till you're on an even keel again. I know you've had a lot going on, and maybe it's all been a bit too much.'

327

'We don't want you backsliding,' Caz adds bitchily. 'Getting overwrought like you did with Roger Lewison. I hear last time was awful.'

I suddenly feel as if all the air has been sucked out of my lungs. *She's going after my children.* It's the last card she has left to play. That's why she set me up with the police; a drink-drive conviction would be a huge black mark against me if Andrew ever contested custody. She wants to take my children from me.

'Dad, I've got to get to school,' Bella urges from the car. 'I'm super late already.'

Andrew can't even look at me as he gets in the car. I watch him drive away, trembling with suppressed rage. How *could* he tell her about Roger? That was private, personal information! It cost me a great deal even to tell him, and I only did that because I wanted to be totally honest with him before we got married. How many times does he have to let me down before I wise up? Just hours ago, this man was in my bed, telling me he'd never stopped loving me. Now, he's using the most intimate details of my past to suggest I'm so unstable my own children aren't safe with me. I don't think I've ever hated him before, but I do right now.

I pull up the camera roll on my phone, and scroll to the one I want. My secrets are out in the open. It's about time Caz's were, too.

Chapter 36

Caz

I can't even bear to breathe the same air as Andy as we drive the children to their schools from the police station. Overnight, my pain and betrayal have hardened into cold, unrelenting anger. I have no idea where we go from here. The thought of sharing my bed with him makes my skin crawl. But the idea of life without Andy opens a yawning pit in my soul. I hate myself for it, but I still love him. How do I reconcile two such warring impulses? How do I fight for him when my first impulse is to throw him into the street and bar the door?

Maybe if he'd stood up for me when this vendetta with Louise kicked off a few weeks ago, things would never have got so out of hand. That woman feeds off his weakness. She'd never have dared do half the things she's done if he'd planted his flag firmly in my corner, instead of trying to please both of us. My bitterness is so thick I can taste it. I'm never going to be free of her. Andy's not going to fight for me, no matter what she does. He's never fought for me yet.

He insists on walking Bella into school, and I watch

as they stop outside the gates, talking intently. Something else is going on with Andy that I still don't know about; something apart from his nostalgic fuck with Louise last night. If he wasn't with her yesterday when he was supposed to be working, then where the hell *was* he? I don't buy his bullshit about Deep Throat anonymous sources for a moment. He's up to something.

'Bella says that policeman was waiting for Louise,' he says abruptly, as soon as he gets back into the car. 'She seems to think it was a farmer with a grudge who tipped them off, but I'm not so sure. You wouldn't know anything about it, would you?'

I say nothing as Andy pulls the car back onto the main road. He was drunk when he came home last night, and by his own admission, Louise was even worse for wear. I was just doing my civic duty, reporting a drunk driver. A mother on her way to school, no less; just one of many up and down the country who hits wine o'clock at six p.m. and keeps on going, never even considering she might still be drunk the next morning. But I should have known Louise would find a way to skate out from under it. Somehow, that woman always comes up smelling of roses. She could shoot someone in Oxford Street, and Andy would praise her for her marksmanship.

'She got away with it this time,' I say. 'But you can't ignore this, Andy. You're going to have to do something about her.'

He sighs irritably. 'Come on, Caz. She was under the limit.'

'*This* time,' I repeat. 'The kids were in the car with her. What if she'd crashed? They're not safe with her anymore.'

He looks sideways at me. 'You really think you can take Bella and Tolly on full-time?' he says sceptically. 'We have trouble managing one child, never mind three. You're not exactly the maternal type.'

'You think I couldn't handle it?'

'I think you wouldn't want to,' he says shortly.

What I *want* has nothing to do with it. But if I can remove the one legitimate reason Louise has to be constantly in our lives by taking the children from her, it'll pull the rug out from under her feet. She'll still have visitation rights, of course, unless we can prove she's certifiable again, which is entirely possible; but if the kids are living with us, the ball will be very much in our court. She'll have to play by our rules if she wants access to them. Andy won't be at her beck and call anymore. We'll have leverage.

My phone beeps suddenly with a text notification from Louise. It's some kind of image. I open it up, and an icy chill sweeps through me as I see the photograph of the peeling sign: *Starr Farm Senior Care Centre*.

She knows.

I drop the phone on the floor of the car, my heart pounding. Louise knows about my mother. She's been to see her. How the hell did she even find her? The only person who knows Ruth exists is Angie, and she'd never breathe a word to anyone. What has Louise discovered? And what is she going to do about it?

My hands are actually shaking as I scrabble for the phone. My mother is a senile old woman; no one will take her lunatic ravings seriously. But what will Andy say if he finds out she's not living in a beautiful Victorian building with a concierge in the heart of Chelsea, as I've told him, but a care home in Essex? He'd never have willingly exchanged the prestige and class Louise brought him for Carol from Dagenham. As far as he's concerned, my father is dead, my mother a wealthy recluse from whom I'm estranged. If he finds out I'm no better than he is, it could be precisely the excuse he needs to run straight back into Louise's well-bred arms.

'Are you OK?' Andy asks, as he parks the car in a side street near our house. 'You seem very quiet.'

I make a quick decision. My battle with Louise over the children can wait. I need to deal with my mother first. 'I'm going back to London after all,' I say abruptly. 'Tell Louise the kids can stay with her for now. I'm sure they'll be fine.'

He looks visibly relieved. 'I think that's a good idea.'

We barely speak on the train back to Victoria. As soon as we reach London, Andy heads off to the taxi rank to go into work, and I take the tube home. I'm not going into Whitefish today; I'm not sure I've even got a job to go back to. I let myself into our empty flat, feeling sick and hollowed out. Stepping over the heap of mail on the doormat without bothering to pick it up, I go straight upstairs, peel off my clothes and pad into the bathroom, turning on the shower and stepping into water as hot as I can bear. As the steam rises around me, I close my eyes and turn my face into the scalding spray. Louise, Andy, AJ, Whitefish, my mother . . . I just want to wash it all away.

The heat sucks the remaining energy from me. I've hardly slept in two days, and I can't remember the last time I ate properly. I long to crawl into bed and shut out the world, but I have dozens of emails clogging up my inbox, at least four of them from Patrick. More importantly, I have to check up on AJ, make sure he's all right. And there's still my mother to deal with. I can't afford to take my eye off the ball for a second.

I step out of the shower, groping for a towel, stumbling slightly in the steamy bathroom. My shin connects with the small wastepaper bin, and I yelp as it goes flying, scattering scrunched-up tissues and strings of dental floss and used cotton wool pads all over the floor. Cursing beneath my breath, I pick up the rubbish and put it back in the bin.

And then I stop.

I stare at the two blue lines on the pregnancy test stick in my hand. The significance of what this means, what Andy has done, drills into my heart. Our cleaner empties the bin every week, which means that since this pregnancy test isn't mine, there's only one other person it can belong to, the only other woman who has been here in the last fortnight.

Bella.

Three days before the party

Chapter 37

Louise

I hear Bella being sick in the bathroom as I'm getting Tolly ready for school. Leaving him half-dressed, I go into the hall and hover outside the bathroom door. 'Darling, are you OK?'

The lavatory flushes. A moment later, the door opens. Bella looks pale, and beads of sweat dot her upper lip. 'Sorry. We had fish tacos at school yesterday. I don't think it was such a good idea.'

'You don't think it's because of your concussion on Monday?'

'Maybe.'

'Do you want to stay home today?' I ask, concerned.

She hesitates. 'I've got a Chem test third period.'

'Mrs Welsh will let you make it up, won't she?'

'I suppose.'

'You get back into bed, and I'll call the school. As soon as I've dropped Tolly off at nursery, I'll come up and sort you out properly.'

I follow her as she shuffles back to her bedroom. I'm not surprised she's sweating: even in the middle of summer, she's wearing long grey sweatpants and a baggy black T-shirt. To my surprise, she suffers me smoothing out her duvet and tucking her in as I used to do when she was little. 'I'll be back soon,' I say, dropping a light kiss on her damp forehead.

'Mum?'

I turn in the doorway, struck suddenly by how vulnerable she seems. Without make-up, her hair pulled back from her face in a loose ponytail, she looks no more than twelve. 'What is it, sweetheart?'

'I'm sorry about yesterday,' she mumbles, looking down and fiddling with a large silver ring on her middle finger. It looks vaguely familiar, though I can't quite remember where I've seen it before. 'Texting Caz. I didn't mean to upset you.'

I come back into the room and perch on the bed. 'You didn't upset me, Bella. It must have been awful, watching your mother get carted off to a police station. I'm so sorry to put you through all that.'

'You were awesome,' my daughter says unexpectedly. 'I'd have freaked out if I got arrested, but you were, like, totally cool.'

'I was?'

'I should've trusted you,' she says. 'I know you'd never drink and drive. Not, you know, after Uncle Nicky.'

He died long before she was even born, but he's still as much a part of our family as my mother or Tolly. 'I was incredibly stupid,' I sigh. 'I should have realised I might've been over the limit from the night before.

I can't bear to think what could have happened with the two of you in the car.'

'You weren't to know,' she says generously.

I hesitate. I don't want to wreck our delicate detente, but I'm aware I may never get a better chance to talk to her while she's in such a receptive mood. 'Bella, I've been meaning to ask you,' I say quietly. 'Three hundred pounds was taken out of my account in cash a few days ago. Was that you? If it wasn't, I need to know so I can talk to the bank about it.'

She stiffens. For a moment, I think I've blown it, but then she exhales slowly. 'Please don't ask me to say what it was for,' she mumbles. 'And no, it's not drugs or anything illegal.'

I manage to stifle a thousand questions I'm bursting to ask as Bella picks fretfully at her nails, which are already bitten down to the quick. 'You always told me if someone was in trouble, I should help,' she says finally.

'It's a lot of money, Bella. Are you sure you can't tell me what it's for?'

She wavers. I can sense her weighing the options, and I hold my breath, willing her to confide in me. But before she can say anything, Tolly erupts into the bedroom, demanding his breakfast, and I see Bella visibly withdraw into herself, the moment gone.

My stomach churns with anxiety as I finish getting Tolly ready for nursery. She says it's not drugs, but she's lost so much weight recently, and she's so *pale*. This isn't the first time she's been physically sick in the last couple of weeks, either. Something is seriously troubling my child, and I have to find a way to help her – which I can't do unless I have the right information. As soon as I get back from dropping Tolly off at kindergarten, I make Bella a cup of ginger tea to settle her stomach, and take it upstairs. I don't want to push her, but I can't see I have a choice. If she's angry with me, so be it. I want to be her friend, but it's more important that I'm her mother.

Bella's awake, listening to music. She pulls out one white earphone as I enter her room, and I hear the tinny thump of music, one of those awful German electronic bands she likes so much. 'I know what you're going to say,' she sighs. 'I swear on Tolly's life, I'm not taking drugs.'

I search her face. Perhaps I'm foolish, but my maternal instinct tells me she's being truthful. She may be keeping secrets from me, but I believe her when she says it's not drugs.

She makes room for me to sit beside her, and I put the steaming mug of ginger tea on the bedside table. 'So why did you need the money?' I ask gently. 'If it's not drugs, what was it for?'

'Please, Mum. Please don't ask me that.'

I pause, torn. 'You said it wasn't for anything illegal?'

'I swear. And it's done now. I mean, it doesn't matter anymore. And I'll pay you back, I promise.'

'It's not the money.' I choose my words with care. 'Bella, I'm worried about you. Is there *any*thing you can tell me? I won't shout or get angry, I promise. And I won't tell Dad, if that's what you're anxious about.'

I watch her worrying the silver ring around her middle finger, back and forth, back and forth. She hasn't taken it off since she got it. It's like she—

Of course! Metaphorically, I clap my hand to my forehead. How did I not see this before? There's only one thing that makes you lose weight and throw up with nerves and swing wildly from joy to misery in the space of a moment: *love*, the oldest drug in the world.

I remember where I saw that ring. Or rather, on *whom*.

'Bella,' I say softly. 'Have you met someone?'

She nods.

'Taylor,' I say. 'That's what all this is about, isn't it?'

She gulps and then nods again, and my heart aches for her. 'Oh, Bell,' I sigh. 'Why didn't you tell me?'

'I wanted to,' she blurts. 'But Taylor made me promise not to. Her parents are really strict, they'd totally freak. And . . . it's complicated.'

How long has she been carrying this secret around? I've been so wrapped up in myself I haven't been paying attention to what's going on in her life. How could I have missed this? 'Did you think I wouldn't understand?' I ask.

She shrugs, pleating the duvet cover with nervous fingers.

'Bella, I don't mind who or what you love, as long as it makes you happy,' I say seriously. 'You can bring home a polar bear, and it'd be welcome at my table.' I pause. 'Well, perhaps not at the table. From what I gather, polar bears aren't particularly well mannered. But if you fall

341

in love with a polar bear, we'll find a way to make it work. Some sort of alfresco picnic, perhaps.'

'*Mum*,' Bella says, but she's laughing.

'Does Taylor know how you feel?'

She bobs her head.

'But she doesn't feel the same way?'

'It's not that. She was seeing someone else. Not anymore. But she thinks it's too soon. She wants some space. It's OK,' she adds quickly. 'I'd rather be friends than nothing.'

'Is this why you've been so upset recently?'

'Mostly. But not just that.' She looks up at me, and then quickly away. 'It's Caz.'

'You don't need to worry about—'

'I *like* her,' she interrupts, startling me into silence. 'I like it when she's there at weekends and stuff! I don't want her and Dad to split up. I don't like it when it's just Dad on his own. I want things to stay as they are.'

I take a moment to digest this. 'What happens between your father and Caz has nothing to do with me.'

Bella pulls up her long legs and wraps her arms around her knees, pressing her face into them. 'That's not true, Mum.'

'What do you mean?'

'I know what happened with you and Dad the other night,' she says, threading her fingers together unhappily. 'It's not fair, Mum. You blame her for stealing Dad and breaking up our family, but that's not true.' She suddenly looks straight at me, her eyes unnaturally bright. 'I know about Tolly. I know my dad isn't *his* dad.'

The room tilts and spins. My mouth gapes stupidly. I am literally speechless, unable even to breathe.

Andrew swore he'd never tell anyone; that was our deal. He'd keep my secret, he'd never breathe a word to Bella or Tolly or anyone else, not to Caz, *especially* not to Caz, and in return, I agreed not to contest the divorce, and to accept the financial pittance he offered me.

'Mum?' Bella says. 'It's OK. I get it. Dad had met Caz; he was cheating on you. I don't blame you.'

I blame me.

I cover my face with my hands, choking on a sob. I've been running from this moment, from this truth, for nearly five years. Memory is a tricky thing. It doesn't just recall the past; it remakes it, as we desire it to be. You can push an unwelcome reality to the back of your mind and bury it behind a wall of wishful thinking, and in time, you'll forget the truth is even there. And then, when you least expect it, the wall is breached and you're forced to face a truth grown far more powerful and terrifying for its long imprisonment.

'Did you love him?' Bella asks quietly. 'Tolly's dad?'

I look away. I don't know how to begin to answer her. When I met Tolly's father, I'd just found out Andrew was having an affair, and I'd wanted to get back at him: to even the score. Revenge at its most basic level. And I'd also needed reassurance I was still lovable, still desirable. I'd yearned for someone to see me in a way Andrew no longer did.

But our affair was so much more than that. From

the first day we'd met, we'd shared something I'd never felt with Andrew, a connection that made me feel as if I had found the piece of myself I hadn't even known was missing. Yet I'd barely known him. We weren't even friends. I don't know, even now: can that be love?

For a brief while, I was certainly infatuated with him. He was all I could think about. I got butterflies in my stomach every time he walked into the room. I created opportunities to run into him even when we'd only seen each other the day before; I made too many phone calls, sent too many texts. And I frightened myself. The intensity of what I was feeling had reminded me too much of Roger. I even went to his house one day, afraid he was lying to me and that he was married after all. I saw his elderly mother through the kitchen window, and she saw me, though of course she didn't know who I was. She waved, the way people do when they think they're supposed to know you, and I'd had a sudden glimpse of how she'd see me if she knew I was stalking her son. Because that's what I was doing. At that moment, even I realised that.

I ran. Literally and figuratively. I broke it off with him, and focused all my energies on repairing my marriage. Andrew was the one I really loved, I told myself firmly. The one with whom I had a life, a history, a family. We'd shared a thousand moments, from the small and insignificant, to the life-changing and dramatic: the birth of a child, the loss of a parent, lunch on Sunday, feeding the cat. This was the stuff of life, this was what was *real*, not a romantic novella 'connection' with a man whose full name I didn't even know.

And then the impossible had happened, the miracle that was Tolly, and I'd convinced myself it had to be Andrew's child. Anything else was unthinkable.

'Do I know him?' Bella asks. 'Tolly's dad?'

I shake my head. That much, at least, is true.

'How . . . how did you find out?' I ask.

'We had a Bio project about blood groups, and Mrs Lockwood told us to find out about our family. You were in London so I just looked in the file in your office.' She looks up, flushing. 'I wasn't prying. I didn't know it was private. I found the tests they did after Tolly was born, when you got so sick, and they thought it was some kind of Rhesus antibody reaction.'

I should have burned them. Or at least put them under lock and key.

'Your blood group is A, and Dad's is O, like me,' Bella says. 'Tolly is group B. Which means he can't be Dad's. That's how he found out, too, isn't it?'

I nod, blinded by tears. My daughter will never forgive me for this. How can she? I can't forgive myself. It's one of the many reasons my anger at Caz is so bitter and unrelenting. She didn't just take Andrew from me: she destroyed my better self. I would never have betrayed my husband if not for her. I would never have betrayed myself.

I haven't told anyone about Tolly, not even my mother, though I think perhaps she's guessed. As he's grown older, he's started to look more and more like his biological father. Secrets have a way of finding their way to the light.

'I'm so sorry,' I say thickly, knowing how hollow it sounds. 'I understand how angry you must be. But please, don't tell Tolly. Your dad is the only father he's ever—'

'I'd never do that,' Bella says sharply. 'I love him. He's my *brother*.'

'If you want to go and live with your dad and Caz, I won't fight it,' I say bleakly.

Bella twists the silver ring on her finger. 'Gree said something the other weekend,' she says, staring at her lap. 'When we were talking about Uncle Nicky. She said love is like water: if something blocks its path, it always finds another way through.' She pauses for a long time, and I suppress the urge to fill the silence. 'I figured it must've been like that for you, when Dad met Caz,' she adds finally. 'You needed somewhere for love to go, and Tolly's dad was there.'

I stare at my wise, extraordinary daughter, over-whelmed with conflicting emotion. Relief, pride, shame, regret. She has behaved better in all of this than any of the sorry adults in this saga.

'Caz isn't the enemy,' Bella says softly. 'Please, Mum. Can you just stop hating her now?'

I nod. 'Yes,' I say. 'I'll stop.'

Date:- 25/07/2020
Duration:- 31 Minutes
Location:- Kingsbridge Police Station

Conducted by Officers from Devon & Cornwall Police

(cont.)

POLICE   So what you're saying is that Mrs Page – your daughter, Louise Page – *wanted* the other Mrs Page there?

BR   I wouldn't say that.

POLICE   Forgive me, Mr Roberts, but you just *said* she

called your wife two days ago and told her she wanted her ex-husband and his wife at the party.

BR   Yes.

POLICE   Are you saying now she didn't?

BR   No, she did.

POLICE   Were you there when she called?

BR   Yes. Celia said Lou told her it was OK.

POLICE   Meaning she *did* want Andrew and Caroline Page to come after all?

BR   That's right. [Pause.] She wasn't too happy at first, mind.

POLICE   What do you mean, at first?

BR   When Celia first invited them.

POLICE   That would be back in June? [Pause.] If you could speak for the tape instead of nodding, Mr Roberts.

BR   Sorry. Yes.

POLICE   Could you expand on that a little?

348

BR	Well. Lou wasn't too happy.
POLICE	So you said, Mr Roberts. [Pause.] Can you clarify that at all? Did she say anything, or do anything, to make you think she wasn't happy?
BR	Lou isn't one to rock the boat.
POLICE	Did she discuss it with you?
BR	I know my daughter.
POLICE	Right. Your wife and Andrew Page were on good terms, is that correct?
BR	Yes.
POLICE	Did that bother your daughter?
BR	You'd have to ask her that.
POLICE	What about you? How did you get on with your former son-in-law?
BR	Lou isn't perfect, but she's a good girl. He'd no need to go carrying on behind her back.
POLICE	With Caroline Page, you mean?
BR	Yes.

POLICE	Why did your wife invite her to the party, do you think?
BR	You'd have to ask Celia that.
POLICE	So, just to be clear. Your daughter wasn't happy when she initially found out her mother had asked both Andrew Page and his second wife to the party, but she accepted it, is that right?
BR	Yes.
POLICE	But then she and Mrs Page fell out. The police were called to an altercation at Andrew and Caroline Page's flat two weeks ago, isn't that right?
BR	You'd have to talk to them about that.
POLICE	What I'm getting at, Mr Roberts, is that the previously civil relationship between your daughter and Caroline Page had clearly broken down in recent weeks.
BR	Yes.
POLICE	Yet you're telling us your wife then got a phone call from your daughter saying she *wanted* her ex-husband and his wife to come?

BR   That's what Celia said.

POLICE   Were you surprised?

BR   [Pause.] Celia usually gets her way.

POLICE   That's quite a turnaround, though. Can you think
            of a reason your daughter changed her mind?

BR   I don't know.

POLICE   Is it possible, do you think, that she wanted
            Andrew Page at the party for a particular reason?

BR   I couldn't say.

POLICE   Might she want to get him alone?

BR   What for?

POLICE   Well, that's what we're trying to find out.
            [Pause.] The thing is, Mr Roberts. Less than
            forty-eight hours after that rather surprising
            phone call to your wife, Andrew Page was dead.

Chapter 38

Caz

If you didn't know her, you might think my mother deserves a little joy, stuck all day in that wheelchair and parked in a miserable beige prison smelling of damp biscuits and disappointment. No friends or family to visit, except me, and we both know I don't come to brighten her day. I don't blame her for taking her pleasure where she can find it, spilling her guts to my worst enemy out of sheer malice and boredom. But that's not going to stop me bursting her little revenge fantasy bubble.

'No one's going to believe it,' I say, almost fondly. 'You can tell them whatever you want. The more terrible it is, the crazier you'll seem.'

Her black eyes are sharp as knives. 'That so? Why d'you come rushing over here, then?'

'I find you amusing. Tell me,' I add conversationally, 'how did it go with Louise?'

'Now we get to it,' she says, with relish.

'She must be pretty desperate, coming to you.'

'*You* must be pretty desperate, coming to me.'

I take a seat opposite her wheelchair as we both regroup, sizing each other up. I don't fool myself my mother loves me; although perhaps, in her wizened walnut of a heart, something flickers. But I am *known*, and I'm constantly surprised by how much that matters. There is no pretence between us, no shame. She has seen my worst and I have seen hers.

'Come on,' I say after a moment. 'Tell me about it. You know you want to. What did you think of her?'

'Not as pretty as you, of course. Not as smart.' She pauses, reconsidering. 'No. She's smart. Smarter than you. But not as cunning.'

'Thank you.'

'It wasn't a compliment.'

'Yes, it was.'

'I can see why she's a good journalist. She makes you want to talk to her. I liked her.'

I smile coldly. 'You don't like anyone.'

'I liked *her*.' She jerks her wheelchair closer. She's like a shark, scenting blood in the water. 'Gone back to his wife, has he?'

There's no point lying, not to her. 'It doesn't matter.' I shrug. 'He returned to *me*.'

'Ha!' she jeers. 'Poor Carol. Still love him, don't you? Even though he ain't never loved you.'

Despite myself, I flinch as the barb finds its mark. *Love him, hate him, hate him, love him.* I've never really forgiven Andy for making me love him so much more than he loves me. He's an anchor, weighing me down. His narcissism, his neediness, his children, his baggage, his ex-wife. My life would have been so much simpler, so much cleaner, without him.

'Ain't why you're here, though, is it?' my mother says, narrowing her eyes. 'There's more, ain't there? There's *worse*.'

'There's worse,' I acknowledge.

Her malicious gaze pins me in my seat like a butterfly beneath the glass. 'Spit it out, girl. What's the real reason you're visiting a poor, senile old woman?'

We both know she's not senile. There was a time, after her suicide attempt, when she chose to withdraw into a world she found more bearable, when depression and medication confined her to a twilight limbo where she was unreachable. And it suited me to keep her there. I couldn't have Caroline's shiny new world muddied by my vicious, over-medicated mother. So I got her committed and stuck her in a private nursing home until I met Andy and the money ran out. Now the government puts a roof over my mother's head and food on her table. And no one cares enough to ask inconvenient questions, like whether she should even be there.

Of course she hates me. It's my fault the world thinks she's mad. But after what she allowed to happen to me, it's no less than she deserves.

Her expression suddenly changes. It's like she has a satanic sixth sense for rooting into the darkest parts of the soul. 'He's like your dad, ain't he?' she says abruptly.

I want there to be another reason for Bella's cutting, for the pregnancy test in our bathroom bin. For twenty-four hours my mind has fought like a rabbit in a gin trap; I'd bite through my own leg to be free of the truth.

I stare at my hands. 'He's nothing like Dad.'

'Don't lie to me, girl.' Her stringy grey hair falls across her face as she looks away, reinforcing the witchy resemblance. 'I should've stopped him,' she mutters. 'I knew. I told myself I didn't, but I knew. I heard him creep out of bed. I knew where he was going, what he was doing.' She sucks her teeth. 'But I didn't care, because it meant he stayed. Till you got too *old* and he left us.'

'Dad died,' I say. 'He didn't leave me. He *died*.'

She jerks her chair forward suddenly and grabs my hands, gripping my fingers like steel. 'Enough,' she says roughly. 'You're not a child anymore, Carol. Your father *left*. He could've taken you with him; I wouldn't have fought him. I was a *drunk*, girl. He could've taken you, and I wouldn't have lifted a finger to stop him. But you got too old for him. Too old for his *tastes*.' I snatch my hands back, and she laughs mirthlessly. 'It was the only good thing he ever did for you. You've made a success of your life, girl. You shook the dirt off your feet, and you moved up in the world. He ain't fit to lick your boots. Never was.'

My father loved me. He *loved* me long before I was old enough to understand this wasn't the way most fathers loved their little girls. *Our secret*, he whispered in my ear, as he stroked me in places he wasn't supposed to touch. *We can't tell anyone, not even Mummy, or they'll spoil it. They'll take you away from me, because they won't understand how much I love you.*

355

I don't know how old I was when he raped me the first time. Seven, perhaps? Eight? So much of my childhood is a jumble of repressed images, it's hard to recall. There was a big storm that night, I remember that much, the lightning illuminating my bedroom in horror movie snapshots. I woke up to my father in my bed, on top of me, crushing the breath out of me. I didn't stop him, because I thought my daddy was perfect, so perhaps it was meant to hurt. He looked into my eyes with an expression I'd never seen before, and then he smiled. *You're such a grown-up girl,* he said. *I love you so much.*

I never said a word to anyone, not once. Daddy would never hurt me, I told myself. He loves me. This must be my fault. Sometimes, I'd catch my mother's eye at breakfast, and she'd look away, and pour herself another vodka.

Then a month before my eleventh birthday, I got my period. A week later, I came home one day from school, and my father had gone.

He left you behind.

Daddy would *never*—

He left you.

The ten-year-old child inside me covers her ears with her hands. Easier to believe he died than that he abandoned me. If he left me, he couldn't have loved me. And as warped as it sounds, I have to believe he loved me for the horror to be bearable.

My mother lunges forward. For a brief moment, as she pushes her crazed face close to mine, her eyes wide with fear, I see the woman she was, the mother she could have been. 'You have to stop him,' she says fiercely. 'Do what I was too weak to do. *Stop* him.'

There's no point pretending anymore. I came to her for a reason, because she's the only person to whom I can unburden my scarred soul. 'If I go to the police, I ruin Bella's life too,' I say. 'Exposing her to that kind of scrutiny. A court case. Who knows what that would do to her—'

'Not the police. Stop him yourself.'

A sudden silence falls. I've seen her worst and she's seen mine.

'You know what has to be done, Carol,' my mother says slyly. 'You know what you have to do. You come here so I'd tell you. You're stronger than I was.' Her hands tremble as she clutches the arms of her chair, and there's a tiny drool of spittle at the corner of her mouth. 'You need to do what I couldn't.'

It's crossed my mind. Fleetingly, hypothetically. The thought dismissed as quickly as it occurred. Almost as quickly.

'I can't,' I say sharply.

'You can. You have it in you. You've got what it takes. There's ice in your heart.' She laughs mirthlessly. 'I should know.' She wheels her chair back and forth, back and forth on the linoleum, the rubber tyres squeaking, until I want to scream. 'I heard about the cat,' she adds, her eyes suddenly bright with glee. 'Poisoned with antifreeze. Louise thinks you did it.'

I look away. 'The cat was old.'

'We had a cat,' my mother says craftily. 'Pissed on your new jacket, d'you remember? Couldn't get the stink out. Washed it three times.' Back and forth, back and forth. *Squeak, squeak.* 'Found the cat in the yard a week later, stiff as a broom. Froth on its mouth. Looked like it'd been poisoned.'

'We're not talking about a cat,' I say. 'This is my *husband*. I can't—'

'It's just us now,' she hisses venomously. 'No need to pretend in front of me. You could do it. Save the girl. And you could take him away from *her* for good.'

I stare at my mother. She is the portrait of my soul kept in the attic, growing ever more hideous and deformed with my sins, as my youthful skin stays soft and clear. I come here to face the raw truth of who I am, deep beneath the polished veneer. Here, I can admit to myself what I can't anywhere else. *Love him, hate him, hate him, love him.* If I can't have him, no one else can.

He doesn't deserve to live. After what he's done to Bella. After what he's done to me.

I pick up my mother's blanket, which has fallen on the floor, and tuck it neatly over her knees. I wheel her back to her favourite position beneath the window, locking the brakes into place, and lift the sash a couple of inches to let some fresh air into the stale room. The day my mother tried to kill herself, I got home from school earlier than I told the police. She must have only just kicked the chair away. I stood in the hall for a full minute, watching her struggle, jerking like a marionette. She wet herself as she scrabbled at the tie around her neck; I can still remember the sound of her urine splashing against the tile floor. I waited, and she watched me wait.

I bend and drop a soft kiss on her forehead. 'I'm glad they cut you down,' I say. 'Death would've been too good for you.'

Two days before the party

Chapter 39

Louise

I pull up at the entrance to the Burgh Island Hotel car park, and root around in the centre console for the piece of paper on which I wrote down the security code for the metal gate. With a patient sigh, Bella locates it and hands it to me, and I lean out of the window to punch in the numbers. 'Could you get our bags, while I wake Tolly?' I ask, as the gate rolls open. 'And try not to let them drag on the ground. It looks like it rained earlier.'

After parking the car, I get out and stretch my aching back as Bella opens the boot. It's a four-hour journey from our house to the Devon coast, but there's no direct train, so I had no option but to drive. I stare across the narrow stretch of water between the mainland and the island itself, inhaling a deep breath of cool, salty air. The sea glitters in the late afternoon sunshine, and gulls swoop and squawk above us. London and Whitefish seem a long way away. It feels good to escape from everything. I'm glad I came down a day earlier than everyone else; I need to hit the reset button and regroup before I'll be fit company for a party.

As I'm getting my sleepy son out of his car seat, a man hails us from the other side of the car park in a thick Irish brogue. 'You the Page party?'

'Mr Connelly?'

'Everyone calls me Ryan,' the Irishman says, coming over and taking the bags from Bella. It's the middle of summer, but he's wearing wellingtons, corduroy trousers and a thick knitted bobble hat. 'Tide's in, so I'll be taking you over on the sea tractor.'

Tolly's eyes light up like pinwheels when he sees the sea tractor parked on the sand. It looks like something from a BBC period drama, with a metal staircase leading up to the covered platform resting atop huge tractor wheels. He yanks free from my restraining hand and bounds up the steps, leaning over the platform railing for a better view. 'We're driving through the water!' he cries. 'Mummy, Mummy! We're driving through the sea! Will we go underwater?' he adds, turning to Ryan, who's taken the wheel in the centre of the sea tractor.

'Don't be stupid,' Bella sighs. 'It's not a submarine.'

I shoot her a reproachful glance, and she rolls her eyes, but puts her arm around her little brother and points out the hotel as Jack drives us across the sands. The water's no more than a few feet deep, but at high tide like this, the island is completely cut off, and I can see dangerous currents at play beneath the surface.

The trip takes no more than five minutes, and Ryan helps us down the metal steps once we reach the island, leading the way up a steep path to the hotel. 'That's the Pilchard Inn,' he says, pointing to a small pub hugging

364

the coast by the tiny quay. 'It's haunted by Tom Crocker, the leader of a band of vicious pirates in the fourteenth century.' He leans down to Tolly, whose eyes are now as wide as dinner plates. 'Crocker and his men looted and plundered ships for years, till he got caught.' He points to the top of the hill behind us, and drops his voice to a sepulchral whisper. 'He was dragged kicking and screaming for his life to the highest point on the island, where he was hanged by his neck until he was declared dead. It is said' – his eyes rest on each of our faces in turn – 'that his restless ghost walks again on the anniversary of his death every year. Folks see him, standing in the door of the Pilchard Inn, waiting for his men to return.'

'Oh, great,' Bella mutters. 'Tolly will be up all night now.'

'You're safe, young man.' Ryan grins, straightening up and ruffling Tolly's hair. 'Old Tom's anniversary's not till August. He won't be appearing while you're here.'

I'm slightly relieved when Ryan leaves us in reception. He seems nice enough, but I don't need him putting any more ideas in Tolly's head. A porter takes our bags up to our rooms, and I turn to the kids. 'I thought I might have a cup of tea before we do anything else,' I say. 'Either of you two fancy anything?'

'Ice cream!' Tolly shouts.

Bella smiles. 'Ice cream works.'

She leads the way into the spectacular Art Deco Palm Court, with its high, domed glass ceiling, and we settle in some pale blue shell-shaped armchairs with a view of the water. The waiter comes over with a pair of menus, and I fight to suppress a grin. The man has long, winkle-picker shoes, a fuchsia-pink embroidered waistcoat, and a shiny bald pate encircled by thick grey ringlets reaching down to his shoulder blades. He looks like an extra from *The Rocky Horror Picture Show*.

The waiter takes our order – high tea for me, and ice cream for the two children – and sidles away. 'I'm guessing the staff here don't get off-island much,' Bella says dryly.

'Ssssh,' I reprove, trying not to laugh.

When they've finished their ice cream, we go for a long walk around the island, which is bigger than I remembered. A combination of the long journey and fresh sea air has tired us all out, and after a light dinner in the restaurant downstairs, I tuck Tolly up in the double bed he'll be sharing with me, while Bella and I go outside onto the terrace to watch the sunset.

'I can see why Gree wanted to have the party here,' Bella says, leaning on the railing and gazing down at the sandbar we crossed earlier on the sea tractor, which is now revealed by the receding tide. 'It must've been a cool place to go on honeymoon. It's like the rest of the world doesn't exist.'

'Nice feeling, isn't it?'

'Did you speak to her?' she asks, after a moment. 'You know, about Dad and Caz?'

I squeeze her hand. 'Don't worry. I told her it's OK with me if they come.'

Mum probably now thinks I'm falling in with her

diabolical plan to wrest Andrew back, but the truth is, I've barely given him a second thought in the last few days. I feel as if I've just awoken from the grip of a feverish obsession. I can't believe I let myself get sucked back into a soap-opera melodrama I thought I'd left behind years ago. The whole vendetta with Caz suddenly seems ridiculously petty.

Bella was right: Caz isn't the enemy. She never has been. My cheeks burn every time I think about my mad dash to London with poor Bagpuss on the seat beside me. Of course Caz didn't poison him! She may be many things, but she's not a sociopath. He was just unlucky. He must have wandered further afield from our house than I thought and got access to antifreeze on one of the nearby farms. The nonsense with Caz made me paranoid. She didn't behave well four years ago, having an affair with a married man, but I know better than anyone you can't choose who you fall in love with. If anyone's to blame, it's Andrew. *He's* the one who made solemn promises to me.

'I'm just going to check on Tolly,' I tell Bella now. 'I'll be right back.'

I let myself back into the bedroom, smiling when I see Tolly sprawled in the centre of the bed, arms and legs thrown wide like a giant letter X. I pull the covers over him, and he turns over without waking. At that moment, catching him in profile, I'm struck once again by his striking resemblance to his father. Tolly is the spitting image of him. They have exactly the same nose, mouth and chin.

I've never told Patrick that Tolly is his son. No one knows the truth, not even Andrew. He knows Tolly isn't his biological child, of course, but he has no idea who is, and has always treated Tolly as his own. Perhaps one day, if the time is right, I'll tell Patrick, but not until Tolly is old enough to understand.

Ironically, it was through Caz that Patrick and I met; a karmic closing of the circle, perhaps, that began when Chris Murdoch introduced Andrew to Caz. After I'd discovered Andrew's secret phone and learned about his affair, I was desperate to know everything about the other woman in his life. Partly to discover something terrible about her, something damning, a weakness I could use to undermine her attempts to steal my husband; but also because I had a visceral, masochistic craving to know who she was, what she was like: everything from her shoe size to her favourite restaurant. It was like picking a scab; even though I knew it'd hurt, I couldn't stop. So I tracked her to Whitefish, and then used my position at the *Daily Post* to cultivate Patrick as a contact, an unwitting informant. But our relationship soon became a great deal more personal than that.

The day I found myself standing outside his house, his mother waving to me through the window, was the day I realised I was in way too deep. Patrick asked me to reconsider after I broke it off, but when I wouldn't, he took it on the chin. We ran into each other several times professionally over the next few years, and he was always warm and cordial, but never tried to push it any further. If he felt the same undercurrent of unfinished business between us that I did, he never gave any indication. He's been the same throughout my brief stint working for Univest at Whitefish, though when I told him last week I was leaving, his regret seemed genuine. 'I'm going to miss you,' he said. 'I've liked having you around.'

I should stay in touch with him, I think now, dropping a kiss on Tolly's cheek and returning to the terrace, where Bella is sitting in one of the uncomfortable iron chairs, focused on her phone. If and when I decide to come clean about Tolly, it'll make it so much easier if Patrick and I are friends.

Bella glances up as I come out. 'Mum, can Taylor come to the party on Saturday?'

'Won't that be a bit boring for her?' I ask in surprise.

'Please, Mum.'

'If she really wants to, I'm sure Gree won't mind.' A thought occurs to me. 'Actually, Bella, why don't you have her come down tomorrow, instead of Saturday? Auntie Min and Uncle Luke are bringing their boys in the morning, so you'll be a bit outnumbered otherwise.'

'What about Gree's dinner tomorrow night? I thought that was just supposed to be family?'

'I'm sure they can fit one more in.'

She nods, but she's not as enthusiastic as I thought she'd be. It's clear something else is on her mind. She puts her phone down on the small side table, tucking her hands into the long sleeves of her ubiquitous black

369

T-shirt in the familiar way she has. Immediately I pay attention: that phone is rarely out of her hands, which means she's nerving herself to tell me something. 'Mum,' she says, then stops and bites her lip.

I wait. For a moment, I think she's changed her mind about whatever she was about to say, and then her words suddenly come out in a rush. 'Mum, do you believe in abortion?'

I'm genuinely taken aback. Of all the questions I expected her to ask, this wasn't even on my radar. My stomach plunges, and it takes all my effort not to let my shock show on my face. *Dear God, please don't tell me my sixteen-year-old daughter's pregnant.* 'Why do you ask?' I say, somehow keeping my tone even.

'It's for a debate we have to do for school,' she mumbles, not meeting my eye. 'We have to give the pros and cons. Do you think it's, like, taking a life?'

'This is a complicated subject,' I hedge, my mind racing a mile a minute. How does this fit in with what she's told me about Taylor? Does Bella like boys, too, after all? Is this the reason she said things with Taylor were complicated? 'You know you can tell me anything, Bella,' I say steadily. 'I'm here for you, no matter what—'

'I'm not pregnant, Mum!'

I'd have noticed if my own daughter was pregnant, surely? But then I've been so obsessed with my feud with Caz, I've let it overshadow everything else. And, oh, God, Bella *has* been sick a lot recently. Those dark circles under her eyes, the weight loss – the same thing happened to me when I was expecting her, until the morning sickness abated. But I just can't believe she wouldn't have told me. I know we've had our problems, but she wouldn't have kept this from me, surely?

'All right,' I say.

Bella knits her fingers together in her lap, her body taut as a bow. Clearly she needs more from me.

'Is this why you borrowed the money?' I push gently. 'For a termination?'

'Do you think they're wrong?'

'I don't think abortion should be taken lightly, if that's what you mean,' I say carefully, aware I'm treading on eggshells. 'But I think, in certain circumstances, it can be the right thing for both a mother and the child.'

A tear splashes on her hand, and a fist squeezes my heart. She's just a child herself. I crouch down beside her. 'Bella, darling, talk to me. I'm not going to judge. I just want to help you. I'm your mother, I *love* you, no matter what.'

'Taylor thinks people who have abortions go to hell,' she says miserably. 'Her parents are Catholic, they're really strict—'

'No one's going to hell!' I exclaim angrily. 'Bella, Catholics may be strict, but they believe in forgiveness, too. I can't believe Taylor's been telling you this nonsense. Of course you're not going to hell!'

'Not me, Mum!' She raises her tear-stained face. 'It's *Taylor* who was pregnant. Not me.'

I hate myself for it, but I can't help a brief, selfish

371

surge of relief. I feel desperately sorry for her friend, of course, but my daughter is my first concern. 'Oh, Bell. I'm so sorry. Poor Taylor.'

'You won't say anything, will you?'

'Of course not.' I hesitate. 'I take it she hasn't told her parents?'

'I told you, they're super strict. They'd never forgive her.'

'This is a pretty big secret to hide, darling. You'd be surprised what a mother can forgive—'

'No! You can't say anything!'

'It's OK. I won't break your confidence.' I sigh, sadder than I could have imagined at the thought of such a young girl going through something as traumatic as an abortion without her mother by her side. 'What about the baby's father? Where was he in all of this?'

'I don't know. I don't even know who he is. All she said is, he's married. I think it's one of her dad's friends – that's another reason she can't tell her parents.'

I hope my shock doesn't show on my face. Taylor is only seventeen. An affair with a married man twice her age, a secret abortion – it's a lot for a child who's still at school. And no matter how grown-up Taylor may seem, that's what she is, legally and morally: a *child*. What kind of man gets a vulnerable teenager pregnant? Bella's right: no wonder the girl's afraid to tell her parents.

If it were my daughter in trouble, I'd want to kill him.

The day before the party

Chapter 40

Min

I feel like I'm herding cats. No sooner do I get one of the boys clean and presentable, than another spills toothpaste on his new shirt or splits his trousers doing cartwheels down the hall.

'Luke, could you watch Archie while I see what the twins are up to,' I pant, corralling our youngest son in the corner of the hotel room and liberating a complimentary pot of boot polish from his sweaty hands. 'Archie, I want you to sit on this chair and *not move* until I come and get you.'

There's a sudden wail from the bathroom. 'Mum! The loo roll fell in!'

'Sidney! Don't you dare try to fish it out!'

'Mu-u-m! There's poo all over my hands!'

Luke holds up one hand to me like a traffic policeman. 'I've got it, Min.'

'Sidney's got poo on him!' Archie shouts, leaping up and running into the corridor to find his brothers. 'It's *disgusting*!'

I open the emergency suitcase I brought with me.

Fifteen years of motherhood to four sons has taught me to bring backup outfits, a stash of gin, and plenty of wet wipes. I find Sidney's spare polo shirt, and take it through to Luke, who has managed to get our son stripped naked to the waist in the bathroom. It's very generous of Celia to treat us all to a weekend away at a five-star hotel, but I'm going to be on tenterhooks for the next forty-eight hours, trying to ensure the priceless Art Deco artefacts aren't used for target practice, and that none of my children fall off the cliff or drown in the sea. It would've been so much more relaxing, on multiple fronts, if she'd just made the party adults-only.

Eventually, we manage to get the four boys suited and booted, though I'm not entirely sure Dom's Whitesnake T-shirt could be considered appropriate evening wear, but in comparison to the expletive-ridden hoodie he *was* wearing, it's progress. I change into a forgiving navy linen cocktail dress, and go into the bathroom to sort out my hair, which has turned frizzy in the humidity.

'Fancy a quick drink before we go down?' Luke asks, appearing in the doorway.

'Who'll watch the kids?'

'I bribed Dom and Jack to mind the other two for five minutes. A tenner each, and I'll turn a blind eye to a beer later.'

'In that case, make mine a double.'

Luke hands me the large sweating glass of gin and tonic he was holding behind his back. 'Thought you might say that.'

I twist my unruly hair up into a loose chignon, and apply the finishing touches to my make-up, then join Luke out on the balcony. The breeze is a little cooler than I expected, and I'm grateful when my husband wraps his arms around me, the two of us gazing out across the sea like Kate and Leo on the prow of the *Titanic*. It's possible to see the white horses breaking on hidden rocks between us and the mainland, and I can't help a shiver. The thought of a boat hitting one of those deadly rocks in the dark, the poor souls on board lost to the treacherous currents, makes me feel oddly dizzy, as if I've just peered over a high ledge.

'You looking forward to this weekend?' Luke says, gently kissing my neck.

I sigh. 'I'm looking forward to it being safely in the rear-view mirror.'

Luke gives me a reassuring squeeze. I rest the back of my head against his chest, hoping my sense of foreboding is misplaced. Lou has moved out of Andrew's house, and given up the job at his wife's office, both of which are steps in the right direction. As far as I know, she hasn't seen him alone again, so there can't have been a repetition of that disastrously mistaken kiss, but the last thing either of them needs is to be thrown together on an island for the weekend like this. I wish for the hundredth time Celia hadn't got us all into this mess with her meddling. According to Luke, Lou actually phoned her mother yesterday and said she *wanted* Andrew and that woman to come. I don't like to attribute any sinister motive to her sudden change of heart, but how can I not? A week ago she was accusing the woman of poisoning her cat, and now she wants her at her mother's anniversary party?

'Stop fretting,' Luke murmurs. 'I can read you like a book.'

'I can't help it,' I say moodily. 'Something bad's going to happen, I can feel it in my waters.'

'Give over, Gypsy Rose. It'll be fine.'

I'm about to argue, when I spot Andrew and his wife coming up towards the main hotel from the Beach House below us. Moments later, Tolly and Kit rush down the slope of the lawn towards them, the pair of them brandishing cheap plastic windmills.

'Lou looks good,' Luke says in surprise as his sister emerges onto the terrace to greet them. 'Has she done something to her hair?'

'I got her an appointment with Stephen on Wednesday,' I say, taking a look. He's right: Stephen's taken off at least six inches and put in some highlights, and the blunt bob looks great on her. She's wearing the stunning red dress I badgered her into buying, too. I wish now I hadn't. Even from up here, I don't miss Andrew's double take when he sees her, and from the boot-faced look on his wife's face, neither does she. I don't have to be psychic to scent trouble ahead.

'Come on,' Luke says. 'We'd better go down before the boys kick off again. A tenner each only buys you so much peace and quiet.'

We round up the troops and clatter downstairs to the Palm Court bar, where everyone is already waiting for us. I'm busy trying to prise Dom and Jack's phones out of their hands before their grandmother has a go at them, so for a moment I don't notice Bella and her friend sitting quietly near the piano, locked in earnest conversation.

And then suddenly I *do* notice them, and everything makes dreadful, shocking sense.

Chapter 41

Caz

'Could you pass me my cufflinks?' Andy says, fiddling with his shirt sleeves.

I hand them to him. 'I take it the whole family is going to be there?'

'Of course.' He tweaks his tie in the mirror. 'That's not going to be a problem, is it?'

'Not for me.'

I leave him to finish dressing and go out onto the deck, leaning on the railing and gazing across the vast, empty stretch of beach in front of me. A warm breeze lifts my hair as the tide washes over the rocks below, and I'm briefly soothed by the susurration of the waves on the honey-coloured shingle. The rest of the Roberts family is staying up in the main hotel, but for some reason Celia has put the two of us down here at the separate Beach House, in the most breathtaking accommodation of all. Nestled into Burgh Island's rock face, the villa has stunning panoramic sea views, and absolute privacy. I couldn't have chosen a location to suit my purposes better myself. To paraphrase Ridley Scott's famous *Alien* tagline: At the beach, no one can hear you scream.

Andy finally emerges onto the balcony, looking suave and debonair in his black tie. The real monsters aren't seamy, sleazy oddballs with lank hair and dead eyes who lurk in back alleys and dark corners. They're pleasant family men who live among you, handsome and charming, the last people you'd ever suspect.

'Ready?' he asks.

I smile. 'Looking forward to it.'

But it's all I can do not to flinch when he takes my bare arm. The touch of his hand on my skin makes me want to vomit. *Another few hours*, I tell myself. It will all be over in a few hours.

Oddly, for such an important decision, I don't remember actually making it. There was no internal debate, no moral dilemma. A lorry hurtles towards your child, and you fling yourself unthinkingly in its path. A bottle is thrown at you, and you duck. There's no thought, no weighing up of options. Your survival instinct kicks in, whether you want it to or not. *Stop him yourself*, my mother said. The part of me that is Kit's mother and Andy's wife recoils in horror from what has to be done, but the other part of me, the darkest, most honest side, feels only recognition at its inevitability: *yes, of course*. This is how my story ends, how my story has always ended. I didn't stop my father, but I can stop Andy.

We walk up the cliff path to the hotel, and I feel oddly weightless and detached, as if I am watching myself from a distance. There is Caz, in her long grey silk column of a gown, arm in arm with her handsome husband in his black tie and gold cufflinks. Here comes their gorgeous little boy, running across the grass towards them, his russet-haired half-brother whooping in his wake, the two of them joyously brandishing plastic seaside windmills. Look at Caz bend down, exclaiming over her son's toy. Look at her husband scoop a child up beneath each arm, whirling them around before placing them, laughing and stumbling, back on the ground. The perfect, photogenic, modern blended family.

Stepbrother, I correct mentally. I've no idea who Tolly's biological father really is, but it certainly isn't Andy.

'Mummy!' Kit cries, thrusting the windmill at me. 'Look what Gree gave me!'

'How lovely, sweetheart. Have you and Tolly been having fun?'

'He let me play with his mini-drone!' my son exclaims. 'You can make it fly in the air with just your hand! And he says I can play with his robot puppy later. Can I have a robot puppy, Mummy?'

'We'll see,' I say noncommittally.

'Can Kit stay in my room tonight?' Tolly asks.

I smile at the little boy and ruffle his thick curls. Such gorgeous hair; I wonder if he gets it from his father. 'Of course, if Mummy doesn't mind.'

Louise is standing in the doorway to the Palm Court, a carefree smile pinned to her face for Andy's benefit.

She's clearly made a serious effort with her appearance this weekend. She's had a new haircut, a razor-sharp reverse bob, which makes her fair hair look much thicker, and takes years off her. I detect Min Roberts' hand behind both the hair and the stunning scarlet dress she's wearing. Louise never usually wears colour. Her go-to palette favours drab greys and boring neutral sludge shades, what Celia would no doubt call 'taupe' and 'bone' and 'ecru', but which the rest of the world knows as beige. I shoot Andy a sideways glance, and see his eyes nearly popping out of his head.

She steps out onto the terrace as we reach her. Andy goes to kiss her cheek, but for some reason, Louise subtly pretends not to notice and evades him.

My eyes narrow. What does she know, this woman who was married to my husband for more than a decade? Does she have any idea what he's done to her daughter? I would say it's not possible, no woman would knowingly let this happen to her child, but of course I know from bitter experience that isn't true.

'How are you settling in down at the Beach House?' Louise asks me as we watch the two boys chase each other around the lawn. 'It's such a lovely room. I know it's a bit of a walk up to the main hotel, but so worth it, don't you think?'

I'm not about to admit this to Louise, but actually, I don't think I've ever stayed anywhere this beautiful. According to the leaflet in our room, Agatha Christie wrote and set two of her novels at the Burgh Island Hotel. ('It's pronounced "Bear" Island, dear,' Celia told me scathingly, when I called to confirm we'd be coming). When the books were turned into movies, they were filmed on location; I remember Hercule Poirot crossing the beach at low tide on the sea tractor. The romance of the image stayed with me, but I never dreamed I'd ever stay here. Sometimes I forget just how far I've come in the last ten years.

'Where's Bella?' Andy asks, clicking his fingers to summon a waiter out onto the terrace. Normally I hate it when he behaves like that, but tonight, it barely registers. 'She is joining us for dinner, isn't she?'

'She's gone down to the cove to meet her friend off the sea tractor,' Louise says.

'I thought it was just family tonight?' Andy says irritably.

Louise shrugs. 'Bella wanted some moral support. Kit and Tolly have each other, and it's a bit boring for her on her own, so Mum said it was OK for her to have her friend come early.'

His jaw tightens. 'Which friend?'

Louise is distracted by the waiter hovering discreetly at her elbow, waiting to take our order. 'We'll have drinks inside,' she says with patrician authority. 'My mother hates sitting outside in the summer.'

We follow her into the hotel. I can't help a slight gasp as we enter, taken aback by the exquisite beauty of the high, domed Art Deco glass ceiling above our heads. 'I know, isn't it wonderful?' Louise laughs, as if the credit for its breath-snatching loveliness belongs entirely to her.

There's the sound of chatter and laughter from the hotel reception. Moments later, Celia and Brian Roberts come into the Palm Court, followed by Bella and Taylor. I sense Andy stiffen beside me. Celia's always made him oddly nervous. I suspect he's afraid she'll see right through his cufflinks and handmade shoes and pretentious middle-class veneer to the working-class boy beneath.

'Andrew, darling, how lovely to see you,' Celia says, ignoring me completely as she kisses Andy's cheek. 'You look marvellous with that tan. Min and Luke are just getting the boys ready for dinner upstairs; they'll be down in a minute. Champagne, I think?' she adds to the waiter, not bothering to wait for anyone to reply. 'A bottle of Krug, please. We'll need glasses for six.'

She's dressed head to toe in pale gold, with a wispy chiffon scarf trailing across her neck and down her back. For a woman of almost seventy, she's in good shape, whippet-thin, her arms sinewy and muscular from hours every day in her garden. She looks like an Oscar statuette, and about as warm and welcoming.

'Seven champagne glasses,' Louise corrects. 'Doesn't Caz look lovely in that dress, Celia? Is it Armani?'

Celia's gimlet gaze sweeps me insultingly from head to toe. 'Clever you. Thrift shop chic is so fashionable right now.'

I smile. It doesn't matter. Celia doesn't matter. I'm floating free as a bird above them all, the Roberts clan with their secret codes and knowing smiles and ineffable air of superiority. They can say what they want,

385

think what they want. In a few hours, their reign will be over.

Andy abruptly pulls me to one side. 'What's that girl doing here?' he hisses, indicating Taylor. 'I thought it was supposed to just be family tonight?'

'Louise already told you,' I say, freeing myself from his grasp. 'It's boring for her if there's no one else her own age here.'

He looks as if he's about to say something, but then Min and Luke arrive with their phalanx of sons, and I'm spared further contact. The waiter brings out the champagne, and I drink mine too fast. I have no qualms about what I am going to do, but it will take physical courage. The gap between intention and action is significant and bloody. I don't want my nerve to fail me now.

Ironically, Louise ensures I don't get stuck in social Siberia at the kids' end of the table this time, presumably to burnish her credentials with Bella, which means I have no choice but to make polite conversation with the adults instead of being left alone with my own thoughts. Perhaps it's just as well. The less time I have to think about tonight, the better.

I'm not the only one on edge. Andy is particularly twitchy, shooting Louise furtive glances when he thinks I'm not looking. Bella and Taylor barely eat, the two of them whispering together and pushing their food around their plates. I wonder if Bella has confided in her friend. I notice Louise looking at them with concern in her eyes, too. She knows more than she's letting on. How can she stand by and do *nothing*? She's Bella's mother! She should be protecting her daughter. If she knows what Andy has done, and has stood idly by, she deserves to burn in the same pit of hellfire as Andy himself.

The dinner seems interminable, and I'm relieved when it ends. The six boys disappear in a scrum upstairs, but to my surprise, Bella and Taylor opt to stay with the adults and join us for coffee. We withdraw back into the Palm Court bar and settle in a group of chairs with a view of the sea. The sky is inky, studded with stars, and a full moon hangs heavy in its black velvet shawl. At Celia's behest, the waiter leaves the coffee and cups on a side table, and the two girls help to pass them around.

'Shall we order another bottle of Krug?' Celia says, squeezing Brian's hand. 'I know it's not done to mix coffee and champagne, but it's our anniversary.'

'Why not?' Brian says amiably.

'Can I have some?' Bella asks her mother.

Louise jumps, as if miles away. 'Yes, if you'd like,' she says absently.

I don't know if it's too much wine with dinner, or my preoccupation with what I have to do, and why. The words are out of my mouth before I can stop them. 'You can't drink when you're pregnant,' I tell Bella unthinkingly.

I want to snatch back the words, rewind, but it's too late. Everyone turns to Bella, eyes wide with shock. Even Celia is rendered speechless.

'I'm not pregnant!' Bella cries. 'I'm *not*,' she repeats, as the horrified silence stretches.

387

'Of course she's not!' Louise exclaims furiously. 'I'm sorry, Bella,' she adds, shoving back her chair, 'I've tried to be understanding, I really have, but this is the final straw. I can't be in the same room as this woman at the moment. She's either wicked or insane. I don't want to spoil your evening, Mum, but I have to get some air. I'll see you in the morning.'

Bella stares at me, her face white, trembling with anger and betrayal. For a moment, I think she's going to say something, but she simply takes Taylor's hand and the two of them leave without a word. I feel sick to my stomach as everyone else follows them. I have only ever wanted to help Bella. She will never forgive me for this.

But forgiveness isn't important. Saving Bella from her monster of a father is the only thing that matters.

I slip back to the dining room and go over to our table, still cluttered with our dirty plates and glasses. There's no one to notice me palm the steak knife Louise was using, with her fingerprints all over it, and slip it into my bag.

LOUISE PAGE
PART 1 OF RECORDED INTERVIEW

Date:- 25/07/2020
Duration:- 51 Minutes
Location:- Kingsbridge Police Station

Conducted by Officers from Devon & Cornwall Police

(cont.)

POLICE   So that was the last time you saw your ex-husband alive? On the beach last night?

LP   Yes.

POLICE   What time was that?

LP	I don't know. About eleven p.m.?
POLICE	You didn't see him at breakfast this morning?
LP	No. I didn't see him till I went to the Beach House and . . . and found him— [Sobbing.]
POLICE	You have my deepest sympathies, Mrs Page. Can I get you anything? Are you in pain?
POLICE	The doctor has already seen her about her arm, sir. He said Mrs Page is fit for interview.
LP	Please, can we do this later? I need to be with my children. They've just lost their father— [Sobbing.]
POLICE	I'm so sorry, Mrs Page. We'll make this as quick as possible, but we do need to talk to you now, while everything's still fresh in your mind.
LP	I'm never going to be able to forget it.
POLICE	So sorry, but just to clarify, Mr Page didn't come up to the hotel at all?
LP	I didn't see either of them all morning.
POLICE	'Them' meaning Andrew and Caroline Page?

390

LP   Yes.

POLICE   Were you surprised not to see them?

LP   Not after last night. Andrew often goes for a run
            in the morning, and I kind of assumed Caz was
            just staying out of everyone's way. [Pause.] We
            were all pretty upset after what she said.

POLICE   The comment to your daughter?

LP   Yes.

POLICE   Was Mr Page upset with his wife?

LP   I don't know.

POLICE   You didn't discuss it when you talked shortly
            afterwards?

LP   No.

POLICE   What did you talk about, then?

LP   Nothing, really. [Pause.] Just plans for my
            parents' party the next day. My mother had asked
            him to say a few words, and he wanted some
            anecdotes to use in his toast.

POLICE   Your mother had asked your ex-husband to give

a toast, rather than your brother? Did that strike you as odd?

LP   No. Luke's very shy, but Andrew's used to public speaking. And he is – was – really close to Mum. Oh, God. [Sobs.] Sorry. I'm OK.

POLICE Did you and Mr Page go to the beach together last night?

LP   No, I left the hotel first. I wanted to clear my head. Andrew joined me on the beach five or ten minutes later.

POLICE And what about when you returned to the hotel? Were you together then?

LP   I came back first. I wanted to check Tolly was in bed. Anyway, I was staying in the main hotel and Andrew was at the Beach House, so we were going in different directions.

POLICE Did you see anyone else on your way back to the hotel?

LP   No. Everyone had gone to bed.

POLICE Including Mrs Page?

LP   I don't know. I didn't see her.

392

POLICE	Why did you go down to the Beach House this morning?
LP	[Silence.]
POLICE	Mrs Page?
LP	I needed to talk to Andrew.
POLICE	What about?
LP	[Pause.] Our daughter. I thought Caz was at the beach, so it'd be a good time to catch him.
POLICE	What made you think she was at the beach?
LP	I saw her. Well, I thought I saw her. She has a bright red bikini, you can't miss it.
POLICE	You admit you wanted to get your ex-husband on his own?
LP	It's no secret Caz and I don't get on. Things have been . . . [Pause.] I just thought it'd be better if she wasn't there. I went down to the Beach House— [Sobs.] I'm sorry. I can't.
POLICE	It's OK. I know this is upsetting, Mrs Page, but I need you to tell me exactly what happened next.

LP   [Sobbing.]

POLICE   Would you like some tissues?

LP   Yes, thank you. I'm sorry. [Pause.] I just keep
            seeing him *lying* there.

POLICE   When you got to the Beach House, did you
            knock on the door?

LP   No. I was going to, but I heard shouting from
            inside, and realised Caz was there after all, so I
            stopped.

POLICE   You heard raised voices? Could you tell whose
            they were?

LP   Andrew and Caz.

POLICE   You're sure about that? Mr Page was alive when
            you first arrived at the Beach House?

LP   Yes.

POLICE   Could you make out what they were saying?

LP   Not really. I mean, they were angry. I could hear
            bits of it. It was mainly Caz. 'How could you?'
            that sort of thing.

POLICE   Did you have any idea what she meant?

LP   No.

POLICE   What did you do?

LP   I didn't want to get in the middle of it, so I
           started to go back up to the hotel. I was about
           halfway back, and then I heard a scream.

POLICE   Was it a man or a woman?

LP   It sounded like a woman, but it might have been
           Andrew. I don't know, I've never heard a man
           scream before. It was terrible. I kind of froze,
           at first. And then I heard another scream, and I
           ran back, and then when I went in—

POLICE   The door was unlocked?

LP   It must have been. I ran in and saw . . . and
           saw . . . [Sobs.]

POLICE   Just take your time, Mrs Page.

LP   I'm so sorry. [Pause.] Andrew was on the floor,
           and Caz was holding a knife, kind of bent over
           him. There was blood everywhere. And then she
           just kind of *came* at me.

POLICE	She attacked you?
LP	I tried to get to Andrew, to see if he was all right, and I must have slipped on the . . . on the blood – that must've been when I hurt my arm – and I was trying to get the knife away from Caz, I was screaming. It all happened so quickly.
POLICE	Did you actually *see* Mrs Page stab her husband?
LP	He was already on the floor when I got there. If I'd been [inaudible] maybe I could've . . . [Sobs.]
POLICE	Was anyone else there?
LP	No.
POLICE	And you didn't see anyone else enter or leave the Beach House?
LP	No. *She* killed him! Ask her! Go on!
POLICE	The thing is, Mrs Page. She tells us exactly the same story as you, with one important difference. She says *you're* the one who killed him.

Chapter 42

Louise

It is the way she makes his coffee that gives it away. She doesn't ask him how he takes it, she simply makes it with the merest dash of cream and two sugars, exactly the way Andrew likes it, the kind of way you would only know if you had done it many times before, the kind of way you would do if you knew someone intimately.

As I watch her hand him the cup and saucer, I know, in that second, and without a shadow of a doubt: Bella was telling the truth when she said it was Taylor in trouble, not her. And the father, the predatory *married* father who got a seventeen-year-old schoolgirl pregnant, is Andrew.

That's what he meant when he came to my house and said he'd been a fool. *That's* who he's been having an affair with: his daughter's teenage best friend.

I'm almost grateful when Caz's faux pas breaks my shocked paralysis. Seizing the excuse, I flee the hotel and race along the cliff top, heedless of where I'm going. I'm grateful for the full moon that illuminates the path, finding my way across the rocks and down to the lagoon almost by instinct. There is something primeval about the sound of the waves crashing on the shore in the darkness, the tang of salt in the air, and I stand on the empty beach and let the sound sweep through me, riding the tide of my anger, the release so intense it's almost erotic.

Now that I know, I can't imagine how I didn't see it before. It was all too evident in the furtive, guilty glances Andrew was throwing Taylor all evening. It was written all over the girl's pale, lovesick face whenever she looked at him. But it's obvious Bella has no idea what's gone on between them, and I hope to God it stays that way. The double betrayal would break her heart.

Andrew's always liked women: *women*, not girls. He's never been able to say no to a pretty face. But Taylor is just a teenager! She's thirty years younger than he is! I know he's a narcissist, but this is a low watermark, even for him. Their relationship may be legal, but morally and ethically, he's just put himself beyond the pale for every parent I know.

I don't hear Andrew come up behind me, and jump when I turn and see him standing just feet away. We stare at each other for a long moment in silence. He can tell instantly from my expression that I know. You don't live with someone for the best part of a decade and a half and not learn to read in their face that the past has caught up with you.

Fear, guilt and calculation play across Andrew's features, but I realise suddenly I haven't once seen surprise since Caz's gaffe. Not *shock*. He must have

398

known about Taylor's pregnancy already. The son-of-a-bitch. He *knew*, and instead of taking some responsibility and helping Taylor decide what to do, or at least paying for the poor girl's abortion, he left her to figure it out alone. All he cares about now is that he doesn't get caught. I don't think I've ever hated anyone more than I hate him in this moment.

'Get away from me,' I say, my voice hard and unforgiving.

'Lou, let me explain—'

'There is nothing you can say,' I bite, '*nothing* that excuses this.'

I can't imagine how I ever found him attractive. There is no substance to him, nothing of any worth. The precise qualities that make him such a brilliant television presenter also conceal the fact that he's an appalling human being.

'I've been an idiot, I know that,' Andrew pleads. 'You don't know, Lou, you weren't there. It wasn't something I planned. If I could take it back, I swear to God I would. It was the biggest mistake of my life.' He realises from my stony expression his opening *mea culpa* gambit isn't working, and abruptly changes tack, his tone freighted now with accusation. 'Look, we all make mistakes. You let me think I was Tolly's father when—'

'Taylor is *seventeen*!' I interrupt angrily. 'She's still a child!'

'She knew what she was doing,' he says, a sullen sneer creeping into his voice. 'It wasn't her first time, trust me.'

My fury and outrage boil over. I slap his face, hard, and even in the darkness I can see the red imprint my hand has left. 'Don't you dare!' I shout. '*You* did this! She's the same age as your daughter! That's not an affair, it's *abuse*! How would you feel if one of your friends had done this to Bella?'

He looks repelled. 'Don't be disgusting.'

'Can you hear yourself?' I demand incredulously. 'How could you, Andrew? She's still at school! How could you *ever* think this was OK?'

Finally, he has the grace to look discomforted. 'Look, it just happened a few times,' he mutters. 'She was always hanging around, making eyes at me. She asked me to show her around the studios, but she made it clear what she really wanted. It's not like the girl wasn't willing.' He rubs the side of his face with an injured air. 'Fuck, you could have broken my nose, Louise. I can't go to work on Monday with my face like—'

I swear to God, if we were on the cliff top instead of the beach, I'd push him off. 'You got that girl *pregnant*,' I hiss. 'And then you left her to cope with it on her own. Bella paid for her to have a termination, did you know that? Your sixteen-year-old daughter had to arrange to abort her own half-brother or sister! Can you imagine what that'll do to her if she ever finds out?'

'She won't unless you tell her,' Andrew says sulkily. 'The problem's sorted now, isn't it? The girl will get over it. I've told her we're finished. I don't know why she's here this weekend, to be honest. She'd better not be thinking about telling Caz,' he adds nastily. 'Now she's got rid of it, it'll be her word against mine.'

I literally have no words. The man has no shame or remorse. I never thought I'd pity Caz, but I do now, married to this amoral bastard.

'Taylor is a *child*,' I repeat bitterly. 'You can't rely on her to keep your secret forever. I'm not even sure she should.'

'Look, Lou. I get it,' Andrew says quickly. 'But there's no need to be jealous. She honestly didn't mean a thing. It was just a stupid fling.' He takes a step towards me, pouring every ounce of charm he can muster into his gaze. 'You're the only woman I've ever cared—'

'Stop,' I interrupt, sick to my stomach. 'Just stop. I don't want to hear it. Stay away from Taylor or you'll have *me* to deal with.'

I leave him standing on the shore, filled with a loathing so visceral I can taste its acrid bitterness at the back of my throat. I feel dirty by association, as if I need to go home and scrub myself clean. I slept with this man just a few days ago! I enabled him, as I have done for so many years. That makes me part of his grimy story.

My foot hits a loose stone, and I slip, my ankle turning as I stumble. It takes me a moment to regain my balance, and when I do, I suddenly see my mother hidden in the shadows of the cliff.

'Mum! You startled me,' I exclaim. 'What are you doing down here?'

'I was worried about you,' my mother says. Her

delicate gold scarf flutters behind her in the breeze. 'You disappeared. Min said she thought you'd gone down to the beach, so I came to see everything was all right. This path can be dangerous, especially at night.'

Her expression is unreadable, but there's something in her eyes that gives me pause. Voices carry across the water. What might she have heard?

'How long have you been there?' I ask her.

'Long enough,' Mum says.

CAROLINE PAGE
PART 1 OF RECORDED INTERVIEW

Date:- 25/07/2020
Duration:- 48 Minutes
Location:- Kingsbridge Police Station

Conducted by Officers from Devon &
Cornwall Police

(cont.)

POLICE   Are you sure you're all right to continue, Mrs
           Page?

CP   I'm fine.

POLICE   You're not in any pain—

CP   I said, I'm fine. Can we please get on with this?

POLICE   You'd gone for a swim, you said. Can anyone
            else confirm that?

CP   I don't know. It was pretty early. I didn't speak
            to anyone, but someone may have seen me from
            the hotel.

POLICE   What time did you leave the Beach House?

CP   I didn't check.

POLICE   Approximately, Mrs Page?

CP   I don't know. About eight, I suppose. Andy was
            still asleep when I left.

POLICE   And you swam for how long?

CP   Twenty minutes, maybe. But I stayed at the
            lagoon for a bit afterwards. [Pause.] Andy and
            I had a row last night, over something I said at
            dinner. It was stupid—

POLICE   This would be when you suggested your step-
            daughter, Bella, might be pregnant?

CP   [Pause.] Yes.

POLICE   Why did you think that? [Pause.] Mrs Page?

CP   It was just a stupid misunderstanding.

POLICE   And that's what you argued about?

CP   Partly.

POLICE   Was this in the hotel, or when you got back to your room?

CP   Back in our room. But that was later on, after Andy got back from the beach.

POLICE   Why did your husband go to the beach?

CP   He went after Louise. She was furious about what I'd said, she stormed out of the hotel, and Andy went to calm her down. But then I heard them shouting on the beach as I was walking back to the Beach House—

POLICE   You heard them shouting? They were arguing?

CP   Sounded like it.

POLICE   Do you know what it was about?

CP   No. They were too far away, I couldn't hear.

405

POLICE   So you went back to the Beach House alone?

CP   Yes. Kit was staying up at the main hotel with
          Louise's son. I went to bed, but I was still awake
          when Andy got back.

POLICE   What time would that have been?

CP   About half an hour after me, about midnight.

POLICE   And you say you then had a row with him your-
          self? What about?

CP   Louise, mainly.

POLICE   Why did you argue about Louise?

CP   [Inaudible.]

POLICE   For the tape, Mrs Page.

CP   Sorry. I said, I told him he needed to be careful.
          She's obsessed with Andy, she's never been able
          to accept it's over. [Pause.] Look, I don't expect
          you to take my word for it. No one else has.
          She's got a police record, you can look it up.

POLICE   Did Louise Page ever threaten your husband, as
          far as you know?

CP   No, she's too clever for that. But—

POLICE   If we could just stick to the facts, Mrs Page.

CP   In the end, Andy said he was going to sleep on
          the sofa. [Pause.] That was the last time I talked
          to him.

POLICE   I know this must be upsetting for you, but can
          you tell me what happened when you got back
          to the Beach House this morning after your
          swim?

CP   I heard shouting on my way back from the
          lagoon. I stopped for a minute to try to figure
          out where it was coming from, and then I real-
          ised it was the Beach House—

POLICE   You're sure?

CP   There wasn't anywhere else it could have been
          from. You've seen how isolated it is. So I started
          running, and then I heard screaming. It was really
          awful. I knew something terrible was happening.
          When I got there, the door was wide open and
          I could see Louise just standing there, and Andy
          was on the floor, and there was blood every-
          where.

POLICE   Was your husband still alive?

CP   I don't know. I tried to get to him, but she came at me with the knife—

POLICE   Mrs Page was holding the knife?

CP   Yes. I tried to get it away from her, and then we both slipped and fell, and I hurt my arm. She was shouting and yelling, and we were both struggling to get it. And then somebody burst into the room, one of the groundsmen, I think, and she let me go.

POLICE   Did you see anyone else at all? Anyone enter or leave the Beach House?

CP   No.

POLICE   Mrs Page, you are aware that Louise Page says it's you who killed him? She says *she* heard shouting, and discovered *you* with the knife.

CP   Well, she would do, wouldn't she? But why would I kill him?

POLICE   You seem very calm, Mrs Page, if you don't mind me saying.

CP   Because I knew something like this would happen in the end. [Pause.] Louise always said if she couldn't have him, no one else would. I guess she meant it, didn't she?

The day of the party

Chapter 43

Caz

I stand by the sofa, watching Andy sleep. People are always supposed to look defenceless and innocent when they're asleep, when their guard is down, but all I see is a liar. He's betrayed me so many times, in so many ways. I've always come second to Louise. Second wife, second choice. *Always*. But that's not why I'm doing this. I made peace with my place in Andy's life when I married him. This is about *justice*. About doing what I should have done years ago, in a different time and in a different place, to a different man.

My mother wasn't strong enough to do what needed to be done, but *I* am. I should've done it last night, but the commotion my stupid blunder caused knocked my plans off course. I still have some instinct for self-preservation: I'll go to jail if I have to, but it's not my first choice. I'll come under suspicion no matter what; the spouse is the first person the police always suspect. But in this case, there are *two* of us. All I need to do is create reasonable doubt. My intention had been to do that by acting during a period of time in the evening

411

when no one knew exactly where everyone else was, but thanks to the furore I kicked off, that didn't happen. So Andy earned another twelve hours of life he didn't deserve.

He didn't even speak to me when he finally got back last night. His contempt is more embarrassing than a row would have been. I'll tell the police we fought; it'll sound more believable.

It'd be easy to kill him now, while he's sleeping, but I need to be seen out this morning, to establish a clear window of time when Andy was alone and give myself an alibi. So I make sure I'm remembered going down to the beach. I throw a scarlet linen tunic over the top of my red bikini, and then saunter up the path to the hotel. I wouldn't normally give the two middle-aged tennis players limbering up for a match the time of day, but this morning I go out of my way to comment on the glorious weather and wish them luck. Two bored waiters straightening chairs on the terrace get the benefit of a wide smile. I can feel their eyes follow me all the way down the wooden steps towards the lagoon.

The tiny beach is surprisingly busy this early in the morning, with a number of swimmers already in the sea. I strip off, and wade out into the lagoon, diving below the surface and swimming underwater until my lungs feel tight. Even in July, the water is cold. Adrenalin courses through me. *I'm not a victim anymore.* I'm finally taking charge of my own life again, and it feels good.

When I emerge from the waves, a woman about my own age is coming down the wooden staircase in a red bikini very similar to my own. It's an unexpected stroke of good luck: one blonde in a red swimsuit looks much like another. Another sign the gods are on my side. I wait till she's swum out to the floating pontoon in the lagoon and settled herself in the sun, then tuck my wet hair up under a nondescript baseball cap and throw on a plain denim dress from my beach bag, which now holds the eye-catching red tunic. Reasonable doubt. That's all I need.

As I climb the stairs back to the Beach House, I spot Celia Roberts walking briskly away from the hotel, dressed in jeans and a T-shirt that should look way too young for her, but don't, the gold chiffon scarf from last night knotted stylishly at her throat. I duck quickly out of sight as I reach the top of the staircase, and she disappears around the side of the terrace without seeing me.

For a fleeting moment, I consider going to her and telling her what Andy's done to Bella. Instinctively, I know she is the one person who'd understand what needs to happen now, and would be ruthless enough to do it. She likes Andy, loves him, even; but her protective love for her children, her grandchildren, is primal and far stronger. Perhaps losing a child shapes you in ways you don't expect.

I dismiss the thought. She might not believe my story, and I'm not willing to risk her raising the alarm. I wait until I'm sure she's not coming back, and then head quickly down to the Beach House. Andy is still snoring on the sofa, sleeping off the half-bottle of Scotch he

413

put away last night. I go into the bathroom and change back into the red tunic I've been so careful to be seen in, and take a deep, steadying breath as I get Louise's steak knife from my bag. This is it, then. It's time.

Now that the moment is at hand, I feel oddly calm and clear-headed. The decision has been made; the sentence has been passed. All I have to do now is carry it out.

My alibi is far from rock-solid, the timings of my comings and going to the lagoon imprecise, but I just have to hope Louise's fingerprints on the murder weapon are enough to muddy the waters. I don't want to frame her. Not exactly. But she and I are bound together in this, whether she knows it or not. It's her daughter I'm protecting. We both have a motive; we both have means and opportunity. If they can't tell which of us did it, they'll have to let us both go. Reasonable doubt. That's all I need.

I return to my sleeping husband and eye his neck, picturing the knife slicing through the soft skin, the bright vermilion jet of arterial blood as his life and lies drain away from him. It can't be that hard to find the jugular. I'm not a medic, but I learned how to take someone's pulse on a first aid course at Whitefish a year or two ago. Presumably you cut in the same place.

I grip the knife a little more tightly. I'm so close I can smell the stale whisky on his breath. Now is the perfect time. Andy deserves this. I didn't think twice over the cat, and Bagpuss was far more worthy of life. *Now. Strike now.*

My hand shakes. I exhale sharply. I can't do it. *Goddammit, I can't do it!*

Rage seizes me with all the power and momentum of a contraction during active labour. I drop the knife with a clatter onto the side table and flee out onto the balcony, despising myself for my weakness. I've failed Bella. I'm no better than my mother. The fury pythons its way around my body, constricting my chest so tightly I can't breathe. I have to grip the railing to stop myself from leaping over it. I hate Andy with all my being, but love is stronger, even now.

I don't know how long I stand there: a minute, or twenty. I'm brought back to myself by the sound of a door slamming, as if caught by the wind. And then a quiet, terrible, rasping, mortal sigh.

I spin round. Andy is standing in the centre of the room, his back towards me. Even as I watch, he staggers backwards, clutching at his neck like the victim in a B slasher movie. Gouts of shocking red blood spill between his fingers. I see the knife, the knife I dropped a lifetime ago, sticking from his throat like a grotesque toy.

And then I see Bella.

Her head swivels towards me like a marionette's as I stand frozen in horror on the balcony. She stares at me blankly, catatonic with shock, as Andy collapses to his knees on the floor between us, gurgling and choking on his own blood. I gape at her, aghast, and then rush to Andy's side. The light is already fading from his eyes. 'Dear God, Bella, *what happened*?'

She just looks at me. And then she screams, a high, unnatural sound that sends chills down my spine. It sounds as if she's burning from the inside out.

Moving faster than I'd have thought possible, I leap up and grab her by the arms, forcing her back towards the front door, away from the gory sight of her father dying on the floor. Bella didn't mean to do this. She must have finally snapped, and the knife was just *there*. Right where I left it. She did what I couldn't. What I *wanted* to do. I refuse to let anyone else's life be ruined by this monster.

'Go,' I say roughly, propelling her towards the door. She has blood on her shorts and bikini top; my own bloodied hands leave grisly smears on her bare arms. 'Go to the beach,' I tell her. 'Swim in the sea. You need to get the . . . you need to be *clean*.'

She looks at me, her eyes glassy. I have no idea if she understands.

'Bella, you were never here,' I press urgently. 'I'll deal with this. It was an accident, it wasn't your fault. Swim in the sea, then get back to the hotel, do you understand? *You were never here.*'

Finally she starts to stumble down to the sand. I slam the door shut and rush back to the sitting room. Vomit rises in my throat as I lean over Andy's body, but I can't afford emotion now; he is not the man I once loved, the father of my son, but a problem to be solved, a crisis to be handled. I pull the knife from his neck, wiping the handle on my tunic to remove Bella's finger-prints. Someone will have heard her screaming. It won't be long before they raise the alarm. I have minutes, at most, to make it seem like she was never here.

I don't even get that.

I'm struck from behind by a blow between the shoulder blades so powerful it knocks the breath out of me. I pitch forward onto Andy's body, instinctively curling my hands over my head to protect myself. I get a glimpse of Louise's face, contorted with fury, but I don't have a chance to explain. She slams the lamp into me again, and I scream in agony as the heavy marble makes contact with my upper arm. Suddenly I'm parrying a flurry of vicious blows as we struggle in mortal combat. She's got the element of surprise; she's winning. I actually think she might kill me.

She raises the lamp to strike yet again, but as I cower, she suddenly slips in Andy's blood. The lamp falls from her hand as she loses her footing, and lands heavily on her back.

I shuffle backwards away from her before she has a chance to regroup. Searing pain shoots through my shoulder as I push myself upright against the wall, panting, my arm hanging uselessly at my side.

The knife lies on the floor between us. I lunge for it, but Louise gets to it at the same time, knocking it from my hand. The knife skitters away from both of us, coming to rest in a glistening ruby pool of blood by Andy's body.

My breath is coming in tight, painful rasps. I think she may have broken some of my ribs, too. I hear shouts outside, and the distant sound of running feet. Sound carries across the water; Bella's screams were blood-curdling.

Louise hears the voices too. She rocks back on her heels, and pushes her hair out of her eyes with the inside of her wrist, leaving scarlet smears on her face. We are both drenched in Andy's blood.

I glance towards the beach, praying Bella reached the hotel unseen, that she keeps her head. I nearly pass out from the pain in my shoulder, but I force myself to concentrate. There's only one way we can save Bella now. But to do it, we're going to have to trust each other. *If they can't tell which of us did it, they'll have to let us both go.*

'Louise,' I say quickly. 'We don't have much time.'

Five months later

Chapter 44

Louise

I read the email twice, and then close my laptop, and go into the kitchen. It's what I expected, but it's still hard to see it written in black and white.

Pouring myself a glass of white wine, I lean lightly against the tall kitchen window, staring down at the bustling street below. Last-minute Christmas shoppers throng the rain-slicked pavements, weighed down with carrier bags, and I can hear the sound of Slade's 'Merry Christmas' drifting up from one of the shops nearby. I love being back in London, in the centre of things. It's like I was never away.

After Andrew's death five months ago, I couldn't face the thought of staying in Sussex. Our house held too many memories of our life together, of everything that went so horribly wrong. Besides, without his financial support, I needed a better income than I could generate freelancing or teaching. Moving to London has enabled me to take a full-time editorial position at the *Daily Sketch*. I couldn't quite face selling the house, though, not yet, so I put it on Airbnb, which is bringing in far more than I'd dreamed possible, and rented a tiny two-bedroom flat in the shabbier end of Primrose Hill. Bella didn't want to leave her friends and her school, not with just one more year to go before uni, so she decided to live with my parents during the week, and come up to me at weekends. Not that Tolly and I see much of her; she's too busy taking advantage of all the city has to offer a teenager. She deserves it, after everything she's been through.

Abruptly, I put down my wineglass and go back to my computer, pulling up the email again. *Re: Police Investigation 47130060126. We regret to inform you . . .*

The words start to blur before my eyes. *The reviewing lawyer at the Crown Prosecution Service . . . difficult decision not to progress the matter to court. Your word against hers . . . no third party material corroborating either party's version of events . . . case will remain open . . .*

She got away with it. Caz literally got away with murder.

Caz lied. I knew it then, and I know it now. My daughter didn't kill her father, even in a desperate moment of madness. It's not that I don't believe her capable of such an act; I know better than most how thin is the line between *normal* and *crazy*. In extremis, we can all be driven to do something we'd never have thought was in our nature. But I also know Bella could never lie to me, not about something like this. Not for five months; not to me. I'd *know*.

Except she lied to me about where she was that

dreadful morning, I think uneasily. She wasn't swimming in the lagoon, like she said. I saw her leaving the Beach House, just moments before I got there.

Bella was *traumatised*, that's all. She's probably just blanked the horror from her mind. No point mentioning it to anyone. After all, Caz is the one who's guilty.

Bella has always refused to discuss what happened that day with anyone, and on the advice of the counsellor we found to help her through her father's brutal murder, I've never pressed it. I don't know what she saw at the Beach House, but she certainly saw me, covered in her father's blood, being taken away in a police car. Of course it scarred her, but she's recovering. Her therapist is very skilled, very kind, and Bella is almost back to her old self again. Almost.

I take a gulp of wine. All these months later, the metallic smell of blood still lingers in my nostrils. I can still see the messianic fervour in Caz's eyes when she concocted that ridiculous story to save her own skin, accusing Andrew of the most appalling wickedness. 'There's only one way to throw them off Bella's scent,' she said feverishly, in those last few moments before the groundsmen burst through the door. 'We have to blame each other. They won't be able to prove which of us did it, but they'll be so busy trying, they won't even look at Bella.'

In the street below, Christmas lights wink in the darkness. A young man in a Santa suit lets himself into an alley behind a department store, pulling off his long white beard and shoving it in his pocket so he can light

423

a cigarette. I turn away from the window. No one is ever what they seem.

The familiar doubt gnaws at me as I pour myself a second glass of wine. I wish I hadn't agreed to let the children spend the weekend at my parents'. Even now, I still don't know why Caz would tell such an outrageous lie about Bella, unless lying is so much second nature to her, she no longer knows how to tell the truth. Why not just blame an intruder? Why tell me it was Bella?

I put my empty wineglass in the kitchen sink, and frenetically start to wipe down countertops that are already clean. Who knows why Caz lied, I think bitterly; maybe she's so delusional she actually believes what she said is true. But *she* killed Andrew. She murdered him as surely as she poisoned my cat. I caught her, literally red-handed, covered in his blood! There's no doubt in my mind she did it. No doubt. And thanks to me, she got away with it. I was the one who contaminated the crime scene; my fingerprints and DNA were everywhere. How could any jury decide which of us had struck the fatal blow? If it hadn't been for our bitter history, the police might even have concluded we were in it together.

For a fleeting second, I wonder what I would have done if Bella *had* been guilty. My first instinct would be to protect my daughter, of course, but would covering up for her really be the best thing in the long run? I'd wreck her moral compass for life. Our actions, accidental or not, have consequences. Even if I'd believed Caz, I don't think I could have gone along with her plan to blame each other to save Bella, though judging by the way things have played out with the CPS, the ploy would've worked. But it's easy to be morally upright in theory. None of us ever truly know what we'd do until we're put to the test.

My mother has no such qualms. 'Of course you'd cover up for her,' she said briskly, when I confided what Caz had told me. 'You're her *mother*. A mother would do anything to protect her child. *Morality* doesn't come into it.'

She's been an absolute rock, my mother. She grieves Andrew's loss herself, I know that, but her only concern has been for Bella and Tolly. Thanks in no small part to her, the children are both doing better than I dared hope. I'm the one who can't seem to get past Andrew's death. I despise him for what he did with Taylor, but I would *never* have killed him and deprived my children of their father. No one deserves to die the way he did, drowning in his own blood.

Perhaps, if the police had been able to *prove* Caz did it, if I knew, beyond a shadow of a doubt, that Bella wasn't involved—

I straighten up and throw the kitchen sponge into the sink in frustration. Every time I let myself go down this insane rabbit hole, I give Caz what she wants. She told me that ridiculous story to mess with my head, and I'm letting her.

Thank God I never have to see the woman again. She moved to New York with Kit as soon as the police

425

returned her passport. She's working at a very cutting-edge ad agency, Patrick tells me. No doubt she'll go far. The further from me, the better.

I pick up Tolly's toys from the sitting room floor and return them to his room, the maelstrom of doubt and fear quietly dissipating as it does whenever I think of Patrick these days. He and Tolly have become firm friends in the three months since Patrick and I started seeing each other again. If he's done the maths around Tolly's birthday and our affair, he hasn't said anything, but things are going so well between us, I think I may tell him the truth soon. Tolly needs a father, and Patrick needs a son, even if he doesn't know it yet.

Bella gets on well with him, too. I thought she'd be really hostile to the idea of me dating again, especially so soon after her father's death, but to my surprise, she was encouraging. 'It's been four years since you split up, Mum,' she said, when I tentatively broached the subject. 'It's about time you met someone else.'

I tuck Tolly's *Star Wars* trainers neatly at the bottom of his wardrobe, and try to close it, but the door jams on something. Kneeling down, I wrestle the canvas strap of a small holdall from beneath the runner. Bella borrowed it from my mother when she came up to stay the other weekend. No doubt it's filled with dirty washing. I must remember to make sure she takes the bag back to Mum next weekend.

Opening the laundry closet in the hall, I empty the contents of the bag onto the floor. Out tumble a pair of grubby jeans, the sweatshirt Bella lost two weeks ago and which caused a hurricane of hunting, and half a dozen dirty T-shirts and odd socks. Not a single item is black. That phase has finally passed, thank God, along with her friendship with Taylor. I think she's met someone new, though she hasn't actually said anything; she gets a lot of texts from a girl called Alice. It seems much less intense than her relationship with Taylor, much less dangerous. I'm hoping she'll be ready to bring her home to meet us soon.

I throw everything into the washing machine, and shake out the holdall to make sure I've got every last sock. A crumpled pair of denim shorts falls onto the floor; they smell damp, as if they've been put away wet. I check the pockets, inhaling the briny tang of salt water, and toss them into the machine. They've probably been sitting in the holdall since the summer. None of us have been back to the beach since Andrew's death. That's a demon we'll all need to face at some point, but not just yet.

My breath suddenly catches in my throat as I fold up the empty holdall. Caught in the zip is a long, tangled wisp of pale gold chiffon. It must have lain forgotten in the bottom of my mother's canvas holdall, along with the shorts.

I ease the delicate fabric through my fingers. *My mother's chiffon scarf.* She was wearing it that fateful morning at the hotel. I remember Bella teasing her at breakfast: *Are you going to wear that gold scarf all weekend, Gree?*

427

You only get one golden wedding anniversary, Mum said, laughing. *Might as well make the most of it.*

Splashed across the chiffon, faded but unmistakable, is the dull rust arterial spray of my husband's blood.

Chapter 45

Celia

I think we can all agree: if ever a man deserved to be murdered, it was Andrew Page.

There was no shortage of women in his life with a motive. Louise, Caroline, Bella, Taylor, even Min; any one of them might have done it. Teenage girls can be very emotional, very *passionate*. They're a maelstrom of hormones and feelings they don't know what to do with. Louise knows that better than anyone. All that nonsense with Roger Lewison when she was nineteen; she stabbed herself that night at his house, but it could just as easily have been his wife. Or Roger himself.

She may tell herself now she'd never have killed the father of her children in cold blood, but I saw the look in her eyes the night before he died, on her way back from the beach. She can lie to herself, but not to me. I'm her *mother*. She went down to the Beach House that morning for a reason. It was just luck I got there first.

I didn't kill Andrew to punish him, though he'd certainly earned it. I did it to save my daughter, and my granddaughter, from themselves. Any mother would have done the same. And I've had my life. It ended when Nicky died. I'm just marking time now, until the end.

Losing a child changes you in ways you'd never have believed possible. The person you thought you were is gone. There's a shadow that covers the world, even as you are forced to still live in it. You cannot imagine the depth of pain to which you are taken unless you've gone through it yourself. It's every parent's worst fear, every parent's nightmare. But your deepest fear of losing a child, is just that: a fear. Your fear is my story.

Everything looks different where I am; it even has a different smell. There isn't a part of you that can possibly relate to this feeling. That's a good thing, trust me. It's not a feeling you want to have. You want nothing to do with this world. I'm like a prisoner in a cage; you can't even come and visit me here.

I know what it's like to bury my child. I know what it's like to have to pick something out to wear to my child's funeral. I know the feeling of having to force air into my lungs, just so I can breathe. The feeling of having to keep on living when there is nothing left to live for. I know what it's like to put all my child's belongings in a box. I know the feeling of bringing flowers to his grave. I can't ever forget the smell of freshly dug dirt. I know what it's like to have the whole world pity you, and in the same moment be glad they are not you.

Grief leaves you hollow and shattered, but when the pieces re-form into a misshapen, distorted approximation of the person you used to be, you find yourself

430

stronger. Capable of doing *anything* to protect the ones you love.

I refuse to lose Louise, or Bella. They may mourn Andrew, but they will move on. Human beings are designed to absorb loss and heal. Except for the loss of a child. We are not meant to survive that.

Andrew was sleeping when I got to the Beach House that day. The knife was right there, on the table next to him; I didn't have to use the one I'd brought. His death wasn't quite instant: somehow, he staggered to his feet as I left, but I think he deserved a little pain, a moment of *knowing*, before he died. I hadn't realised Caz was outside on the balcony until afterwards, I'd thought she was still at the lagoon, but she didn't see me slip down the path to the beach. I must have missed Bella by just seconds as she came the other way. I'm so sorry I had to put her through that: walking in on her father in his last, bloody moments. But it could have been so much worse. Her friend, Taylor, had just told her that Andrew had been the father of her baby. Who knows what might have happened if Bella had been the one to find the knife.

I don't know if she saw me leave the Beach House. She's never mentioned it, but she's also never told anyone she was there that day. I don't know if she suspects me, or Caz, or even her mother, but if she does, she isn't going to tell.

After all, the Roberts women are good at keeping secrets.

Acknowledgements

I am extraordinarily lucky to have two editors to thank for making this book so much better than I could have managed alone: Rachel Faulkner-Willcocks, who was working on the manuscript right up to the moment her beautiful daughter arrived a little earlier than expected, and Tilda McDonald, who seamlessly picked up the baton and carried the book across the finish line. I am truly blessed to have you both.

Thanks also to Rebecca Ritchie, who is, without question, the best agent in the world. Thank you for holding my hand, calming my terrors, and championing my writing with faith and passion.

Thank you to Sabah Khan, my brilliant and dogged publicist, and Helena Newton for copyediting. Your eagle eye prevented some excruciating howlers.

And thanks to all at Avon and HarperCollins for their tireless support behind the scenes, doing all the unglamorous heavy lifting that actually puts books into readers' hands.

Thanks to Georgie Stewart, for reading the manuscript at lightning speed to check I'd got the details of the advertising world right; and to Wikipedia for some of the technical medical detail. Any errors are my own.

Thanks, too, to the NetGalley readers and the many bloggers and book lovers who review my novels and give them a headwind as they sail out into the world. It makes such a difference, it really does.

And across the globe, thanks to all the readers, to all the buyers and sellers and lenders of books who ensure that a good story, well told, will always find an audience. You set a high bar, which is as it should be.

Last, though never least, thanks to my family, Erik, Henry, Matt and Lily, for riding the rollercoaster that is life with an insecure, paranoid, narcissistic writer, for holding on hard and never letting go.

You trust your family...
But should you?

"Dark, twisty
and addictive."
LISA JEWELL

A
MOTHER'S
SECRET

A NOVEL

TESS STIMSON

Out now